WITH P9-BZU-888

The Mysterious Death of Meriwether Lewis

ALSO BY RON BURNS:

Roman Nights

Roman Shadows

ONTARIO CITY LIBRARY

NOV   1993

ONTARIO, CA 91764

The Mysterious Death of Meriwether Lewis

A N O V E L

Ron Burns

ST. MARTIN'S PRESS
NEW YORK

THE MYSTERIOUS DEATH OF
MERIWETHER LEWIS. Copyright ©
1993 by Ron Burns. All rights
reserved. Printed in the United
States of America. No part of this
book may be used or reproduced in
any manner whatsoever without
written permission except in the case
of brief quotations embodied in
critical articles or reviews. For
information, address St. Martin's
Press, 175 Fifth Avenue, New York,
N.Y. 10010.

Production Editor: David Stanford Burr

Design: Judith A. Stagnitto

Library of Congress Cataloging-in-Publication Data

Burns, Ron.
      The mysterious death of Meriwether Lewis / Ron Burns.
          p.   cm.
      "A Thomas Dunne book."
      ISBN 0-312-09347-0
      1. Lewis, Meriwether, 1774–1809—Fiction. 2. United States—
History—1801—Fiction. 3. Explorers—United States—Fiction.
I. Title.
PS3552.U73253M97   1993
813'.54—dc20   93-4109
                                                CIP

First edition: August 1993

10 9 8 7 6 5 4 3 2 1

Dedicated to Frank Swertlow and Mary Murphy

The Route of the
Natchez Trace

Missouri River

St. Louis

Nashville TENNESSEE

• GRINDER'S STAND

Memphis

Mississippi River

THE NATCHEZ TRACE

• Jackson

LOUISIANA

MISSISSIPPI

Natchez

• New Orleans

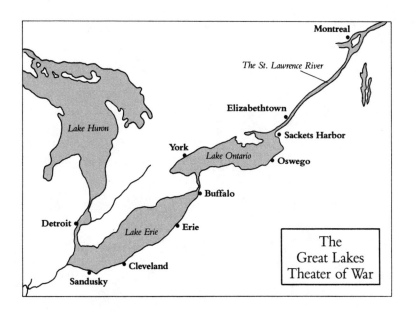

Montreal

The St. Lawrence River

Elizabethtown

Sackets Harbor

Lake Huron

York

Lake Ontario

Oswego

Buffalo

Detroit

Lake Erie

Erie

Cleveland

Sandusky

The
Great Lakes
Theater of War

In 1806, Meriwether Lewis returned a hero from the triumphant Lewis and Clark expedition to America's Pacific Northwest. But within three years, his career was mired in controversy and his life came to a violent and mysterious end . . .

The
Mysterious
Death of
Meriwether
Lewis

C H A P T E R

One

Of course it was murder," the old man said, and I looked at him with a sympathetic nod.

As before, when he said it his eyebrows leapt excitedly to the uppermost reaches of his high, brilliant dome of a forehead, and his tone, more fervent than ever, crackled with indignation. This time, however, as he spoke he took a healthy whiff of snuff in each nostril, involuntarily pinching his nose and accentuating even more the arching leap of his grand, gray, bushy eyebrows.

"Of course it was!" he repeated, stretching out each *s* with an angry hiss. He took two more whiffs of snuff, and as usual I could not quite hide a faint smile: after all, snuff was so wildly out of character for him. It was his one and only affectation—a distinctly European one, at that, indeed, one favored most particularly by the hated English. Otherwise, there was only the distant remnant of his Scottish burr to give away his foreign birth. Nowadays, those old rolled *r*'s of Scotland were nearly subsumed by a flatter, earthier lingo that somehow matched his plain, baggy suits. All in all, he had the sound and look of a noticeably un-European man—in truth, a man of the people, a Jeffersonian man.

An American man.

Not a man who, of all things, snuffed.

"Well, dammit, Harrison, don't you agree!" he demanded, glaring at me insistently. "Don't you think suicide is out of the question?"

In fact, it suddenly occurred to me that his snuff was his only vice—outside of a rare indulgence in slightly colorful language. For unlike myself (and nearly everybody else I knew), the old man did not smoke and never touched liquor in any form.

"Yes, Alexander, I do. Very much so," I said.

"Well . . ." His bluster faded within that one short word, and the anger in his eyes faded, too. He even managed what passed from him as a smile—taciturn but not unkind. It was, I thought, a Scottish smile. (Or was it, I wondered, a Yankee smile after all?)

"That's more like it," he said with an approving nod.

"I was only trying to keep an open mind," I said, "and familiarize myself with the evidence, such as it is."

"And now you have?" he asked.

"And now I have," I answered.

"So now you agree with me. That's your decision?"

"Irrevocably," I said.

He snuffed again, as if in a gesture of goodwill, and sneezed loudly several times. I poured myself a glass of Madeira, drank it down and poured another.

"To justice," he said.

"To capturing the killers," I said, and drank my wine.

I called him the old man, but he was not so old in years. In truth, at the moment of our talk in a candlelit drawing room of a wealthy friend's town house in Philadelphia, Alexander Wilson was only forty-four.

Somehow, though, he *was* old in other ways: in his stern demeanor, for one, and in his unyielding rules of conduct, for another. But it was his unforgiving *self*-appraisal that aged him most of all—as if he turned his merciless glare upon all his own words and actions, revealing his every foible, his every shortcoming.

"How little have I done, how small is my accomplishment for the human race," he was fond of saying lately, quoting the words of our late friend—the one we'd decided had been murdered.

One other thing: Wilson's health had begun to fail—and that did worry me. It worried him, too. Indeed it was one reason he wanted me along for the dangerous and strenuous undertaking at hand. For now that I had agreed, it was at least implicit that we would embark on our remarkable adventure together.

"God, I wish I had back that dozen years," he said with a weary sigh.

"What dozen years is that, Alexander?" I asked, though of course I knew the answer.

"The dozen years that you're younger than me, that's what!" he growled. "As if you didn't know!" He shook his head thought-fully. "I've walked all over this country, and now . . ."

He shrugged and let his voice trail off, and I smiled at him agreeably. For as I well knew, he had indeed traveled by foot over almost literally the length and breadth of the great United States, clear west to Buffalo on one occasion that I knew of, and south to the Carolinas on another.

It was all part of what he saw as his mission in life—or at least his mission until now: to find and catalogue every North American bird in existence. Indeed he had in a sense accomplished it, for the first two volumes of his work had recently been published, and he was now the country's preeminent ornithologist—and I was his assistant.

"And now what?" I said. "And now you need help; you need a friend. Is that it? Well, so what. So you need one. Don't we all once in a while? So you have one; you have me. And we'll go together, you and I, on this terrible *new* mission—the mission to solve the mystery of our friend's death."

And he frowned while I drank yet another glass of wine.

★　★　★

Meriwether Lewis was the man whose death by violence Alexander Wilson and I so ardently discussed that candlelit evening in Philadelphia. I'd known Lewis before he became great and famous, serving under him with the troops called out to put down the Whiskey Rebellion out by Pittsburgh back in 1794.

I'd known him only briefly, but liked him at once. I was a mere babe then, a man-child soldier of seventeen, while he was a dashing young lieutenant, only twenty himself, but impeccably dedicated and serious beyond his years—another one (it suddenly occurred to me) who'd grown old before his time. But I'd admired his serious ways and dashing manners; even then, you see, Meriwether Lewis was something of a dandy.

We served together, and that was about it until we became reacquainted through Wilson a few years later. By then, I was a young lieutenant myself, and Lewis had moved on to no less a job than secretary to the president of the United States. That's what Tom Jefferson told the world he was, but it seemed he didn't use him much for that. It seemed Tom Jefferson had other things in mind—specifically for Meriwether Lewis to lead what would soon come to be thought of as the most remarkable land exploration in the history of the world: Lewis, Jefferson proposed, would command an expedition through the uncharted lands of the far western portions of the continent all the way to the Pacific Ocean.

Lewis eagerly accepted—it seemed that he and Jefferson had talked informally of this for years—and immediately selected William Clark as his colleague and co-captain. Lewis and Clark were then charged with charting the rivers, lakes, mountains and valleys of the unknown region. They were also to catalogue the wildlife and send or bring back samples whenever possible. This included birds, of course—and that was how Lewis and Wilson first met.

For under Jefferson's guidance Lewis prepared for his journey for more than a year. In particular, he visited Philadelphia at least a dozen times for talks and seminars with a variety of scientists, including, among others, the distinguished Alexander Wilson.

"Corvus cristatus—the blue jay to you, sir," Wilson said during one of Lewis's first visits. With a somewhat melodramatic flourish, he pulled back the muslin covering to reveal a handsomely stuffed sample of the species. "You've seen it before, of course—the distinctively pointed head feathers, the slightly wider than usual beak, and of course the coloring: light gray belly, royal blue back, speckled blue and gray wings."

"Beautiful, yes," Lewis said.

Wilson nodded with a touch of triumph flickering in his eyes. "So then, why do I bother to point out this rather commonplace specimen?" he asked.

"Because there are other members of the jay family out West that you'll want me to recognize and be able to categorize properly," Lewis said at once.

Wilson's mouth dropped open, though just for an instant; clearly he had not expected any answer at all to his question, let alone the right one.

"Yes, that's correct," Wilson said, and even let loose his typical hint of a smile. "The Canada jay is certainly one. The forehead and lower parts are said to be dirty white, while the wings and tail are supposedly dark leaden gray, the back of the head is black, and, as with the blue jay, the feathers on the crown are full and crested."

By now Wilson's eyes were bright with excitement, for though he'd told and retold his description of the bird (I had heard it dozens of times), now he was telling it to a man who might actually see one one day soon enough.

"A drawing would be wonderful, of course," Wilson said, "but if you could get a specimen . . ."

He trailed off, apparently with sheer ecstasy merely at the thought. "It would be thrilling," Lewis put in. And I suddenly realized that Lewis was as genuinely excited as Wilson.

I sat in on their sessions, for as I say I was Wilson's protégé—struggling to become an ornithologist in my own right, something I still do in my spare time. And that was how I came to know Lewis again, know him much better, really, more as an equal—or at least more so than as a soldier in his company back in '94.

Lewis was an apt student—I could see that much—and old Wilson loved it, loved his unswerving sense of purpose. Truth be told, if I were a lesser man I might have become jealous of the old man's new favorite. But I did not—not so much because I so nobly rose above it all, but because I was enthralled with Lewis in my own way. He was strict and meticulous and disciplined, and yet garrulous and flexible and friendly. And he held an immediate and powerful attraction for all who met him—or at least those who met him with an open mind.

"You may also see birds of this type," Wilson said at a later meeting. "Picus auratus—or woodpeckers, in this case the gold-winged woodpecker."

Lewis nodded admiringly. "The gold wings, of course," Wilson went on, "the speckled breast, the touch of scarlet on the back of the head, but most important, the unusually long beak—probably twice the length of your usual land bird."

"You really think so, Alexander? Woodpeckers out West?"

Wilson bristled slightly: the student was already asking more knowledgeable questions. But as always, at least with Lewis, Wilson when he spoke was calm and respectful. "It's possible, yes, Meriwether. Not so likely as with some of the others, but possible."

And then came a moment when Meriwether Lewis gave me the thrill of my young life. "Why don't you join us," he asked Wilson and me one quiet morning over breakfast of grits, fried eggs and scrapple.

I struggled to swallow my mouthful of food. "Join you?" I stammered.

Lewis looked over at me with a kindly smile. "You're both still young and fit, you have a great knowledge of birds and other elements of the wild. Come with us on our expedition."

I recall more stuttering on my part, and then, when I finally settled down a bit, I saw Wilson shaking his head. "Too much to do here first," he said matter-of-factly. He meant of course that there were still far too many birds in the United States that needed to be catalogued before he could go traipsing off to unknown parts of some unknown country.

Lewis looked away a moment, then slowly shook his head. "Well, it would be wonderful to have you," he said with a degree of sadness that surprised me. I also took note that he seemed to be speaking at that moment just to Wilson. Did he realize, I wondered, that I might be caught in an awkward middle ground if he posed the invitation solely to me? Or was it Wilson he really wanted, caring little whether I went along or not?

I never knew for certain, for the question never came up again. Still, I have thought many times over the years how close I came to joining that historic journey through the uncharted lands of the West.

Lewis also extended us one other rare privilege. Not long before his departure, he showed us his private letter of instructions from President Jefferson. Needless to say, we read it with great interest:

"The object of your mission," Jefferson wrote,

> is to explore the Missouri River as, by its course and communication with the waters of the Pacific Ocean, may offer the most direct and practicable water communication across this Continent for the purposes of Commerce.
>
> Your mission has been communicated to the ministers from France, Spain and Great Britain, and through them to their governments, and such assurances given them as to its objects as we trust will satisfy them.
>
> In all your intercourse with the natives, treat them in the most friendly and conciliatory manner which their own conduct will admit; allay all jealousies as to the object of your journey, satisfy them of its innocence, make them acquainted with the position, extent, character, peaceable and commercial dispositions of the U.S., of our wish to be neighborly, friendly and useful to them, and of our dispositions to a commercial intercourse with them.
>
> Other objects worthy of notice will be the soil and face of the country, its growth and vegetable productions, the animals of the country, the remains or accounts of which may be deemed rare or extinct, mineral productions of every kind, but more particularly metals,

limestone, pit coal and saltpeter, salines and mineral waters, noting the temperature of the last and such circumstances as may indicate their character; volcanic appearances; climate, as characterized by the thermometer, by the proportion of rainy, cloudy and clear days, by lightning, hail, snow, ice, by the winds prevailing at different seasons, and the dates of the appearance of particular birds, reptiles or insects . . .

The president also went on at length about the importance of gathering plant, bird and animal specimens, and of learning in every detail the occupations, traditions and customs of the Indians. And Lewis was to be certain, he added, to record all this in a daily journal.

"A further guard," Jefferson wrote, "would be that one of those copies of your journal be on the paper of the birch, as less liable to injury from damp than common paper."

Jefferson, afraid the expedition might find itself stranded on the opposite coast on the shores of the Pacific Ocean, thought the men might be forced to return by ship with stops at foreign ports along the way. So he also gave Lewis this letter of credit:

I hereby authorize you to draw on the Secretaries of the Treasury, War and Navy monetary draughts which will be most negotiable for the purpose of obtaining money or necessaries for yourself and your men. And I solemnly pledge the faith of the United States that these draughts shall be paid punctually at the date they are made payable.

I also ask of the consuls, agents, merchants and citizens of any nation with which we have intercourse or amity to furnish you with those supplies which your necessities may call for, assuring them of honorable and prompt retribution.

And our own consuls in foreign parts where you may happen to be are hereby instructed and required to be aiding and assisting you in whatever may be necessary for procuring your return back to the United States. And to give more entire satisfaction and confidence to those who may be disposed to aid you, I, Thomas Jefferson, President of the United States of America, have written this letter of general credit for you with my own hand and signed it with my own name.

Finally came the big day: Wilson and I had traveled to Washington for the occasion, though there was no special ceremony. It was in truth a very simple, informal, private moment on the fourth day of July in the year 1803 when we rode out with Lewis a few miles into the Virginia countryside, along the Old Wilderness Road, to see him off on the start of his journey.

"The president approve your new attire?" I asked with a smile, for somehow we were amazed at his dress—though of course we shouldn't have been. He was all in buckskin, frontier style—so different from his Beau Brummel look of the parlor and drawing room where he nearly always wore the latest in wool trousers tucked nattily inside the tops of his boots, smartly tailored coats and sometimes even ruffled shirts imported from England.

Lewis answered merely with a shake of his head and a roll of his eyes. For Jefferson was well-known for doing official business dressed in house slippers, worn and baggy pants, and ill-fitting coats.

We exchanged a few more awkward pleasantries, and then: "Goodbye Mr. Wilson, goodbye young Mr. Hull," he said in his most formal tone of voice—which could be impeccably formal (and formidable!) indeed. And then he rode off across the trail with only a single servant in tow.

It would be months after that before he completed preparations for the trip, including the purchase and construction of several boats, the acquisition of provisions and the recruitment of all his men. He would not even meet up with William Clark until late the following autumn. And then they would all winter at St. Louis before beginning the true journey of exploration up the unknown and uncharted waters of the wide Missouri. We would not see him again for more than three years.

"How little have I done, how small is my accomplishment for the human race," Lewis wrote on the occasion of his thirtieth birthday while far from civilization on his journey through the wilds.

Rather like Julius Caesar, I thought, whining a bit over his supposed lack of accomplishments at about that same age. But then Caesar was comparing himself to Alexander the Great, who had conquered the world before he was twenty.

Caesar, though, wound up doing rather nicely, I thought. And so, it seemed to me, did Meriwether Lewis. Yet his wistful, perhaps even slightly melancholy, reflections have been used again and again by those who for whatever reason seek to dismiss his violent death as the suicide of a man in a state of derangement.

And though Meriwether Lewis, I came to realize, was hardly perfect and could be many things—cold and ambitious and even ruthless at times—one thing he was not was deranged.

Never that; nothing like it.

Meriwether Lewis, Wilson and I told ourselves repeatedly as we read over the so-called evidence again and again, did not take his own life. Meriwether Lewis was murdered, and Wilson and I decided we would prove it or die trying.

C H A P T E R

Two

The life of Meriwether Lewis ended at a place called Grinder's Stand, an inn so ridiculously crude and desolate as to be hardly worth the name. It sits about seventy miles southwest of Nashville, Tennessee, on a road (another overstated description) called the Natchez Trace, which is really nothing more than a well-worn rut—albeit a rut that stretches hundreds of miles.

At the time of his death on the eleventh of October, 1809, Lewis was more than three years back from his Pacific expedition and in his second year as governor of the Territory of Upper Louisiana. When he died at Grinder's, he was traveling from the territorial capital of St. Louis to the city of Washington.

The popular account of what happened there is based entirely on the report of a certain major of the Tennessee Militia named James Neelly, who in turn based his description almost solely on the statements of one Betsy Grinder, wife of Peter Grinder, the owner of the stand.

"It is with extreme pain that I have to inform you of the death of His Excellency Meriwether Lewis, Governor of Upper Louisiana, who died on the morning of the 11th and I am sorry to say by suicide," Neelly wrote.

Neelly said he had joined Lewis on his journey at Chickasaw Bluffs outside Natchez after the governor became ill with fever. Lewis had been traveling downriver by boat and had planned to make the entire trip by water when he changed his mind and headed inland—specifically, northeast along the Natchez Trace toward Nashville and beyond.

"His thinking a war with England probable," Neelly continued in his report, "and that his valuable papers might be in danger of falling into the hands of the British, he was thereby induced to change his route. I furnished him with a horse to pack his trunks and a man to attend to them."

Neelly insists that Lewis "appeared at times deranged" during the journey. Yet he says Lewis arrived at Grinder's alone except for two servants (one of them Lewis's, the other Neelly's) in the late afternoon hours of October 10, because "where we encamped three nights before we lost two horses, so I remained behind to hunt them while the governor proceeded on with a promise to wait for me at the first house he came to that was inhabited by white people."

"He rode up and asked me for quarters for the night," Betsy Grinder was said to have told Neelly, "but my husband away and I alone there, seeing he was deranged, I gave him up the house and slept myself in the one near it, the guest cabin. The servants slept in the barn.

"About three o'clock in the morning," she continued, "I heard two pistols fire off in the governor's room. I awakened the servants and went in, but too late to save him. He had shot himself in the head with one pistol and a little below the breast with the other. When his servant came in, the governor said, 'I have done the business, my good servant, give me some water.' The servant gave him water, and, Mr. Lewis died a short time after."

This was Neelly's version of Mrs. Grinder's account, which Wilson and I managed to piece together from newspaper dispatches and the help of a certain friend of ours with access now and then to the private letters of Thomas Jefferson, to whom Neelly had written. This was done, I might add, with no help from Neelly, for after his initial report he became unavailable to us or to anyone regarding this matter, and he would remain so for a long time to come.

"Unacceptable! Unbelievable! Absurd!" Wilson had snarled as we studied the account again and again, and I could only agree.

"The only two-shot suicide in history," Wilson growled with a shake of his head.

Most galling of all, Jefferson himself, by then in retirement at Monticello, had issued a statement indicating his complete acceptance of the account. And given his exalted status, particularly as Lewis's most ardent mentor, his opinion for all practical purposes had put the matter to rest.

Wilson and I had only grown angrier because of it. Thus, six months and nine days after the death of our friend—on the twentieth of April, 1810—he and I arrived at Grinder's Stand to pursue an investigation of our own.

The inn, as I say, was small and primitive, consisting of just two little log structures—one the house for the Grinder family, the other the so-called guest cabin. The two buildings stood just a few feet apart, with a well off to one side and a barn about fifty yards to the northeast.

"What a funny little place," I said, trying to sound cheery, I suppose, as we came upon it. Truth be told, there was an oddly savage and melancholy cast to the surrounding forest: the tall trees blocked most of the sunlight; the rugged terrain grew more dangerous with each step, especially in the dimness; there were treacherous swamps of deadly, foul-smelling water, and the small clearing and the little "stand" inside it did nothing to lift the gloom. In other words, there was nothing the least bit funny about it.

It was nearly twilight, a handsome spring sun just lowering over the treetops. About the same time of day as Lewis must have arrived, I thought, though of course he had come in from the opposite direction with the autumn sun flickering faintly behind him.

"I'm so tired," was Wilson's only response to the gloom of Grinder's Stand.

I studied him a moment, and indeed he appeared gray and exhausted, his skin sagging and his eyes milky with fatigue. As I was well aware, it had been a long day, but I knew it was more than that: the arduous journey was taking its toll.

Riding up, we saw a man bent over some tool or other, apparently trying to fix it. Approaching him from the rear, we pulled up, waited politely and even cleared our throats. But after a long moment, when he still gave us no greeting, Wilson and I exchanged slightly startled glances, and finally I said, "Howdy do" in a tone of deliberate good cheer.

Slowly, the man stopped what he was doing, turned around and spat out a plug of tobacco. He was a rugged-looking man, as most frontiersmen are: thick through the middle and shoulders, sinewy in the arms. He nodded carefully, his expression sternly disagreeable, and looked us over, making an appraisal of his own.

And I thought, This is more than foul temper or frontier moodiness on his face. These are careful, darting eyes and a hard, tight mouth with odd little scars at the corners. Scars of some injury? I wondered. Or marks of the man. Taken all together, I decided, they gave him the look of someone in a state of chronic, nagging suspicion.

"Peter Grinder," he said in a tone so menacing that for an instant I didn't quite know what he meant. But then I realized that he was simply introducing himself—albeit in his own peculiar way.

"Put us up for the night?" I asked with a tone I can only describe as chirpy. Indeed, my own show of agreeability was un-flagging.

"See the missis," he growled and walked off into a nearby field.

Wilson caught my eye and shook his head with a sigh of what was very nearly disgust. I started to mutter something equally disapproving when walking up slightly behind us and to our left came the woman I presumed to be "the missis," and my mind went quite suddenly and completely blank.

It wasn't that she was glamorous, understand. She couldn't

have been, living the way she did out in the wilderness working the land. Her clothes were grimy and tattered, as work clothes generally are, and her hands looked decidedly strong and unwomanly.

Even her face was smudged in a spot or two and her own expression was grim enough, but there was something about her, some strength that showed through the ugliness of that place: Her eyes were wide and bright and brown, and her skin, I realized looking beyond the grime, appeared smooth and soft and somehow feminine.

It was, I decided, a face of depth: a beautiful face.

And when she spoke, her own weariness and traces of suspicion suddenly vanished, and her whole expression came to life with a light she could not hide—a light that shone almost, it seemed, in spite of herself.

"Betsy Grinder," she said, and I nearly flinched, for in that brief moment I had nearly forgotten that she was no doubt "the missis" of the dour-faced man who was slowly edging his way back toward us—though it seemed to me trying not to act as if he were.

"I'm Harrison Hull," I said, "and this is Alexander Wilson."

She nodded with a faint smile, and, wishful thinking though it might have been, I swore I saw just the trace of something more when she stared up at me. A twinkle in her eyes, perhaps? Or a slight telltale throbbing in her throat?

"Staying the night?" she asked, and we nodded. "Dollar apiece," she said, and that time Wilson flinched—not so much because the price was indeed a bit high but because of the blunt manner in which she asked for hard cash.

Cash, after all, was the one thing they were always short of on the frontier, partly because it wasn't around, but mostly because there wasn't much use for it anyway.

"I'll pay a Spanish doubloon for each of us," Wilson said, somehow getting a bit more Scottish into his *r*'s than usual. Ah, I thought, he's negotiating.

"Fine with me," she said at once, cutting short the fun. "That's still mostly all we see out here."

We dismounted and a Negro slave girl took the horses to the barn. Mrs. Grinder showed us the "guest room," as she called it—Wilson called it the "guest hut"—a small, airless cabin with a dirt floor and one tiny window cut in the rear wall.

"Want some bedding?" she asked agreeably enough.

"We have our own," Wilson and I both said at once.

We turned around, still standing in the cabin doorway, and faced the setting sun. The suspicious-looking man had stopped about thirty yards off and was puttering in some noticeably inconsequential way.

"Your husband?" I said, though of course I knew the answer.

I watched her carefully. Her left cheek twitched and she blinked with an unhappy-sounding intake of breath. "Mmm," she said finally, and I took that for a yes.

"Shall I . . ." Wilson started to say, fumbling for his purse.

"Pay him," she said, nodding toward her husband with a shake of her head. "He'll get it from you later, at supper, if you want it."

We both nodded again—a definite yes to the invitation—and she abruptly turned and walked off, away from us—and him—without another word.

As it turned out, Wilson was too tired to eat. He fell asleep almost at once, and I paid for the lodgings, ate my meal with a kind of methodical lethargy, and was soon wrapped in my bearskin and sound asleep as well.

It was the time of day when everything always starts on the frontier—the very early morning with a chill in the air and the sky gray and heavy with predawn mist. I shivered and wrapped my buckskins tight around me, while Wilson struggled to come awake. We were in the main house (or hut!) having breakfast, and Peter Grinder, predictably unfazed by it all, downed his eggs and smoked pork in huge, brisk mouthfuls and headed for the barn without a word or even a smile for his handsome wife.

A moment later, Wilson said quietly to Betsy Grinder: "Meriwether Lewis was a close friend of ours."

She stopped what she was doing—or more accurately she paused. What she was doing was carrying a bucket, and after an instant she resumed her task, carrying it out to the well and lowering it down. Then, straining at the rope, she raised it slowly until it emerged above ground and carried it, water sloshing over the sides, back to the house.

"We wanted to ask you some questions about the night he died," Wilson went on matter-of-factly, quite as if there had been no interruption at all—though his tone was still quietly respectful, almost too respectful for my taste.

"It's months ago now," she said, "and I told the man then what happened."

Her tone surprised me, for I was half expecting defiance, or at least impatience, with the question; instead, her back partially toward us, staring down into the pailful of water, there was a softness, almost a girlishness, in her voice that I had not heard before.

"Neelly?" I asked, and she nodded her silent answer.

And I thought: She doesn't want to talk about it—that much seems clear. But why? I wondered. Is the memory of it all so unpleasant? Or is there more behind her reluctance? Is there a trace of fear, perhaps, in that soft, new voice?

"Well, if it's all right we'd like to ask you about it again," I said, my own voice suddenly so softly gentle that it surprised even me.

She put down the bucket and stood there, apparently thinking it over. Her face was suddenly transparent to me: Should she say anything at all? she seemed to be asking herself. And if so, what?

When it seemed as if she'd finished her little self-questioning, she sat down between us at the crude wooden table where Peter Grinder had just eaten his enormous farmer's breakfast. And then, her features suddenly composed and her voice strong and regular again, she gave with very little prodding the following report:

"Governor Lewis came here alone at about sunset and asked if he could stay the night. I told him yes, and he got down from his horse and brought his saddle into the house. He was dressed in a loose gown, white with blue stripes. When I asked if he came alone, he replied that there were two servants behind who would soon be up. He called for some whiskey and drank a little. When the servants arrived, he inquired for his gunpowder, saying he was sure he had some in a canister. The servant gave no distinct answer, and in the meanwhile Mr. Lewis walked backwards and forwards by the door, talking to himself.

"Sometimes it would seem as if he were walking up to me. Then he would suddenly wheel round and walk back the other way. He sat down to supper, but only a little while later he started up again, talking to himself in a violent way, his face flushed. Then, suddenly, he was calm again. He lighted his pipe and said very politely, 'Madam, this is a very pleasant evening.' Finally, he retired to the guest room for the night.

"But I could still hear him pacing and talking, and I was afraid; I could not sleep. He talked loudly, sounding like a lawyer to me. Then I heard a pistol shot, and then something heavy fell to the floor. And I heard the words 'Oh, Lord!' Then I heard another shot, and then I heard Governor Lewis at my door. He scratched at the door and called out, 'Oh, madam, give me some water and heal my wounds.'

"I looked through the cracks between the logs—they're open and unplastered, you know—and I saw him stagger back against a tree stump. He crawled for some distance and raised himself by the side of a tree where he sat for about a minute.

"Then he came scratching at the door again, but did not speak. And then I heard him scraping in the bucket with a gourd for water, but there was none."

At this point, I heard a loud gasp from Wilson. I turned to face him and saw a single teardrop slowly sliding down the left side of his face.

"At first light," Betsy Grinder went on with almost eerie smoothness, "I sent my two children to the barn to bring the servants. They went inside the guest room and found him in bed. Mr. Lewis uncovered his side and showed them where the wound was. Also, a piece of his forehead was blown off and had exposed the brains, though there wasn't much blood."

There was a much louder gasp then, and Wilson suddenly looked clammy and deathly pale. Mrs. Grinder, noticing his condition, drew him a cup of water, and he sipped it slowly; I took a sip or two myself.

"Mr. Lewis asked the servants for water, and they gave him some," she resumed, again without so much as a missed breath. "Then he begged them to take the rifle and blow out his brains, and he said he would give them all the money he had if they would do it. He said several times, 'I am no coward, but I am so strong and it is so hard to die.'

"The servants didn't shoot him, of course, and the governor finally died about two hours later, just as the sun rose above the trees."

Though Wilson was still in a state, I couldn't take my eyes off Betsy Grinder. But now I was more fascinated than enthralled. What sort of creature is she really? I asked myself. And how different her story is today from her story of last autumn to James Neelly.

"So . . . your two children were with you then?" I said. I spoke as offhandedly as I could, not wanting to alarm her. For according to Neelly, she had said she was home alone when Lewis died and that she, not her children, had awakened the servants.

"Oh yes, they were here," she said, her tone almost cheerful. "Like I say, I sent them to the barn for the men."

"And . . . you just let him . . ." It was poor Wilson, still gasping and upset. I smiled faintly and held up a quieting hand. Mrs. Grinder looked at us quizzically.

"You say the governor was out there for . . . what?" I asked. "Two hours? Three? Staggering and crawling?" I was still trying my best to sound casual about it, though I was starting to crack a bit myself under the strain. Also, there was nothing in Neelly's account of her statement to indicate such a delay. To the contrary, reading his version, I would have thought that she'd acted at once upon hearing the gunshots.

"Like I say, I was frightened," she said, suddenly a touch defensive. "I don't know how long it was. But, yes, two hours sounds right. Maybe longer."

"Maybe lo—"

I reached over and put my hand on Wilson's forearm, and he obligingly stopped himself midword, so to speak.

"So you did stay in the house that night?" I asked smoothly, in any case wanting to get off that most terrible part of the ordeal—and also wanting Wilson to calm down. Besides, I had suddenly remembered Neelly's version: that Mrs. Grinder was so alarmed by Lewis's supposed "derangement" from the moment he arrived that she gave up her own house to him and spent the night in the smaller guest room.

"Of course I did, I slept right here, just like always," she said.

"You talked about the servants finding him, you described that very well," I said with a smile. I wanted her to take it as a compliment, but it didn't work.

"That's right," she said, and that was all she said.

"What I mean, Mrs. Grinder . . . that is, you say the servants found him, and then you talk about it so . . . vividly . . ."

"What?"

"So . . . much in detail," I managed. "So . . . did you go in there, Mrs. Grinder? Did you see him for yourself?"

She looked at me then with a wide-eyed expression, as if really seeing me—really taking me seriously—for the first time.

"I don't get you," she said, a faintly puzzled look in her eyes—or at least that was the look she intended to be there.

"Well, it's simple enough, ma'am," I said in my gentlest tone yet. "You talked in all this detail, and I was just wondering if what you're telling me is what the servants told you, or if you went in there and saw it for yourself."

She hesitated for a very long moment, her eyes directly on me, never wavering for an instant, but her mind plainly chewing hard on some distant bone.

"Course I didn't go in there myself," she said at last with almost savage abruptness. "Woman like me. The servants told me, that's how I know."

She kept on staring at me, while I looked from her to Wilson and back again. Wilson seemed very much himself again and, suddenly in his quiet tone of earlier, said, "Forgive me, madam, but there's one thing I don't understand."

He paused, and she slowly moved her dark eyes to him.

"How did you know it was a pistol?" Wilson asked.

"I . . . wha-a-a-?"

"You said you heard a *pistol* shot, Mrs. Grinder," Wilson went on, "and I was simply wondering how you knew what sort of weapon it was."

Then it was *her* breathing that took a slight turn for the worse: I could see a throbbing in her neck and a slight heaving in her chest.

"Well . . . I . . . that is, I don't. I didn't," she said at last. "I meant it was a shot, and I said pistol because that's what it turned out to be later. Didn't it?"

"Oh yes, Mrs. Grinder," Wilson said with a grand smile. "Quite right, that's absolutely what it turned out to be."

And with that we ended our questioning of Betsy Grinder, at least for the time being. We were saving for later our biggest question of all—the one about the second gunshot.

C H A P T E R

Three

I paid for another night's lodging and left Wilson behind to rest while I borrowed a horse from the Grinders (to let mine rest a day) and rode off at a meandering pace. I wanted to look anything but purposeful and determined, which was what I very much was— hoping instead to seem like a man taking a casual look at the country while his friend rested up for the journey ahead.

Even so, Peter Grinder eyed me carefully as I left, and without, I might add, attempting to conceal it. Indeed, as my backward glances told me, he watched me till the last as I disappeared into the forest several hundred yards away.

I would, I had decided, visit another farmer or two (or three) just to get some hint of what the rest of the neighborhood thought of this Grinder fellow and his wife. As things turned out, I got an earful and then some.

"Grinder, eh?" one neighbor said. His name was James McFarlane and he was as tree-branch thin as Grinder was wide.

"Grinder, eh?" he said again (and then, as I recall, again and then again).

"Yes, Grinder," I said with a smile I couldn't quite hide.

"Yeah, well . . . somethin' funny happened, all right," McFarlane said, "with Governor Lewis, I mean. I mean, ask me and I'll tell you, Lewis was murdered." He shuffled his feet and lowered his eyes. "Now don't go tellin' Grinder I said that, Mister, uh . . ."

"Hull," I said. "And don't worry, I won't."

" 'Cause he's mean, that fellow. Grinder, I mean."

I gave him a minute, hoping he would calm down just a little. "Think Grinder did it?" I said. "Murdered Lewis, I mean?"

Poor McFarlane flushed dangerously red. "Now I said nothin' like that, mister," he fairly wailed. Then he abruptly turned on his heels and walked off, yelling back over his shoulder, "Nothin' like it, didn't say it," over and over again as he headed toward his house, or as far from me as his feet would take him— whichever came first.

It was the same at the next place, except that farmer, a man called Bakeless, said flatly, "Grinder killed him, sure he did. Wanted his horse, I hear. And his cash. Mean man, that Grinder. Watch out for him."

I nodded agreeably, thanked him and told him I would. Then I rode off a mile or so to a third neighbor's place, and that was where events took a truly unexpected turn.

Alfred Cooper's farm was typical of the area, a ten- or twelve-acre affair nestled on a flat spot among the rugged Tennessee hills—a spot that was littered, as so many of them are, with tree stumps too large and stubborn to uproot. There was a log house about twice the size of the Grinders', though still far from large, a barn, and a separate shed for tools and a plow. For crops, they grew mostly tobacco and cotton, plus some beans and a little corn.

Cooper himself was agreeably middling in size (for a change!) with a flat, friendly face and even a hint of a smile. His wife was a pleasantly plump and dithering woman surrounded by her children—a noisy crew of nine, I think. At first glance, she seemed quite flighty for the frontier, but then it occurred to me that with so many youngsters to help with the chores she simply was not in the state of perpetual exhaustion so common to pioneer wives.

"Cooper's the name," Mr. Cooper said as I rode up, and actually held out his hand, which I shook with pleasure.

"Harrison Hull," I said.

"And these two are neighbors," Cooper said amiably, pointing to two men standing beside him in front of the barn. "They're here for the day to help me put up a new shed."

"John Moore," one said with a wave.

"Frank Moore," said the other.

I assumed they were related, but never did find out for sure.

"And this here's the postman, R. O. Smith," Cooper said, indicating a third man just riding toward us across the field to the north.

"What brings you here, Mr. . . . uh . . ."

"Hull," I said again.

"Hull, yes sir," Cooper said.

He was friendly but to the point. After all, these men had little time to waste. Also, like all farmers, especially out here, he could tell easily enough that I was a visitor to the wilderness.

"I'm on a visit," I said.

"Oh? Family out here?"

"Not really, sir. You see, Meriwether Lewis was a great friend of mine, and . . ."

I paused briefly as I realized they were suddenly staring at me intently. Indeed, I had their undivided attention.

". . . And I'm making inquiries into the circumstances—"

"Of his death," Cooper put in.

"Ask me, he was murdered, sure," one of the Moores added.

"Yep," the other one agreed.

"That's right," Cooper said, "and here's just the man to prove it."

By then, postman Smith had dismounted, walked up to us and handed Cooper a single letter. "All the way from New Jersey," Smith confided. "From your sister, I imagine."

"I imagine, yes," Cooper said with a smile. He fingered the

letter nonchalantly, making no move to open it. "Tell Mr. Hull here about Governor Lewis," Cooper went on.

Smith's eyes opened wide, and he cocked his head as if to say, Yes indeed I will! "That was somethin'," he drawled, then launched happily into his tale; it was plainly a story he'd told with relish many times before:

"I was on my regular route, see, coming up the trace about ten that morning, coming from the east where it's closest to the Grinders, about two hundred yards north. I had nothing for the Grinders, almost never do, and I was riding right by when what do I see but a man lyin' in the road. He looked beat up somethin' awful and his clothes was torn and raggedy.

"I stopped, turned the man over on his back and tried to get him to talk, but he couldn't, on account of he was dead. So I rode into the Grinders—they was closest, of course. And I said, 'Pete, you got a dead man on the road up here.' And he and Betsy looked at each other, and then he come up pretty slow you ask me, and he didn't seem surprised.

"Then, when he got there, Pete says, 'Oh Lord, it's Mr. Lewis,' like now he's surprised. And I said, 'Who?' And he said it was Meriwether Lewis, the great explorer, had stayed the night at his stand, and now here he was dead in the road, and how could this terrible thing have happened.

"Well, then we got the body back to the stand, and Grinder said some friends of his, of the governor's, would be along soon and they would attend to everything. So I just said all right and rode off. And that was it for me, except the next thing I heard was a whole different story coming out about what happened, and it didn't sound like nothin' I saw."

Well, all the way from Maine to New Orleans, if anybody was surprised right then, it was me. I hadn't expected much of anything from this little foray, except to pick up the local gossip and maybe get some idea of who liked the Grinders, if anybody did, and who didn't, which seemed to be just about everybody. And now here was this whole new story to deal with—yet another version of how my friend had died.

"What do you think happened, Mr. Smith, if you don't mind my asking," I said.

He shuffled his feet, lowered his eyes and shook his head. "No, I don't mind . . ." He hesitated again. "Who'd you say you were, mister, don't mind *my* asking?"

I repeated my name and explained I'd been in the army with Lewis and had studied scientific matters with him before he'd gone on his expedition.

Smith nodded and cleared his throat—evidently a signal that he accepted my story. "Well, yeah, what I think, Mr. Hull, is that Grinder shot him for his money and left him for dead, and next thing he knows, his 'body' up and crawls off on him." Smith shook his head again and rubbed his fingers over his eyes. "That Lewis was a helluva man, they say, a strong man. Probably hard to kill. So he crawled off, and I found him. And that's what I think happened."

We chewed over some of the same ground for a while, and then I thanked Smith and the others and rode off, heading back to Grinder's Stand. The short ride seemed to take forever, for my head was spinning, but luckily I arrived in one piece: The Grinders' horse had led the way.

"Astonishing," Wilson said when I told him all I'd heard, saving the best—the postman's account—for last.

I sipped a bit of rum I'd been saving for a special moment— either of celebration or commiseration, whichever came first. Not to be outdone, Wilson pulled out a bit of snuff and took a fat whiff up each nostril. It was the first he'd done since Philadelphia, and predictably enough he started to sneeze. They were loud sneezes, very loud, and he must have been on his twentieth or so when the door creaked open and Betsy Grinder peered in.

Wilson obligingly sneezed again, then in a voice half strangled by an obviously plugged nose, said, "Madam, excuse me, my apologies." Then—what else?—he sneezed again. The woman shook her head and quickly backed out of there.

"Do it again and the militia will be here," I said, trying not to smile. But it made him laugh, and it was another minute or so before the sneezing finally stopped.

"What do you make of it?" I said, and he shook his head.

"Well, presumably the mailman has no reason to lie, so if we accept what he says, then Mrs. Grinder is lying."

"Well, I thought she was lying anyway. But now?"

"I know, Harry, so did I. After all, all those differences from the first version."

"If we can believe Neelly," I put in.

"Of course. But now it's as if she's trying to make herself look bad. I mean, admitting that she let him crawl around helplessly like that all that time. So why is she lying? Is she protecting someone? Or trying to implicate someone?"

"Her husband?" I said.

"Or this . . . Neelly?" he answered, putting a distinctly disdainful emphasis on the name.

"Don't like him much, eh?" I said with a wicked smile.

"Never met the man," Wilson said with a snappish tone. "And you do, I suppose?"

"I'm . . . keeping an open mind," I said, strictly to annoy him.

I swallowed another drop and offered him one, but of course he shook his head. "Vile stuff," he added.

"Well, you can't snuff again, you'll cause an earthquake," I said with a laugh. "They have those around here, you know."

He looked at me askance and said, "That's in Louisiana, you dolt."

I smiled numbly, but then soon enough that one word sent us both into melancholy recollections: Louisiana. It was so tied up with Meriwether. He'd begun his journey there. He'd finished there. He'd been governor there.

"Louisiana," I said, then took one more large swallow of rum, stretched out on the bearskin and fell asleep.

I awoke to angry voices outside the cabin. Dimly in the disappearing evening light I saw Wilson at the door, peering out. I stood and stepped up behind him and saw the Grinders over by the well about thirty yards away, shouting at each other.

By the time I focused on it all, she had slapped him in the face, and he'd replied by knocking her down. When she tried to get up he slapped her hard across the face. She fell back down, and he stood over her as if to hit her again. Instinctively, I started toward him, but Wilson held me back.

"Just wait," he whispered, wisely it turned out. For even Grinder, lout that he was, seemed to realize he'd gone too far. He picked up a tin cup, pumped water in it, knelt down beside her and made sure she took a sip. Then he put the cup on the ground next to her outstretched right hand and walked off, leaving her alone and crying in the dust. For him, I decided, it was a gracious gesture.

Supper was a short time later, but neither Grinder was there. It was a simple meal, even by frontier standards, of smoked pork and hominy, served by the young slave girl, whose name of all things was Esmerelda.

"How long have you been here, child?" Wilson asked. He was an avowed antislavist and, it seemed to me, felt compelled to show kindness to any slave he met. I agreed with him about slavery, of course, and felt it was bound to end in a few years. (After all, I reasoned, the Constitution had banned any new imports of slaves starting two year earlier, in 1808.) But I never liked to bother them with questions, which were at best annoying, I felt, and at worst condescending.

Esmerelda explained with predictable deference that she had been with the Grinders the last three years and before that had been with a family in Kentucky.

Wilson's eyes lit up, and all at once I realized this was not his usual indulgence of sympathy for the downtrodden. "Alexander!" I said sharply, and I knew that he knew precisely what I meant.

But in a rare indulgence of another sort (excessive curiosity) he ignored me and said, "Were you here the night Governor Lewis was here?"

She looked at him for a long moment with confusion in her eyes, then said, "Oh, the man that died. No, massa, no, I weren't here. I was down at the grandma's house, Mrs. Grinder's mama, down by Columbia." And I breathed a sigh of relief that must have been felt in heaven itself. Mercifully, we finished our supper without further interruption of note.

Wilson fell sound asleep almost at once, but I was restless. I dozed fitfully, then about midnight looked up through the tiny rear window and saw a bright, three-quarter moon beaming down. I felt wide awake.

I wrapped myself in my buffalo robe, stepped outside and stretched. The moon bathed everything in its pale white light, and I walked without hesitation to the well, lowered the tin cup and drew it back. The water was cool and sweet, and I drank most of it down in a few large swallows.

I looked around, not discontentedly, turned back to the well, finished the water and was about to lower the cup for a refill when I saw a pale, gowned figure walking toward me. It was Betsy Grinder.

Without a word, she lowered the cup into the deep water, brought it up and drank several swallows of her own.

"Beautiful night," I said.

"Beautiful," she agreed and drank some more.

I smiled as affably as I dared while she looked appreciatively at the skyful of stars. "Did it ever strike you as peculiar," I said after an appropriate silence, choosing my words with great care, "that there were two shots from the governor's cabin that night?"

She smiled back at me in an oddly impersonal way, as if she were negotiating a price with a local peddler for a new tin pot or a sharper knife. "I must talk with you, Mr. Hull," she said in a bland tone of voice, the meaningless smile still all but frozen on her face.

That face, I thought: it's still strong and beautiful. And then there is the moonlight. And yet something, I told myself, is obviously amiss.

"You mean now?" I said, rather idiotically, I suppose.

She nodded, mostly with her eyes, gripped me firmly by the elbow and led me to the barn.

She stopped just inside the wide front door, where the moonlight streamed in, catching her wide eyes just right, giving them a captivating allure. It was as if she knew just where to stop, out of sight of any intruder, yet still in that light. Indeed, I thought, it was as if she had done it just that way many times before.

"What happened that night with Meriwether Lewis?" I asked, my tone cool.

"Hmm," she said, though not at all as a question. Then: "You don't believe it was suicide, eh?"

I briefly closed my eyes, then stared straight at her. "Mrs. Grinder, my friend was murdered, you must know that."

She stared right back at me, then very suddenly threw her arms around me and said, "Mr. Hull, I'm so frightened."

I muffled an understandable gasp of surprise and looked down at her with sympathy. Evidently she mistook it for something else and started kissing me—once on the side of my face, then on the tip of my nose, then on my lips. I let her kiss me; I let her melt into my arms. Slowly, we moved farther inside, out of the moonlight at last. She kept kissing me, and then I kissed her, and slowly we melted down in the darkness, still kissing and beginning to caress in other places.

"Frightened of what?" I said, distancing myself just a little— though not enough to put her off. Instead it was as if I were saying that I needed to rest a moment, get some air—or, in my gentlemanly way, to let her do so.

"What do you *think!*" she answered, her voice suddenly deep with power again.

Very gently I pulled just slightly away. "What are you saying?" I asked, and then she started to cry.

"Of him, of course," she said very softly. "Of my husband; I'm terrified of him." She threw herself into my arms again. "He did it, Mr. Hull. He killed him. He wanted his horse, his fancy pistols, his rifle, whatever cash he had."

She wept loudly; tears cascaded down her face. "I hate him," she said between the sobs. "I fear him."

I put my arms around her and gave her a firm, affectionate hug—or, rather, a hug that was intended to seem that way. I kissed her gently on top of her head and softly on each cheek. Then I pulled her up beside me and, still holding her, slowly, ever so slowly, eased her out of the shadows back into the light.

You see, I wanted to watch her reaction, to see her face, when I said: "You must, a great deal, to do what you're doing—"

She started to interrupt, no doubt with even more emphatic denunciations, but I softly put the first two fingers of my right hand over her lips in a quieting gesture.

"—to falsely accuse him this way," I went on. "To falsely accuse your own husband of murder."

It was, no doubt, the one thing she was not expecting me to say. For, as if something or someone deep inside her had abruptly closed off a faucet, the tears stopped and a hard glaze suddenly formed over her eyes. It was, it seemed to me, all she could do to keep from laughing.

"So many lies," I insisted. "Did you really let a dying man crawl around half the night begging for water? Did he really take his own life with two gunshots? And now you say your husband did it. After everything else, why should I believe *that?*"

She looked up at me again with those bright, brown eyes flickering in the moonlight. They were beautiful eyes, powerful eyes. Irresistible eyes.

Almost.

"Harrison, I . . ." She paused a moment. "He did do it, Harrison. I swear."

But I shook my head and laughed out loud. Not a real laugh, of course, but a forced outburst that sounded like "Hah!" And I said: "Again, I ask you, Mrs. Grinder, what about the two gunshots? You're the one who said it. You told us yesterday, and you told it to Neelly—"

"Neelly!" She fairly spat out the name, but then, recovering herself as always, she stopped. Apparently, she had nothing more to say about him.

"My friend didn't kill himself, I know that now for certain," I went on. "And I know that you're lying. Now it's only why that puzzles me."

She started crying again, and that time for some reason the sobs seemed real. She reached for me again, but I backed away and there on the soft, dusty ground, bathed in that pale moonlight, she fell to her knees and wept.

And then it occurred to me: she wants to get out of this forlorn place and away from her forlorn husband. She wants some brighter, better place—a place back East, perhaps, a genteel city of fine food and handsome clothes and brick houses. Naturally, what woman would not? I asked myself. Indeed, what man?

And just possibly, I thought, she wants me of all people to take her there.

I almost reached out to her again to caress her softly one more time, but I held back. For somehow I knew it would be a mistake. "I can't help you, Mrs. Grinder," I said from a safe distance.

I started to walk off, then turned back one last time. "I'm sorry," I said, and walked away.

I returned to the guest room and slept my fitful sleep; Wilson and I left Grinder's Stand first thing next morning.

"So she was lying about the two gunshots," Wilson said as we rode off. "And about letting him die that way."

"About her husband, too," I said.

"You think so?"

"Yes, certainly," I answered. "About everything."

He slowed his horse to a walk and give me the oddest look, as if to say, You're always so damn cocksure of everything, aren't you?

"What, you don't agree?" I said, slowing up beside him.

"Well, she wasn't lying about hating him, was she, Harry? She really does feel that way about him, don't you think?"

He stared at me a long moment, then without another word suddenly spurred his horse and trotted off, while I just sat there eating his dust and hoping for once that he was all wrong about everything.

We searched Tennessee for Neelly, but as I say he was hard to find. We doubled back to Nashville, where we'd heard he was staying in a rooming house, but had no luck. We checked at his mother's farm just outside the city, but she said she'd had no word of him for months.

So we headed southwest, down along the Natchez Trace through fiercely rugged country of thickets and snakes and swamps and craggy hillsides. A few days out, by the fire one evening, Wilson solemnly handed me a small scrap of paper on which he'd penned a brief poem of farewell to Meriwether Lewis:

> *The anguish that his soul assailed,*
> *The dark despair that round him blew,*
> *No eye, save that of Heaven beheld,*
> *None but unfeeling strangers knew.*
> *Poor reason perished in the storm*
> *And desperation triumphed here!*
>
> *For hence be each accusing thought,*
> *With him my kindred tears shall flow,*
> *Pale Pity consecrate the spot*
> *Where poor lost Lewis now lies low.*

I read it carefully and handed it back to him with a smile. It was, I felt, the best poem—in fact, the only good poem—I'd ever read about our friend. And I thought how sad it was that it took his death to finally get one written.

We rode on through the gloomy country. At one point we saw a mockingbird which, to our everlasting surprise, was singing its own sweetly melancholy song—a rare event indeed, as mockingbirds mostly pick up and imitate the melodies of others. We stopped right there in the trail, listening for several minutes, and I asked myself, Had this bird sung for Meriwether Lewis? For I knew the legend—that the mockingbird's own song was a signal of impending death.

Finally, we reached our destination: the army post at Chickasaw Bluffs, where Neelly had supposedly first met Lewis. Once again there was no trace of him, but we encountered a Captain Gilbert Russell, commander of the little fort at the Bluffs, who had a good deal to say *about* him.

"This Neelly's never even given back his pistols, you know," Russell declared, indignation dripping from every breath. A large-headed fellow with a handsomely full mane of jet-black hair, carefully waxed black mustache, and equally well-groomed silver side whiskers, or "mutton chops," as people are calling them now, Russell was evidently referring to Lewis's missing weapons, two handcrafted guns imported from England. Indeed, they were just the sort of costly finery that Lewis had so frequently preferred.

So *he* has them? I thought with a start. "Neelly has the pistols, eh?" I said smoothly enough.

"His rifle, too," Russell said angrily. "And his horse."

Wilson and I nodded solemnly, and there was a brief pause while Russell offered Madeira all around. I eagerly accepted—I hadn't had a taste of anything like it in weeks—but naturally Wilson politely refused.

"Just how did this Neelly hook up with Governor Lewis in the first place?" Wilson asked; it was the question I'd been dying to ask somebody for a good long while.

"Well, that's just it," Russell said with a smile that was just a little too smug for my taste. Evidently, I thought, he'd been equally eager to answer it. "Neelly acted as though he made the trip especially to watch over Lewis and take care of him after his illness. But that's absurd! Neelly was going to Nashville anyway. He *had* to make the trip! If you ask me, he thought he'd found a mark, a man under the weather who might easily be taken advantage of. Apparently, he was right, at least in some sense. How easy it was . . . well, we can only judge by the results. Lewis is dead, but from what I understand he didn't go without a struggle."

I lowered my eyes in sad agreement, Russell went on awhile longer and then I noticed to my amazed amusement that the full bottle of Madeira was gone: except for my small glass, Russell had drunk it all as we sat there. Drink is one thing, I thought, but isn't this a bit much? And suddenly I felt Russell's opinions suspect about a matter of such importance.

"So where is Neelly now?" Wilson asked blandly. He obviously had not noticed the empty bottle or anything untoward about the captain's condition.

"No idea," Russell replied. Then he looked at me with an affable smile. "More wine?"

"No, no," I said at once. It was an instinctive reaction on my part: I simply didn't want him to open a new bottle, strictly for his own sake. Naturally I should have known better. In a flash, he produced a fresh one from under his desk, cracked the seal and poured himself another glassful.

Wilson remained happily oblivious to it all. Like most non-drinkers, he only noticed it if you pointed it out, much as I always did when I drank in his presence. Otherwise, only a ranting outburst of the so-called typical drunkard would capture his attention. But except for a slight flush around the nose and mouth, Russell looked nearly sober, even to me. Even so, for whatever reason, I had suddenly had enough of the captain's particular brand of hospitality.

"Thank you for your help," I said. And with Wilson caught more by surprise than anyone, I stood to go, and we left the office without another word.

We had done precious little bird-watching on our grueling journey to the Southwest, but that day, just off our campsite outside the fort, we witnessed a sight remarkable mainly as a ghastly reminder of the power of the wild.

"We are presiding at a singular feast," Wilson remarked dryly as we watched in near-stupefied amazement: More than two hundred carrion crows—*Vultur atratus,* or vultures, as Wilson corrected me—were dining on the flesh of a dead and rotting horse. To be exact, Wilson counted 237 of the birds in the immediate area (as well as five or six mangy dogs).

Now for myself, the smell alone was enough to keep me at a distance, but Wilson edged closer and closer until finally I could see him stretch out his feet and touch the hooves of the mostly devoured animal.

Even that close, as he remarked later, he could barely see an inch of exposed horseflesh for the clutter of birds. "I counted thirty-eight vultures on and within him at one time," Wilson said.

After that, for whatever strange reason, his passion was renewed, and as always in such matters I followed his lead. For the next two weeks we camped out under the stars, a refreshing change in a way from the airless, dirt-floor cabins of the Natchez Trace—most no better than Grinder's so-called inn. And we watched, captured and sketched birds.

We saw more than our share of hawks in the area. We got a wonderful look at a pigeon hawk, a small bird no more than ten inches long with dark brown above the tail, white bars on the tail itself and streaks of dark brown on the belly. We saw the so-called sparrow hawk, or small hawk, a stunning bird with a bright red body handsomely crossed with black stripes, a blue head and red crown.

We saw a different sort of woodpecker with a long pearl-white beak—known, not surprisingly, as the ivory-billed woodpecker. We saw a cuckoo drop its eggs in a crow's nest, leaving its hatching and further management to other birds, as cuckoos will do. We even caught sight of a snowbird, or at least that's what Wilson thought it was—though it seemed impossible that we had actually seen one so far south so late in springtime.

Finally, on the thirteenth day of our dalliance the reality of nature's cruelty intruded again: a bald eagle, its eyes cold and fierce and terrible, swooped down from a cloudless sky and clamped its powerful beak around a helpless baby lamb, then swooped off again—all in eerie, deathless silence.

And that was when I think we somehow finally made our decision, for of course that was what we really had been trying to do all along those previous two weeks.

As we'd worked it out, we had three choices: give it up and go home; go back to Tennessee and keep looking for Neelly; or take a new tack, a bold new turn, as Wilson put it, and perhaps even find Neelly in the bargain.

And so we decided: St. Louis was our next destination. That was where our friend had spent most of the final year of his life, and perhaps, we reasoned, that was where his troubles had begun.

So we rode over to Natchez and took passage on the next boat upriver. Three weeks later, we found ourselves playing by a whole new set of rules.

CHAPTER

Four

Though the streets were laid out evenly enough, St. Louis had a ramshackle look: the houses, stores and other buildings were all of logs or crudely formed timbers; even the old Spanish courthouse and fort weren't in much better shape. Indeed, as we found out later, somebody was just starting to build the first house in town made out of brick.

We tried to slip in quietly, but it was hopeless: the place was just too damn small—around fourteen hundred people living in a space about three miles by two.

The first night there, Wilson ran into of all people James Audubon, his famous bird-watching rival, just coming out of the rooming house next door as we were entering our own.

"Audubon," Wilson said archly.

"Wilson," Audubon responded, his tone much the same.

To add to the awkwardness, Audubon was accompanied by two young men Wilson had taught a few years earlier at the

University of Pennsylvania. There were more stiff nods and false smiles all around, and we went our separate ways.

Then, the next day, coming around a corner onto LaGrange Street (formerly Rue de la Grange), I ran into two old friends from my army days, a Lieutenant (now Captain) Nyles Jackson, and a Captain (now Major) Henry Phelps.

"Harry goddamn Hull, you son of a whore," one of them shouted—Jackson, I think.

Though it was hardly eleven in the morning, they both looked a little drunk to me. "Harry, how've you been," Phelps fairly bellowed and gave me a hug. And then I knew they were drunk. Blessedly, Wilson wasn't with me.

"C'mon up, meet everybody," Jackson said. "Lunch is at one. Will Clark's in town, great guy if you've never met him. Have you met him? And the commander of the fort, Colonel Bently— he's all right, I guess."

"And Bates'll be there, the old sourpuss," Phelps put in.

Naturally, they asked me what I was doing there and why, and I told them I was on a scientific expedition with a friend. And of course they asked me who, and of course I told them it was Wilson. And though I managed to beg off for lunch, sure enough by that afternoon we'd received invitations to a party—in our honor, no less—up at Government House inside the old fort.

I was astonished, though only briefly, for I soon recalled how little there was to do in those frontier towns—except drink, of course. And give parties for nobodies who happen to show up out of nowhere and break the monotony.

Not that St. Louis was a dead place; nothing like it. It was busy and bustling enough considering it was still in a way very much in the middle of nowhere, with trading caravans coming and going almost by the hour on busy days, and plenty of sharks and money types jockeying for angles and advantages over the boom times that clearly were on the way.

"Oh my God!" Wilson blurted out (it was nearly a shriek) when the invitations arrived at our rooming house about four o'clock. Part of his distress was that they were for seven that very evening.

I looked over his shoulder red-faced as he stared at the paper. After all, I hadn't even told him of my street-corner encounter— why should I have? And now here were these unexpected missives. As far as Wilson was concerned, they might have come from hell itself.

"Do we absolutely *have* to go?" he wailed.

By then I couldn't help laughing a little. "Alex, for God's sake, it won't be that bad," I said, but my voice carried little conviction.

Naturally enough, we went, and what began to unfold at that party was far more than we expected.

But first, in order to understand what happened to us and what we learned that evening and in the days and weeks ahead, I think this is as good a place as any to break off for just a little while, go back a ways and pick up the story of Meriwether Lewis at a slightly earlier time:

Lewis's return to Washington in 1806 was triumphant—a return befitting a heroic explorer of the unknown who had carved out new trails, named previously undiscovered rivers and charted vast stretches of land. He'd kept a journal that was thousands and thousands of pages long. He brought back hundreds of samples of soil, rocks, plants, and wildlife—including birds, of course. Birds by the score.

And he had made peace with the Indians. He even brought a great chief with him, Big White of the Mandans, along with his wife, Little Tree, and his son, Little Big Deer.

Word of Lewis's return had been circulating for weeks— Lewis and Clark had reached St. Louis in late September and slowly made their way east. Thus, with so much warning, Wilson and I arranged to be part of his official greeting party when he finally arrived in Washington on the twenty-eighth of December.

In a way, much had changed: Meriwether Lewis had left as a friend. He returned a great and famous man.

Jefferson greeted him formally two days later: "The unknown scenes in which you were engaged and the length of time without hearing from you had begun to be felt awfully," the president said, "and I assure you of the joy with which all your friends here receive you."

There was a garden party on the grounds of the President's House right after with tables full of yams and pies made up by several dozen of the more refined ladies of the city. Whiskey and even rum seemed to flow in abundance, though there was none in public view. (Even so, all afternoon not five minutes would go by without somebody or other offering me some. I refused most of it; indeed, if I had taken a tenth of what I could have, I would not have lived out the day.) To my surprise even Lewis himself looked at one point to be a bit tipsy.

The Marine band played, as it usually does at such gatherings. And I overheard Jefferson saying to someone—the French ambassador, I believe—that he thought they were "sounding a bit better these days." I'd heard rumors in the past that their poor playing had annoyed Jefferson no end, and that now, sprinkled among the military men, were professional musicians imported all the way from Italy to improve the band's quality. "*Much* better, yes, Mister President," the ambassador dutifully replied. To me, they had sounded all right before, and they still sounded all right, but then I didn't have Jefferson's musical ear or training.

That night, Wilson and I joined Lewis for an evening at the theater. Among others in the party were Big White and his wife, as well as five braves of the Osage tribe and their wives who had come to Washington by another route.

The onstage antics included a variety of songs, juggling and acrobatics. But it was an exhibition of rope dancing that seemed to interest the Indians most. They evidently thought it hilarious stuff, laughing at many points, though with admiration. One squaw kept calling each trick "Big Medicine," apparently because she felt the dancers must bear great spirits within. And I heard another squaw whisper that because the dancers' contortions were so extraordinary they must have had most of their bones removed as children. Big White himself, I noticed, kept picking and pulling at his cheeks throughout the dancing, and I finally realized that what he was doing was trying very hard *not* to laugh. Apparently he felt that coming from him, as chief, it might be taken as an insult.

At intermission, several in the audience asked Lewis if he could ask the Indians to perform, and at his request the Osage braves dashed onstage in an abbreviated war dance, whooping and hacking at the air with knives and tomahawks. Then they displayed their pipes and declared peaceful intentions. They actually lit the pipes and briefly smoked them. But the most intriguing, even shocking, part, at least by the way the audience reacted, was that two of the peaceful braves were naked except for loincloths.

The festivities culminated at the President's House on January 14 with a lavish banquet for about two hundred invited guests. There were dozens of toasts, none of which seem especially worth remembering. "To the Constitution, the ark of our safety," came one. And "To victory over the wilderness, which is more interesting than that over man." And "May those who explore the desert never be deserted"—a pun of a toast, though not much fun to my way of thinking.

Finally that night the poet Joel Barlow read his new work in Lewis's honor. The sentiments were noble, of course, but the words fell short, in my opinion. The last two stanzas went:

> *From Darien to Davis Strait one garden shall bloom,*
> *Where war's wearied banners are furl'd;*
> *And the far-scenting breeze that wafts its perfume*
> *Shall settle the storms of the world.*

> *Then hear the loud voice of the nation proclaim,*
> *And all ages resound the decree:*
> *Let our Occident stream bear the young hero's name*
> *Who taught him his path to the sea.*

Barlow, you see, wanted to change the name of the River Columbia to the Lewis, but nobody else seemed to think much of the idea, so it was never done. Soon after, however, Congress gave its reward: sixteen hundred acres each to Lewis and William Clark,

320 acres each to all the other men of the expedition, and double pay for everyone.

Not long after that, Jefferson announced his own reward: he appointed Lewis governor of the territory of Upper Louisiana, and Clark, who had arrived in Washington at last after extended delays, to be Lewis's superintendent of Indian affairs.

Jefferson apparently envisioned a considerable delay in Lewis's actually traveling to St. Louis to assume his new post. As a precautionary move, he therefore named as territorial secretary one Frederick Bates, which would turn out to be a fateful decision.

With the hoopla finally winding down, we at last got a chance to spend time in private with our friend. One afternoon in late March he invited us to the President's House, led us to the basement and began to open box after box from his expedition. Wilson was thrilled, of course: they contained what he'd been waiting for—the feathers, claws, beaks, and in some cases entire heads of scores and scores of birds unheard of east of the Mississippi, along with drawings and written descriptions made by Lewis and Clark.

"This is the first new specimen we saw on the trip," Lewis said. "As you can see, it's a large, crowlike bird, but with a very long black and white tail, and it goes *twait, twait, twait* instead of *caw, caw.*"

"A magpie, of course," Wilson answered with a broad smile, and Lewis nodded.

"Next came this one," Lewis went on, as before holding up the feathers and the drawing beside it. The bird had a remarkable rose-colored breast and dark green head and back.

"A type of woodpecker, of course," Wilson said.

"Not quite," Lewis replied with a huge grin. "This is *Lewis's* woodpecker."

We all laughed, but Lewis wasn't finished. "And this," he went on, "is Clark's nutcracker."

"Aaah," Wilson said in some awe, for this was a truly beautiful creature about the size of a robin with patches of white on its tail and wings that stood out strikingly against its black and gray body.

The two of them went on and on together, like small boys,

really, marveling at the discoveries. There was the black-headed jay, the Rocky Mountain jay, the interior varied thrush, the Steller's jay and many, many more. And there was Lewis's story of the travelers making their way for miles through a virtual flood of mysterious white feathers until finally they stumbled on the source: a great flock of molting pelicans.

Finally, in a rare (for him) burst of melodrama, Lewis put his fingers to his lips and literally tiptoed to an unusually large container. He opened it with slow, gasping flourishes and finally revealed what was inside: there were wing feathers glistening black with a white stripe; there was a naked head and neck covered with bright orange-yellow skin; there were strange pale eyes with red irises and sea green pupils, and a vicious, hooked beak: they were the remains of a California condor.

Lewis smiled with immense satisfaction as Wilson knelt down and softly caressed the parts. The bird had been sighted before, but nothing like it had ever been brought back to civilization.

When Wilson looked up and tried to thank him, tears were streaming down his face and he was too overcome to speak. Later, he told me it was the most wonderful day of his life.

Finally, it was time for Wilson to return to Philadelphia. I would not go with him. I had spent all the time and family savings I could learning about birds and helping him with his work. Now, with no other noticeable means of support, I had wangled a post in an army unit stationed down in the swampy flats of this federal city. Remarkably enough I even managed a promotion: I would reenter military service at the rank of captain.

"My dear, dear old friend," Lewis said the day Wilson was to leave at last. He gave the old man a friendly slap on the back, smiled and said farewell again. For him it was a rare outburst of emotion. As for Wilson, I could see him biting his lower lip to hide the sadness he felt.

Oddly enough, Lewis would see Wilson again well before I did, and much more often, for in the year until he left for St. Louis, he would visit Philadelphia four times while I would make the trip just once—and that to the family farm outside town in Bucks County.

I must say, however, that that one journey of mine turned out to have certain fateful overtones, so it's worth mentioning briefly at this point: It had been months since my last visit, and as usual I was accorded the lavish greeting of the prodigal son. My mother, Alice, lovely as always in her cultivated way, welcomed me with her inimitable display of impeccable grace and good manners and a studied once-over with her sharp, knowing eyes.

"Time to settle down, don't you think?" she said quietly as she hugged me hello, her voice revealing nothing but genuine concern.

My father, Morgan, was his usual self—a grand mix of slightly bumptious bluster and vigor that miserably failed to conceal his fundamental kindness. "You look good, boy," he said in his booming way.

Older brother Edward was there, of course, dour and a bit pompous as always. "Hello, Harrison," he said. (He always called me Harrison.)

But mostly I remember my two lovely, laughing little sisters—nearly grown by then, but at times still childlike and giggling, especially, it seemed, around the dinner table.

"You've had a lot of letters, Harry," Ellen, the older of the two, said one evening with a teasingly pouty little grin.

"And they all smell so sweet," Laura, the baby of the family, said with a grand, throaty laugh. "Aren't you ever going to get married, Harry?"

"Oh, of course he is," said Ellen, "and we know who to. Though I can't imagine why, with all the choices he's got."

By that time I was surprised they hadn't both literally died laughing—that was how uproarious they found it all.

"Letitia," they both said at once, drawing out her name in a really grating singsong way.

"Now that will do," our mother said from down the table, but naturally to no avail.

They went on and on with it—so long that I finally descended to their level, and feeling very much like a child again myself picked up a whisk broom and chased them shrieking from the room.

"Not too old to get spanked," I yelled after them, jokingly of course.

In truth I was indeed engaged to a lovely if sometimes chilly woman named Letitia Greenleaf, whom I admired but wasn't sure I really loved; trouble was, I'd been engaged to her for more than four years. And when I visited her two days later at her family's pleasant little house in Philadelphia, she pretty much gave me an ultimatum to, as they say, put up or shut up.

"But I love you, Letitia," I protested, and mooning as I was at that moment into her deep and beautiful blue eyes, I meant it with all my heart. "But these have been busy years, you know that. And there's still time; I'm only thirty-three."

Those beguiling eyes of hers suddenly took on a hard edge as she glared at me from across the front parlor of her father's house.

"A man can say that," she said angrily. "I'm twenty-seven, and I'm *out* of time."

"End of the year, I promise," I said, and again meant every word.

It was right after that that I managed to stop by Wilson's rooms, but he was on his way out to a conference of some sort, and we chatted for exactly five minutes—no more. And then it was back to Bucks County for me and on to Washington soon after, and that was all I saw of him all that year.

As for Lewis, he went there as I say at least four times that I can remember, mostly to sit for a portrait by the artist Charles Willson Peale. But he always met with Wilson and other scientists, as well, and never failed to return with fine new insights in his mind and fine new feelings in his heart for all his old friends. Indeed I felt Lewis was that rare sort who knows it is the proper condition of man to always keep learning anew.

No European capital could have outdone little St. Louis for sheer intrigue at the time Meriwether Lewis finally arrived to begin his new job on March 8, 1808.

More accurately, I should say, to begin his new job in person, for he had technically been governor for a year and had been trying to run the territory by correspondence. This was impossible, of course, and Lewis found Frederick Bates predictably resentful and grown perhaps a little too accustomed to wielding power on his own. Thus Bates had become a reluctant colleague at best.

"I have assumed full charge at last," Lewis wrote to Wilson soon after his arrival. "I know Bates will work with me, though perhaps in spite of himself."

Just why he wrote that to Wilson, of all people, I never understood. But as far as we were able to learn, it was the one and only time he ever expressed even the slightest hint of dissatisfaction with his second-in-command.

Bates, as we shall see, would not be so laconic.

Lewis got right to work. He immediately confirmed the legendary Daniel Boone as a justice of the peace, an appointment that had languished inexplicably on Bates's desk for months. He brought a newspaper to the frontier by arranging financing for the *Missouri Gazette,* which published its first issue just four months later. He moved quickly to outlaw bold stakery, claim jumping and all other forms of illegal preemption of mining claims. He laid out a road from St. Louis to St. Genevieve, Cape Girardeau and New Madrid. He ordered construction of a new watchtower at the fort and arranged for further exploration of the nearby saltpeter caves.

But first and foremost throughout his tenure he worked to calm the rising restlessness among the Indians. Big White still languished in St. Louis because an earlier expedition to take him home to the Mandans had been set upon and nearly destroyed by hostile braves of the Arikara tribe. Ironically, the Arikaras were angry because their own chief, Ankedoucharo, had traveled to Washington two years earlier and never returned. He had died of influenza, but naturally the Arikaras did not understand such a disease and blamed American treachery for his demise.

But in most other cases, Lewis blamed—and rightly so!—the British and the Spaniards for sowing dissension among the Indians themselves and of trying to provoke their hostility toward the Americans. Lewis reported to Secretary of War Henry Dearborn that "British agents are tampering with Indians as far south as Des Moines and three hundred Sauk warriors are assembling to join the

British on the Great Lakes." Soon after, the British were indeed telling hundreds of Indians gathered at Detroit that the Americans were planning to seize all Indian lands and game without paying so much as a bead or blanket in return.

Meanwhile, the Spaniards were building new forts, and the Osage, Pawnee and Kansas tribes were meeting at a council called by the Spaniards on the Great Saline River. "The result of this council cannot be expected to be favorable to the quiet of our frontier," Lewis wrote. "Some measures are therefore necessary for defense."

Lewis clearly understood that the motivating drive behind all this double-dealing was the vast, largely untapped fur trade, particularly beaver, of the great Northwest—still mostly in British hands. He referred to agents of the British-owned North West Company as "unprincipled and hostile in the extreme to our government. Indeed, they are a fit instrument to mar our best arrangements for the happiness of the Indians and the tranquility of the frontier." A bit later, Lewis would gleefully receive word from Jefferson that John Jacob Astor was preparing to carve a slice of the fur trade away from Britain with a million-dollar American enterprise.

Lewis also understood the desperate need for building up the defenses of the long frontier. He asked for and received authorization to recruit as many as two hundred so-called scouts—actually spies—to keep track of the comings and goings of the British, the Spanish and the various Indian tribes. And the intelligence network he created was second to none—providing him time after time with remarkably prompt and accurate information that saved scores, if not hundreds, of lives.

But he faced astonishing amounts of backbiting and intrigue within his own ranks. Bates, of course, soon became openly unfriendly. "Contrary to my first expectations, you must expect to have some enemies," Bates wrote dryly in a note to Lewis shortly after his arrival. By then, Bates was no doubt one of them.

Lewis had been at St. Louis barely six months when Bates told a colleague, "I lament the unpopularity of the governor but he has brought it on himself." Bates's comment had no basis in fact, at least so far as Wilson or I ever could learn. By then, Lewis and Bates were barely on speaking terms, and at one point Lewis called on Bates and suggested they at least remain cordial in public. Bates agreed to his face, but never let up behind his back: soon after he told a friend, "Lewis has fallen from the public esteem and almost into the public contempt. He is well aware of my increasing popularity." Again, this had no relation to reality that Wilson or I were able to discover.

While Lewis was aware of Bates's hostility, he may not have known its source. Interestingly, it turns out that Bates's father had hoped back in 1801 to get the job of secretary to the newly-sworn-in President Jefferson for his son Frederick. "All my dreams are shattered," father wrote son when Jefferson gave the job instead to Meriwether Lewis.

Lewis also faced impossible pettiness from the regular army. One captain, a George Armistead, told Lewis flatly he would do nothing to enforce his orders severely restricting white settlements on Indian lands and that as far as he was concerned whites could settle wherever they pleased.

The army game drifted toward lunacy when at one point a Colonel Thomas Hunt learned that Lewis's Indian agent, James McFarlane, had convinced some Osages to travel to St. Louis for a meeting with the governor. Not only did Hunt do nothing to help, he tried to get other Indians to intercept them at White River, telling them they were free to kill the travelers. Fortunately, the Indians all considered Hunt to be a liar and they were able to contact McFarlane and tell him: "We know that you are going to see Our Father," meaning Lewis, "and we therefore will let you pass."

In the meantime, the angry Arikaras had to be pacified and the Missouri valley reopened. Denied use of the army and possessing only a poorly armed territorial militia, Lewis decided to use mercenaries in a combined commercial and military expedition. He had already signed an exploration-and-settlement contract with the infant Missouri Fur Company, and he now authorized payment of $7,000 for a force of at least one hundred twenty well-armed men, plus provisions and gifts for the Arikaras and other tribes along the way.

Missouri Fur provided additional support, and the eventual force that left in three sections during May and June of 1809 included one hundred sixty riflemen (eighty of whom were Delaware and Shawnee Indians), one hundred ten traders and an additional eighty scouts and militia officers.

The impressive armada would find the Arikaras suddenly meek as mice, and would eventually prove an overall triumph. But it came too late for Meriwether Lewis: too often in the past, he had overruled plans set down by Washington; he had annoyed military officers in the region; he had behaved flippantly toward officials at the War Department; he had failed to communicate his own plans and programs to his superiors with sufficient frequency and promptness.

Quite simply, Lewis had stepped on too many toes. And it didn't help that by that summer of 1809, his mentor, the visionary Jefferson, had retired. Replacing him was Madison, the little man with the famously elegant wife. With him, of course, came a new cabinet, all good Jeffersonian democrats, to be sure, but all men whose most noticeable attribute was patience. For they had all been waiting in the wings a long time for their rewards for years of party loyalty.

Thus, the men of real vision had come and gone. These were all littler men, one way or another, and perhaps littlest of all was the new secretary of war, William Eustis, a bureaucratic professional who despite an American trade embargo, British warships lurking constantly off our shores, and war itself looming painfully on the horizon, had, by the time Wilson and I traveled to St. Louis in the late spring of 1810, reduced the War Department to a dusty little bureau of eight clerks entirely unprepared for anything but the peacetime preoccupation of pinching pennies.

How what happened next happened Wilson and I could not tell right off, though we knew Bates had been writing dissimulating letters to any remotely like-minded person. In any case, by early July of that summer of 1809 rumor swept St. Louis that Washington was severely displeased with the administration of Governor Meriwether Lewis.

Then came the shocker. On a steamy hot day, Lewis received

a letter of his own back in the mail with these words scrawled across it: "The bill mentioned in this letter, having been drawn without authority, cannot be paid." The note was signed by one T. Smith, a government clerk. The bill in question was for $18.70.

"This rejection cannot fail to impress the public unfavorably with respect to me," Lewis told friends. He also worried about other, larger bills which might also be contested, remarking that his private funds were "entirely incompetent" to meet them, should that become necessary.

The $18.70 was for the cost of translating a section of old territorial law from French to English, without which a particular felony trial could not have gone ahead. Lewis indeed lacked specific authority for such an expenditure, however small, but he remarked, "I did not hesitate to cause the copies to be made. I was compelled to do so, or suffer a fellow to escape punishment."

Lewis paid the translator's bill, by then already five months old, out of his own pocket. But there was more to come. On July 18, he received a letter from Eustis himself reminding him somewhat silkily that the government had already advanced him $7,000 for the expedition up the Missouri and therefore would not pay an additional bill of $500 submitted by Lewis to purchase more presents for the Indians. "It has been usual," Eustis wrote,

> to advise the Government of the United States when expenditures to a considerable amount are contemplated in the Territorial Governments. In the instance of accepting the volunteer services for a military expedition to a point and purpose not designated, it is thought the Government might, without injury to the public interests, have been consulted.

Lewis was outraged. He had long since sent the contract with Missouri Fur to Washington, which indeed clearly stated the purpose of the expedition.

What happened then was more suspicious than ever. Mysteriously, everyone seemed to know almost at once about Lewis's setbacks, most particularly his creditors. They descended on him like wolves, demanding immediate payment of thousands, which he did not have. How had this knowledge become so widespread so quickly? Could the fine hand of Frederick Bates be seen once again? Wilson and I would soon be asking ourselves these and many other questions.

Thus was the state of the Territory of Upper Louisiana in the summer of 1809. Thus also was the personal state of Meriwether Lewis. Taken all together, the events forced upon him a decision about which as a man of honor he felt no choice: he would journey to Washington and confront his tormentors directly.

After weeks of frantic preparations, he left St. Louis on the fourth of September, 1809. One month and one week later, while en route to the capital, he died at Grinder's Stand.

C H A P T E R

Five

So let me see, who was there that evening in St. Louis? Jackson and Phelps, of course, though only after a fashion. They'd been "celebrating" my arrival all afternoon, they told me, and by then Jackson was so drunk his attempts at conversation were laughable—his words no more than unintelligible mumbling. Phelps, on the other hand, was pale as a ghost. He'd become ill around four, he said, managed to reach his rooms and passed out till half past six. He awoke, became ill again, but somehow managed to get into uniform and arrive in the nick of time. Even as he spoke, his hands trembled and very suddenly he had to excuse himself for yet another bout. Smiling to myself, I couldn't decide which of them was worse off. I introduced them to Wilson, but they didn't seem to notice. For his part, Wilson, aghast at their condition, barely maintained a sort of standoffish aplomb.

From the ridiculous to the sublime, William Clark was indeed in attendance and greeted us graciously, remembering us (or at least doing a damn good job of acting as if he did) from our days in Washington following Meriwether's return.

Obviously, we remembered him—though we'd met him only briefly once or twice. He was, I thought, a man of absolutely no pretensions who'd impressed me at first and did so again now with his clear and contented sense of himself. Indeed, laughing and chatting amiably beneath his thick headful of light reddish hair (which somehow accentuated his natural affability), he unfailingly put everyone at ease—as men of that sort usually do.

"Terrible about Meriwether, isn't it?" he said, and from the look on his face I knew that he still felt the pain of losing his best friend.

Wilson and I nodded sympathetically, then stood uneasily silent. We were in a sense afraid of the subject, afraid we would let something slip—accidentally give away the real reason we were there. Not to Clark, understand, but to others who might be listening.

"Terrible, yes," I said at last, clearing my throat with obvious awkwardness.

"Yes, yes, terrible," Wilson added.

We all smiled numbly. "So . . . what brings you here?" Clark finally asked.

"Bird-watching," we both said at once, and at that a bit too quickly and loudly. "Birds of this area and to the west," Wilson went on. "So many undocumented, unnamed, undrawn. It will be fascinating work, though there's still so much to do." Naturally it was a subject he could warm to, and I happily let him take the lead for once. "They have to be sighted, then captured or shot. Did you know, sir—but how could you have known—Meriwether showed us his specimens, so many beautiful new specimens. That was back in Washington, of course, before he died, of course—"

And I thought: Oh Christ, control yourself, old man.

"Of course," Clark said, and put a calming hand on his shoulder.

Wilson visibly took a breath. "And I felt—that is, Hull here and I felt—that there must be so many more to search out, and we thought this would be a good time to do it."

Mercifully he stopped himself, and I breathed a quiet sigh of relief.

"Birds, eh?" Clark said very softly and smiled. "Well, good luck to you both, and if you ever need anything—and I mean *any*thing—look me up. I'll help if I can."

He smiled his warming smile as smoothly and lightly as if he'd just complimented us on our choice of table wine, then slid away into the crowd, suddenly beaming at somebody far across the room about something no doubt infinitely simpler. Or was it? I wondered. How in the world could I tell, after the way he'd just handled us? For all I knew he was talking in that same light and graceful manner about some delicate issue of politics and intrigue. And very suddenly I longed for the simple pleasures of a party at the President's House. That, I decided, would be sanguine stuff indeed compared to this Byzantine confection.

"So you're here for science, eh?"

It was a brisk, affable sort of voice, and I happily turned to face it. The face matched it, glowing amiably red around a wide smile and a larger-than-life headful of shiny silver hair.

Phelps, looking surprisingly recovered, was standing next to it. "Captain Hull, Mr. Wilson, this is Colonel Lawrence Bently, commanding officer of Fort St. Louis," Phelps said snappily.

"Yes, science," I said smoothly enough after introductions all around. I was already starting to get a feel for things in this peculiar place.

"Must be birds then, eh?" Bently said. He looked pointedly at Wilson. "I know you, sir. You're famous. Brother of mine subscribed to your book. Brilliant stuff. Wonderful drawings."

"Well . . . uh . . ." Clearly, Wilson hadn't quite got the hang of it yet. ". . . good . . . glad to hear it. We should . . . uh . . . talk. And now of course, with Hull's help, I want to do the same thing for—"

"Birds of the West," Bently said.

And I thought: One of the games out here must be to stay alert enough to finish the other fellow's sentences for him.

"That's right, birds of the West, Colonel," I said. "In fact, I think you just came up with the perfect title for the book, don't you, Alexander?"

Wilson looked around at me, not nonplussed exactly, but not quite ready for it, either. "Why I . . . yes, Harrison, I do believe he has."

Bently smiled, though as far I could tell without the slightest glimmer of intelligence. "Well, call on me anytime, gentlemen," he said. And he walked off triumphantly.

"Ah, the swaggering of imbeciles," Wilson murmured. I winced a little and shook my head, but Phelps fairly exploded with laughter—indeed, much too loud and free a laugh for that place of masks and double-dealings. And sure enough, a moment later, a very tall man with close-cropped brown hair wearing a plain brown suit hovered over us. His skin looked warm and moist, and his small eyes jerked from spot to spot, covering us as if by aiming darts inch by inch over our bodies. His upper lip shifted nervously, one of the stranger things I've seen on a human face, until I realized after a moment that he was smiling, or trying to. The more he did so, the harder he tried, the more he seemed to sweat—beads of it forming in particular on that shifting, twitching upper lip.

"Captain Hull, Mr. Wilson, this is Acting Governor Bates," Phelps said with a distinct gulp of discomfort in his voice.

We shook hands all around, and I felt the clamminess of Bates's skin. I withdrew my hand with a shiver.

"Just wanted to come over, personally welcome you to Upper Louisiana," Bates said, his voice oozing with . . . what? And I suddenly realized that I had no idea. Was it friendship? I wondered. Or suspicion? Or dislike? There was no way of telling for sure.

I did my best to smile; so did Wilson, from what I could see. Bates nodded, smiled in that very peculiar way, turned and, thankfully, walked off. And that time, judging by the faint smiles from Wilson and Phelps as they turned to face me, even I could not quite conceal my feeling of relief.

All in all there were perhaps two hundred people there, and we met at least another couple of dozen: There was a Major Preston of supply and a Captain Thompson of administration.

There was another captain, one John Brahan, who told us breathlessly he wanted to "talk to us when we had time" about "the strange death of Governor Lewis." There was Bates's assistant, David Bradford, and Bently's aide, a Captain Campbell, and innumerable young lieutenants, Bratton and Goodrich and Heney and Randolph, among others.

There were trappers and traders, too, fur men and money men, factors to finance it all and naturally to keep the fattest share of profits for themselves. In particular there was a Britisher named Robert Dickson, a big six-footer of a Scotsman with flaming red hair and a fiery look in his eyes, whom I wasn't sure if I liked or not, but definitely didn't trust. And there was a Frenchman, Georges Charbonneau, a typically ingratiating type whose oily manner impressed me not in the least.

There were also the ladies of the town, relatively few in number and consigned by custom to remain demurely on one side of the room smiling pleasantly and dishing up refreshments. They were mostly wives of the army men and traders, half of them (no doubt the traders' wives) dressed in dowdy homespun, the others in clothes bought from traveling peddlers or, in a few cases, shipped in from the East.

We nodded from a distance at Big White—another one we'd met just briefly back in Washington—*still* languishing in St. Louis after all that time. We saw Lewis's trusted friend, the Indian agent Nicholas Boilvin, who was one person both Wilson and I wanted very much to talk to—eventually. And we spotted Colonel Thomas Hunt, of all people, whom neither of us cared to speak to ever, if we could help it.

It went on and on for three hours or more until finally young Major Phelps (indeed, he was only twenty-seven, the third youngest major in the whole damned army—the brat!) leapt to the little platform at the far end of the room and yelled for everyone's attention. The room was not small, about fifty feet by seventy, and it was no easy task quieting that boisterous crowd, especially on his own—for Jackson had long since babbled his last and disappeared for the evening. But Phelps finally did it and made the customary toast: "Tonight, we bid welcome to an old friend and a new.

Joining us this evening from the great city of Philadelphia, the splendid Harry Hull and his renowned and eminent colleague, Alexander Wilson."

There were the customary "three cheers," and then the party wound down quickly enough. It was, after all, the frontier, and still very much a place of early to bed and early to rise. Ten o'clock was about as late as the night usually went in those parts.

There were no lights for the streets—as I say, St. Louis was still hardly more than a wilderness outpost in those days, and Wilson and I walked slowly and carefully to our rooms ten blocks away. Our boots clomped noisily on the plank sidewalks—where there were sidewalks. And coming up the last block of LaGrange Street, something made me come very suddenly to a stop and made me stop Wilson, as well. Hearing nothing, I nodded at him and we started again, then stopped, then started, until finally I was certain that I *had* heard it—the sound of a third pair of boots clomping on the walkway behind us. I glanced backward and indeed saw a shadow in the moonlight not a hundred feet away.

Our second night here, I realized, and we were already being followed.

"Stay here," I whispered to Wilson, then wheeled around and ran toward the shadow. But the man was just as quick: Before I could reach him, he saw me coming and took off. I stood and watched his mad dash, then turned back to Wilson and escorted him up the street. We reached our rooms in safety a moment later.

"A robber?" he said, as we softly closed the door behind us.

I shrugged. Very possibly it was. But something inside me insisted it was nothing quite so easily understood.

"Can you dine with me tomorrow evening?" said the note delivered with breakfast next morning. It was addressed to us both and was signed, simply, "Bates." But that was enough.

Wilson looked pained, but I told him, "Look, this is what we're here for," in a somewhat snappish tone of voice, then had to apologize.

"No, no, you're right," he said gloomily. "I just didn't think it would be so hard."

He slumped down in the chair by the dining table and picked at his food. When I looked up twenty minutes later, he had left his seat without, it seemed to me, eating anything at all.

We dined in a room on the second floor of Government House inside the old fort on a gentle hill about five blocks inland from the Mississippi River. It was a not unimpressive room with great dark oak beams along the ceiling and well-polished wood on the floor—also oak. And it took me a moment to realize that we were in the same room as the night before, only now we were partitioned snugly in a corner by a five-foot-high portable wall of thin wooden slats neatly trimmed with a carved molding of surprising intricacy.

There were four of us for dinner—Wilson and myself on one side of the table, and Bates and his assistant, David Bradford, on the other. Bradford was an unusually tall (about six foot four), wide-eyed, gloomy young man who did nothing throughout the meal but eat and glare darkly across the table at us each and every time we spoke.

"To a successful quest for, uh . . . birds, is it?" Bates said, his eyes darting and his upper lip almost undulating in that peculiar way. It was as if he had somehow said something unbelievably penetrating and clever. And I thought, What are we supposed to do now? Confess the true purpose of our visit? Beg forgiveness, perhaps, for conducting ourselves in this blatantly obscure and obstructive fashion? Throw ourselves on his mercy and promise never to set foot in Louisiana again?

We raised our glasses, smiled politely and sipped our wine, or at least most of us did; I was amazed to see Wilson let it so much as touch his lips. For myself, I was thrilled: it was a French Médoc from something called the Chateau Haut-Brion that had a silky, dry, almost chalky taste. Indeed, I'd never sampled anything quite like it and was actually uncertain for the first few sips. But by the end of the first glass I was convinced: it was superb.

"To success all around," I said blandly, and sure enough Bates's smile twitched again in that silly way, and he narrowed his eyes as if to say, What do you really mean by that?

"This will be my best book yet," Wilson said with a grand smile. He raised his glass, and I thought; Is he getting into the spirit of the madness at last?

"I should say so," I put in. "These birds out West—they're truly marvelous." And we raised glasses yet another time.

"Ah yes, birds," Bates said with a smile.

And it seemed to me to be almost laughable—how hard he was trying to be sinister.

Dinner itself was simple fare, as we'd expected: well-done roast beef with potatoes and sweet cakes at the end. Then came the brandy, some cheesy, table-quality stuff—a big disappointment after that wine. We hoisted several more toasts: to birds again, and to Louisiana, and to prosperity, and of course to the United States of America.

Bates made most of them, each time looking around, as if he were waiting for someone or something to catch him by surprise. And I thought; What a truly unhappy man he must be, to always be on guard this way.

"You knew poor Lewis, did you not?" Bates asked us suddenly. And it occurred to me that perhaps that was what he'd been waiting for, for some graceful way to bring that up, and he'd been hoping Wilson or I would do it first. Now, as he finally did so himself, his tone was unctuous and his strained emphasis on *poor* seemed plainly intended to annoy us.

Indeed, from the corner of my eye I saw Wilson on the verge of losing control, but I cut him off by repeating, "Yes, poor, poor Lewis," in a tone that mimicked Bates's own.

While obnoxious, Bates was far from stupid; in truth, like so many men of his sort, he was ever on the alert for slights of the tiniest variety.

"I only meant," he said, his eyes darkening and a trace of actual anger creeping into his tone, "that I pitied the poor man his terrible end."

I nodded and looked across the table straight into his eyes. "Of course," I said airily. "What else?"

His mouth opened and closed, but no words came out, and frankly I was amazed to find him so easily outmaneuvered. Then again, I realized, verbal sparring was not his game; he would always be the dunce at that. But by making him feel even the least bit foolish then, I thought, I risked his enmity later. And it would be later, when my back was turned, when I was out of sight—that's when this man would truly be dangerous.

"Governor, we deeply appreciate your feelings of sympathy upon the death of our friend," I said with every bit of sincerity I could muster.

"Yes . . . well . . . a great man," Bates blustered, and I think that for a while anyway he was almost convinced that I'd meant what I said.

"My God, these people are just awful," Wilson complained the moment the door to our rooms was safely closed behind us.

I nodded at him with a kindly smile and thought, What can I say? I agree with him completely. "All the more reason to believe we'll find something out," I said. "We have to be patient awhile, play their game. And it really isn't that hard a game to play, once you know the rules. And those seem simple enough; in fact, there may be only one: Nobody ever believes what you say. Or, to put it the other way round: Everybody always assumes that you're lying. Whether everybody is actually lying is another matter. I haven't quite figured that out yet."

Wilson looked at me with a sad little smile. "Can you imagine, Harry, how out of place Lewis must have felt here, among such people?"

And I must admit I hadn't thought of it in quite that way until that very moment. "God, yes," I said.

After that there were no more words from either of us that evening.

★ ★ ★

It wasn't too loud a knock—it couldn't have been at that hour without waking the whole house; after all, it must have been three in the morning. Instead, it was just loud enough for Wilson and me to hear.

I jumped out of bed, grabbed a pistol, crept to the door and swiftly jerked it open with my left hand. Then, with my right I instantly brought the end of the gun barrel flush to the dead center of the forehead of the man who'd been knocking on my door at so rude an hour.

"Oh no, oh God, please, sir, spare my life," the man stuttered. He was literally quaking in his boots.

"Who in hell are you!" I demanded. I didn't move the pistol a hair, though the man now seemed harmless enough. And then his face began to look vaguely familiar.

"J-J-J-John Brahan, at your service, Captain Hull," the man said. And I realized: He was the one at the party with the breathless story to tell about Lewis's death.

"It's the middle of the night, come back tomorrow," I snarled. I started to close the door in his face, but he actually stuck his foot inside. "Please, Captain, it's urgent," he insisted, then looked back over his shoulder with fear in his eyes. "It's dangerous, Captain Hull," he said in a loud whisper. "Please let me in."

I pushed him back a few inches, just enough so I could peer down the hallway myself. I watched for a long moment, but saw nothing. I listened, too, but didn't hear a sound.

"All right," I said with a shake of my head, then waved him inside. By then, poor Wilson was awake and lighting a lamp or two. "Sit down, Mr. Brahan," I said, pointing to a hard little wooden chair in a far corner of the room.

"Uh . . . that's *Captain* Brahan, sir," he said with excessive politeness. He was a slightly overweight man with a flush to his face (Who wasn't flush-faced out here? I was starting to wonder) and, so far at least, an absurdly ingratiating manner.

"Then you don't have to call me sir, do you?" I said with a smile that was entirely false—and intended to be taken that way. "Never mind the nonsense, what's this all about?" It was

Wilson, suddenly at his growling best. Brahan slid back in the little chair (if that was possible for him) and gulped.

"I . . . I'm sorry about the hour, gentlemen," he said, breathless as ever, "but there are enemies everywhere. Enemies of Lewis. They won't let up. And I have information. I was there in Nashville. I talked to Neelly not three days after it happened. Talked to the Grinders, too. And there are things I know, stories I can tell you."

As he spoke, his flush deepened and his rapid chatter—as I say, never with sufficient breath for him to finish—left a considerable accumulation of saliva at the corners of his mouth. When he finally paused, he wiped his sleeve across his lips, taking with it a nauseating little mound of drooling liquid.

I closed my eyes in disgust. When I opened them a moment later and looked around, I saw Wilson absolutely riveted—apparently by the sheer repulsiveness of it all.

"What things, what stories?" I insisted. I tried to sound snappish, but was just too tired and instead only sounded bored—and exhausted.

"Well . . . it's hard to explain," he said. "If you can join me at my rooms. They're just around the corner. Then I can show you—"

"You mean now?" I grumbled.

"Well, yes, if—"

"Oh don't tell me you're one of these idiots who thinks Lewis was murdered?"

I nearly gasped out loud, but thankfully muffled it just in time. To my everlasting astonishment, it was Wilson in a brilliant tactical stroke.

"Well . . . that is . . . ." Brahan stammered like that for a long moment before finally composing himself. "Why, yes, actually, gentlemen," he managed—and smoothly enough, at that, I must say. "I used to think it was suicide myself, but now . . . well, as I say, if you examine the information I have, you might change your minds—that is, what do you think? I thought . . . er, don't you think he was? Murdered, that is?"

I shook my head slowly and saw Wilson do the same. "Hmph," Wilson snorted.

"The point is that you now think he was murdered, is that it?" I said.

Brahan nodded emphatically. "I do think so now, yes, Mister Hull, Mr., uh . . . Wilson, is it?"

"Wilson, yes."

"And that's *Captain* Hull," I said.

Wilson sighed with seeming exasperation. "Well, that's the first I've heard in a while of such nonsense," he insisted, his tone flawlessly sincere. "And I don't see why you'd want to rake up this ghastly business anyway."

"Indeed," I put in. "The poor man simply lost his mind and took his own life. Tragic but true." As I finished, I shook my head sadly.

Brahan stared from one of us to the other and back again, then reached up his right hand and scratched his head. "Well, I must say, gentlemen, your attitude surprises me," he said. "I mean, if I had a friend, as I understood you did in Lewis, and if everyone was saying that that friend had killed himself—taken the coward's way out and done it so barbarically, at that—and then someone came to me and said he believed otherwise, well, I'd want to hear what the man had to say. And I wouldn't be bothering about the niceties. Time of day, time of night—pesky matters of that sort, if you see what I mean."

I leaned back against the wall nearest the doorway. I still hadn't sat down, still had the gun out ready to fire. "But we are interested, aren't we, Alex?" I said with a polite smile. Wilson nodded dutifully. "We want to hear you out, old man. So go ahead, tell us. Surely you can give us some idea of your thoughts without having to have your 'information,' as you call it—papers, documents, whatever it is—right here in front of you."

Brahan took a long, wheezing breath, and I had the distinct feeling he was about to unburden himself at length once again. "It's a matter of, um . . . what you might call discrepancies," he said. "As I say, I talked to Neelly and the Grinders and, well, some of what they say doesn't match up."

▲
63
▼

Wilson looked pointedly at Brahan, then at me, then back to Brahan again. "What in the world do you mean?" Wilson demanded. "Match up with what, for God's sake?"

"Well . . . with what they said before, with what they told each other, I suppose." He stopped, took a breath and suddenly began in that rapid-fire way again. "Now you see, that's just it, without the information, as you say, the papers, the notes, right in front of me, it's hard to remember it all. That's why it's best to do it there, where I can refer to the notes I made."

I glanced quickly at Wilson, who nodded with a slight smile. "You, uh . . . you made notes, Captain Brahan?" I said.

"Oh yes, sir—that is, Captain. Piles of them, all in a mess. That's why they're hard to carry. If I brought them here, I'd misplace half what I want to show you, and it would take me hours to find the right pages again."

He babbled on, ever so cleverly trying to get me to go with him at that unseemly hour. And I could only imagine what treachery lay in wait, around the corner or down some alleyway or maybe not until we were well inside his rooms, wherever they really were.

"Enough, Harry, it's late and I'm tired," Wilson suddenly snapped, and at once I said: "It's late and Mister Wilson's tired, so you'll have to go, Brahan." Indeed, my own voice sounded utterly exhausted and without so much as a shred of politeness—or the niceties, as Brahan had called them—remaining in my tone.

Only very slowly did the large captain raise himself from the little chair, and it was all I could do to keep from brandishing the pistol in his face again.

Lumbering across the room, he finally neared the door, and I managed, "Perhaps we can talk of this again," with just the world-weary tone I'd hoped for.

And then at last he was gone, and Wilson and I were so tired we actually went to sleep at once without exchanging a single word about our extraordinary night visitor.

C H A P T E R

Six

Wilson and I had precisely the same thought when we woke up at the proper hour that morning—that we were lucky to be alive. Also, we were both amazed and amused at how tired we'd been.

"I can't believe we went back to sleep," I said, and Wilson nodded with an agreeable laugh.

"And I can't believe marauders of some sort didn't come blazing in here right after Brahan left," Wilson said.

I looked at him with an admiring smile. "You were brilliant, Alex. I mean the bit about him being 'one of these idiots' who thinks Lewis was murdered." I paused, laughed out loud and nodded, letting him bask for a while in the glow of my compliment. "Brahan obviously went back to whoever he was going back to and told them what you said. And that's what did it; that confused them. What you said, Alex—that's what saved our lives."

"And now—"

"And now we're in danger; yes, I know. And the fact that whoever's behind this was on to us so quickly is very frightening.

And there's also no doubt that they'll pursue the matter; they won't just go away. They'll keep on us, all right—no doubt about it.

"But we also have a golden opportunity. *They're* confused now; *they're* off guard. And we're the ones who can pretend to be what we're not; it's perfect for this place, these people."

"So . . . we're two scientists on a bird-watching expedition," Wilson put in, "who just happen to have been friends with Meriwether Lewis and just happen to have turned up in St. Louis a few months after his death. Is that the idea?"

"Well, obviously they don't believe that, or at least they didn't. But now . . . well, now they won't know what to believe. I tell you, Alex, we can drive them crazy just puzzling over it, and all the while we can find out everything."

Wilson cocked his head and looked at me through narrowed eyes.

"Well, maybe not everything, but a lot, and much more easily than we could have before. I tell you, we have nothing to worry about, it's fine, it's perfect, it's—"

Bam! Bam! Bam! came a sudden pounding on the door, and for an instant I literally felt as though my heart would jump out of my body. I grabbed the pistol, stepped swiftly across the room and shouted, "Who goes there!" in an angry voice.

There was a response, but much too faint to make out, so I yelled, "Who, goddammit!" Then I yanked the door open, and fairly leapt into the corridor, pistol in hand.

"Oh please, no sir, don't kill me," came the timid voice of a young girl. It was, to my everlasting embarrassment, the landlady's younger daughter with our breakfast tray.

"Oh God, oh please," she wailed, bobbling the tray, nearly dropping it, in fact.

I helped her inside, all the while apologizing profusely. "It's all right, child, it's all right," Wilson chimed in, and it seemed to help a little. She set the tray down on the table and fussed about with plates and tableware, though still eyeing me fearfully. It was another long minute before I realized that I was still holding the gun in my right hand.

I put it away, and she calmed down a little more. By the time she left she was nearly herself again, though mostly, I thought, because I gave her one of our Spanish doubloons as a tip.

"Everything still so perfect, Captain Hull?" Wilson suddenly asked.

I stopped in my tracks and looked around at him, shocked. For Wilson was a man who abhorred sarcasm of that sort and invariably spoke in words that, if nothing else, were straightforward and direct. Thus for him this indulgence in innuendo was rare indeed. And I thought: This place is beginning to get to him, isn't it?

"The breakfast's not perfect, either," I said with a smile as we settled down to eat: it was a huge concoction of fried eggs, potatoes, salt pork and hominy. "It's too big and too salty," I said.

Wilson nodded over a mouthful of food, and I realized that suddenly he was eating again. In fact, he was eating everything in sight. "Salt's good for you," he said, still chewing as he spoke. "Strengthens the arteries—you know that."

"I'm not so sure," I said, like him, talking with my mouth full—something I avoided as a rule. "Besides, I just don't like the taste. Makes me thirsty."

"Everything makes you thirsty," he said with a terse little smile.

And I thought: Ah-hah, yet another little jab.

"You're very amusing this morning," I said and took a bite of pork, then stuffed a spoonful of eggs in my mouth right after. I smiled across the table at him, but was shocked at the rapid change in his demeanor. Abruptly, he stopped eating and looked quite pale. "Am I?" he said, genuine surprise showing on his face. "Sorry, Harry, didn't mean to be." Then he slowly got up from his chair, walked the few steps back to bed and crawled under the covers.

And I thought, I'm the one who should be sorry. "Didn't mean to upset you, Alexander," I said, but he just shook his head.

"You all right?" I asked, and he shook his head again and stared off thoughtfully.

"Sorry, Harry," he said after a long pause. "Just this place, I suppose. Too much for me. Tires me out."

I felt like telling him, Goddammit, stop apologizing! But all I said instead was, "Tires me out, too."

He closed his eyes, but I could tell by his breathing he was still wide awake. I slid my chair away from the breakfast table; suddenly, I wasn't hungry anymore, either. Maybe this is too hard, after all, I thought. Maybe we're taking on too much for an ailing old bird-watcher and an army captain doing his second hitch.

I heard a faint rustling noise, looked around and saw a note being slid under the door. Do I care what it says? I asked myself. Does it matter if I ever find out? Will any of this in any case bring our friend back to life?

Slowly, very slowly, feeling like an old man myself all of a sudden, I stood, walked over, bent down and picked up the paper. It was an invitation to another party at Government House that evening.

"You go, Harry, I just want to sleep awhile," Wilson said, before I'd even told him what it was.

"How—" I let that much slip out, but no more. He'd just guessed, that's all, that's how he figured it out. It was the sort of good guess, I decided, that a tired man can make sometimes, the sort of guess that comes along to hit the bull's-eye just when everything else seems to be going dead wrong.

I started to say: But, Alex, it's not till tonight. And: But Alex, you should be there with me. I started to say those things and a few others that I can remember, but none of them were worth much, even then. So I just kept quiet.

I'll just let him sleep, I finally decided. And that's what I did, and that's what he did, all that day and all that evening. And all because I had pointed something out that could so easily have been left unsaid altogether.

This party was exactly the same as the first: the place, the people, the drinks, the attitudes.

Except for one man who had not been there last time. His name was James Wilkinson, and he'd had, in a sense, an illustrious career: he'd been territorial governor at this very place just before

Meriwether, and everyone there that evening still called him that. "Evening, Governor." "Governor! Good to see you." "You look wonderful, Governor." If I heard those greetings once, I heard them a dozen times each that night, exploding mirthfully across that dark wooden room at Government House inside old Fort St. Louis.

Before that, Wilkinson had been general. Not *a* general, mind you, *the* general—in truth, commanding general of the entire Army of the United States (such as it was at the time—at just 3,500 men, a mere flyspeck of a military force).

And I heard that title as well that evening. In fact, "General" seemed to please him much more than the other one, seemed to make his eyes really light up.

So how did I describe him? Oh yes: as a man with an illustrious career—*in a sense*. For somehow there had always been ugly side issues—rumors that kept coming up, rumors that for years now just wouldn't go away.

Understand, these weren't silly rumors about dalliances or drink or even dumbness. These were dark reports of conspiracies and plots, of lies and deception. Tales, in other words, about the fundamentals of life—especially public life. About serving as general of the Army of the United States and as governor of this place called Upper Louisiana, a territory so vast it nearly equaled the whole of Europe for sheer breadth of acreage.

And come to think of it, it was little wonder that he preferred "General" to "Governor." For James Wilkinson was not a well-liked man and his appointment to the latter post, by none other than old Tom Jefferson himself, had been extremely unpopular. In fact, Jefferson finally had had to remove him from that more recent of his federal offices.

And now here he is, I thought, in this Government House party room, the personal guest for the evening of no less than Acting Governor Bates himself.

And now I was almost up to him in that damned reception line. For yes, there was a reception line that night—a nicety which had been dispensed with the other evening for a couple of nobodies like Wilson and me. And moving slowly up the line, I took a moment to study him: Wilkinson was a round-faced, clean-shaven man of pleasant enough features, a faint smile and no particular irregularities of facial expression (no warts or tics or undulating upper lips). His only really distinctive mark was a pair of magnificently bushy gray-black eyebrows.

"Good evening, General," I said snappily. "Harrison Hull, Captain, U.S. Army, at your service."

"Hull . . . Hull . . . O-o-o-o-h yes . . ."

"And apologies, sir, from my colleague, Alexander Wilson. Mister Wilson is indisposed this evening and deeply regrets being unable to attend."

"Wilson! Birds! Of course! Heard about you and your friend. Saw his book once at a colleague's house. Wonderful work. My best to him for a speedy recovery, and best of luck to you both in your new endeavor."

Smooth as silk, I thought, as I thanked him and wandered off. And then I thought, Now what? I feel like getting stinking, that's what. But I was worried about Wilson, and besides—that's right! I'd caught a glimpse of that idiot Brahan earlier, and he seemed especially anxious to avoid me. Finding him might be amusing, I told myself, and I might even learn a thing or two.

I carefully looked over the room section by section, didn't see him, then began looking again, this time starting on the opposite side and, as before, moving my gaze around part by part, until . . . ah yes, there he was, over by the whiskey barrel—surprise, surprise!

I hustled over, moving quickly so that I could be casually standing right there when, glass filled, he turned around to face the room again.

"Brahan, old friend," I said with loud joviality, and he nearly lost the swallow of liquor that was already in his mouth.

"Uh . . ."

"Hull," I said. "Harry Hull. Saw you here the other night. You wanted to talk to me, remember?"

"Oh yes, I, uh . . . Did I? I'd had a few, of course. Not sure I recall . . ."

Smiling, I leaned close to him and said in a very quiet but

adamant tone, "Surely you remember, Brahan? Or do you want me to remind you right here and now, right in front of everybody?"

He looked at me through wide, startled eyes. "Oh yes, Hull, I remember you," he said, his tone suddenly imitating the forced politeness of my own. "But really, now is not the time. Perhaps—"

"We can talk now," I said, as before my voice soft but menacing, and told him with my eyes to walk ahead of me. I eased him out a side door onto the open balcony that ran the length of the room. Down the sloping hill, we could see the few flickering lights of the little town and beyond that, reflecting in the moonlight, the shimmering black waters of the Mississippi.

"You treated me like a fool the other night," Brahan complained the moment we seemed to be out of earshot. "I risked my life to bring you important information about your friend, and you sent me off like a . . . like a . . ."

"Lost puppy?"

He did his best to put real anger into those plump, florid features. "Go ahead, mock me, but I know what I know," he said. "I tried to tell you the other night, but you wouldn't have it."

"So?"

"So . . . that's the end of it. I wouldn't tell you a thing now, no matter what. I'll . . . go elsewhere with my story. To the army. To the courts. To the president, if I have to."

"All the way to Washington, eh?"

"Yes, if it's needed. You see, I'm prepared to do that—to do what's needed to bring out the facts of this situation. And by that I mean *whatever* is needed, unlike certain others I could name. It seems, Captain Hull, that I didn't know Lewis so well as you, but I knew him better." He stood there a moment shaking his head, wheezing indignation with every breathless word. "So if that is all, sir, if you don't mind—"

"Who's paying you, Brahan?" I cut in. "Who's behind this charade?"

He jerked his head forward and opened and closed his mouth. "Sir!" he said. "That question is—"

"Insulting?" It was childish, I know, but I somehow couldn't resist finishing his question for him one more time.

"More than that, it's—"

"Whatever it is—that is to say, whatever they're paying you, I'll double it," I said. It was of course a reckless remark, for not only did I have no intention of fulfilling such a pledge, I had no money with which to do it.

In any case, that finally got his attention. He stopped and stared at me, for the first time with real curiosity in his eyes. "I don't . . . it's absurd. Paying me? Why would anyone do that?"

I smiled at last—once again I couldn't help it. It was, after all, very funny, don't you think?

"Well, I suppose for one of two things," I said. "Either for the truth you know, or the lies you can tell. Which is it in your case, Brahan? What truth is there, really, in those documents you say you have? Or what lies are there deep inside yourself?"

I stared at him—we stared at each other, really—for a long long time. Long enough, anyway, for a light or two to flicker out on the hillside below and the moon to grow a tiny bit brighter and whiter on that spring evening at the edge of America.

"Good evening to you, sir," Brahan said at last, then tugged briefly on his army coat, straightened himself with a slight flourish and walked off the balcony, through the side doorway and into the deadening party beyond.

"You think you are right about him?"

I wheeled around in surprise at the voice suddenly emerging from the shadows. It was a deep voice, solemn—dignified even.

"Right about . . . who?" I said, startled, but still managing a disingenuous touch.

"Foolish question," the voice said at once. "Insulting question."

"Oh?" I said. "And just who in hell . . ."

And then a form emerged slowly from the darkness, the form that went with the voice, and I was nothing less than astonished to see that unmistakable figure: the dark, penetrating eyes, the prominent nose, the deep brown skin, the erect bearing:

It was the Mandan Indian chief, Big White.

"Good evening, sir," I said, my politeness entirely sincere for once in that place. "My apologies for being abrupt, sir, but I didn't realize—"

"Do not worry, Captain Hull," he said with his usual graciousness, which I knew of mainly by reputation—I was frankly amazed that he remembered my name.

"Thank you, sir," I said.

And if, as you may already believe, I was being a tad obsequious to Big White, I suppose it was because I had lately encountered so many dreadful people and behaved so badly myself that I was truly thrilled to meet someone entirely outside that nonsense and glad to show him all the respect I could.

"Interesting conversation you had with that man, Hull," Big White said. "Sorry to . . . what is the word? Well, sorry I overheard—"

"Eavesdrop?" I put in.

"Yes, that's it. Anyway, sorry to eavesdrop. None of my concern, really. I just thought . . . Well, no matter."

"You thought I was . . . harsh with him?"

"Yes, a little, perhaps."

I shook my head sadly. "I should have done worse," I said in a raspy whisper, then found myself surprised at my own vehemence and a little ashamed.

"I apologize again, sir," I said. "But that man . . . I don't trust him."

Big White nodded, as if considering what I said, then turned to go.

And I suddenly wondered: Where *does* he go, what does he do with himself after languishing here so long while the government tries to figure out a way to return him safely to his people through hostile tribes?

At first he'd been at little Bellefontaine a few miles outside the city; then, tiring of that after a few months, he'd insisted on taking up residence here in town, in fact, right here inside the fort at government expense—from what I'd heard, to the considerable annoyance of Bates and his cronies.

As an honored guest, and strictly speaking royalty at that, he was of course invited to all the parties and functions, but since, like most Indians, he didn't drink, he was known for lurking about in stately, though lonely fashion (much as I'd just encountered him), contemplating on his own, I suppose, the follies of the white man.

"We . . . we should smoke the pipe sometime," I said, calling after him, suddenly not wanting him to leave. He was, after all, the first genuine person I'd met at St. Louis.

"Sometime," he said in that laconic, unsmiling way.

And then he turned away and seemed to melt almost ghost-like into the darkness.

CHAPTER

Seven

Wilson was feverish when I returned.

I touched his forehead and stood over him a moment, angry at myself for leaving him. Goddamn it! I thought, and sent for the doctor at once.

"Keep him warm, keep him in bed, keep the shutters closed and give him a spoonful of this every four hours," the doctor said matter-of-factly, handing me a little jug of some foul-smelling stuff—a sort of herbal mix, I think.

He turned to leave, and I followed him into the hallway. "What's wrong with him, Doctor?" I said, once we were out of earshot.

Understand, I wasn't necessarily expecting much of an answer; mainly, I was troubled over his apparent lack of interest in my friend's condition and simply felt like annoying him a little. So I was quite surprised when he turned and faced me with what appeared to be a genuinely thoughtful look in his eyes.

"Touch of melancholia, nothing more," he said, "or it should be nothing more." He paused and seemed to study me a moment. "You're new out here, is that right?" he asked, and I nodded.

"Well . . . maybe it's just the sickness people get sometimes when they're in a new place away from home. But with him . . . I don't know. Is something bothering him? Because he seems . . . resigned, I suppose you could say. Not much fight in him. And that frightens me a little because I've seen that before and . . . well, it's always important that the patient want to get well. You understand, don't you, Mr., uh . . . ?"

I was amazed enough that I just stood there open-mouthed a moment, and finally he turned and walked off without waiting to hear my name one more time.

I stepped back into the room and watched Wilson hot and exhausted beneath a pile of bedcovers.

"Get well, old friend," I whispered, but he just lay there, seemingly far out of reach of my good wishes.

They found Brahan's body late next afternoon. It was suicide, they said; he'd hanged himself. And they showed the hangman's noose to anyone who cared to come by and see it at Brahan's rooms on the old Rue de l'Eglise—what everybody by then was calling Church Street. As it turned out, the rooms really were right around the corner from where Wilson and I were staying.

They also found about thirty dollars in the room, mostly in Spanish coins, clothing and the usual personal effects, including two of those new renderings of human heads called silhouettes— one that looked to be of a young girl, the other of a grown woman.

There was a tablet of writing paper, blank, except for the words, "My dear wife," written in the upper left-hand corner of the top page.

And, oh yes, in case I hadn't mentioned it, the body was still there. For of course how could there be such a spectacle without it?

Hanging was the cause of death, all right—no doubt about it: there were rope marks still fresh around the neck, the eyes nearly out of their sockets, the tongue far back in the throat, and the stink of the man's final earthly discharge. A chair, tipped on its side, lay nearby.

What there wasn't was the slightest sign of any papers or notes of any sort. Nor had there been, I was told.

"Saw nothin' like that here, no sir," said a little man in a dirty brown coat with a crude little badge that said "Town Marshal" on it. His name, as best I could understand it over a faceful of chewing tobacco, was Clovis. It was the only name I ever heard him use, and I never even knew for certain if it was his first name or his last.

"Have you notified the army?" I asked him, and he nodded slowly.

"What'd they say?" I said. "What'd they do?"

"Huh?" He stared at me numbly for a moment. Then: "Oh. Well . . . nothin' yet. Sent word up there couple hours ago. Haven't heard back."

I stared at the ceiling where the rope was still looped through a crossbeam. I started to use the tipped-over chair to get a better look, then thought better of it and took a stool from beside the dining table, instead. I got up on it and examined how the rope was rigged: the hole in the beam where it went through was freshly cut.

"Any mechanic's tools here?" I said, stepping down from the chair.

"Huh?"

"A hammer, saw, chisel. Anything that might have made that hole?" I pointed up at the beam.

The marshal gazed upward. "Nope. Nothin'. Just the captain's knife, I guess."

Brahan's knife was still on him, neatly sheathed and strapped to his belt. It was easy to get to without disturbing the body, so I carefully untied the leather lacing and pulled it out. It looked to me to be dull and seldom used, hardly much good for whittling, let alone for gouging through the heavy wood of a crossbeam.

I looked around on the floor near the stool and the body. Where were the wood shavings? I suddenly wondered. Would Brahan really have swept up so neatly before finishing this ugly business? And for that matter, if he did so, where was the broom?

Just like the shavings, just like those now famous papers of his, there was no sign of it anywhere.

"If the army ever comes, tell them Captain Hull was here," I said to the man called Marshal Clovis. There was more than a little ferocity in my tone.

"Hall?" he said.

"Hull," I said, but not so he could hear me, for by then I was well down the corridor, and I knew in any case that I'd told him my name in the first place only out of anger and that maybe it was just as well if he forgot about me altogether.

To my considerable surprise and enormous pleasure, Wilson was sitting up in bed and even spooning hot soup into his mouth when I returned.

"I'm fine now," he said crisply. "I'll be all right."

He still looked deathly pale to me, but of course I smiled and said, "That's wonderful, Alex. You seem much better."

I wondered if he could stand the news about Brahan just yet, so I decided to put that off, at least till later that evening.

And then, almost nonchalantly between spoonfuls, he asked, "What happened, Harry? Landlady says Brahan's dead. Is that right?"

And I thought, Oh God, he knows that much and now what else can I do but tell him the rest?

"Yes, that's true," I answered, trying to put a kind of businesslike crispness into my own tone of voice. And then of course I made the mistake of holding back, and I knew it was a mistake because I knew precisely what his next question would be.

"How'd it happen, how'd he die?" Wilson asked, and I swallowed hard trying to sound as casual as I could about it.

"Suicide," I said. "Hanged himself. At least that's what they say."

And just as I knew he would, Wilson tried to keep up the pretense a moment or so, still briskly eating soup as if I had just told him nothing more vital than a guess at tomorrow's weather.

But soon enough an unmistakable sadness crept slowly into

his eyes and his eating tapered off until he wasn't eating at all anymore. And then he asked me if I would please take the tray away because he suddenly felt very tired and wanted to rest.

Nicholas Boilvin would only meet me at Lacey's, a falling-down pit of a place that the locals called a tavern but which I thought nothing more than a ramshackle room full of hard wooden benches and crudely cut tables. At the far end was a large closet from which the keeper dispensed whiskey by the shot or bottle, depending on your means, and ladled out mugfuls of flat, warm ale or mead.

"Ale," Boilvin called out as we took our seats.

"Two," I said, holding up the first two fingers of my right hand.

"Nobody comes here," Boilvin said with a wink, "who knows anything. Nobody who counts." In other words, he was saying, don't worry about being here with me because nobody who matters will see us.

Looking around the room, I could only agree with him. The dozen or so other habitués appeared to be an odd assortment: a farmer or two, a couple of drunks, a peddler, a few mechanics with their tools, and several bargemen and other riverboat types.

Suddenly, the innkeeper was there with our ales. He put down one mug in front of Boilvin and two in front of me. He had taken my signal the wrong way.

"No, no—" Boilvin started to say, but I held up my hand in a quieting gesture.

"Quite all right, barman," I said and handed him another of my dwindling supply of doubloons. The proprietor smiled gratefully, as I expected he would. It was, after all, more than enough by a long ways to cover the cost of three ales.

"Shouldn't spoil them that way," Boilvin said with a smile, "but thanks anyway." He raised his mug with a toast of good cheer, and I did likewise.

★   ★   ★

Nicholas Boilvin was a not quite gangly man—lanky was the better word for him—of pale complexion (a refreshing change from the typical flush of these parts, though he could certainly drink his share when the occasion arose) and features which, though not disagreeable, could certainly be termed odd when at rest: a high forehead, prominent nose, smallish mouth and chin that gave his face an unusually elongated appearance.

It was when he spoke, however, that he captured your attention in a decidedly agreeable way. His eyes, blue and very clear, came brightly to life, and he talked with an intensity that was quietly comfortable to listen to. He had been, as I've mentioned before, one of Meriwether Lewis's most trusted colleagues.

"So birds are what you're here for, eh, Hull?" he said in a voice that I could fairly describe as skeptical.

I smiled and took a swallow of ale. "Well, yes, that's true. Uh, why? Is it so hard to believe?"

"No, no, not at all," he said, his tone now completely convinced. "If you say it's birds, then it's birds, sir."

I cocked my head, let a faint smile play upon my lips and stared at him almost literally eyeball to eyeball. After a long moment, he turned away and laughed out loud.

"Why . . . what . . . ?" I asked, laughing a little myself.

He shook his head, still chuckling. "It's just that you don't seem like the bird types, you and your friend. He looks more like a minister, you ask me. Presbyterian, probably. And you . . . Well, you look like what you are, a young army officer out for fame and adventure."

"Oh really," I said, smiling broadly. I thought it over a moment. "But Wilson's already famous," I protested, "the most famous bird-watcher in America."

"Yes, but you're not," Boilvin shot back in that deadly serious way of his.

"No, but I've studied with him for years," I came right back smoothly enough, "and I can name you all of them, everything from *Motacilla sialis* to *Fringilla tristis* and a lot in between."

Boilvin abruptly looked at me with a whole new wide-eyed

expression of respect. "Well, as you say, Mr. Hull, it's birds you're here for."

I gave him a triumphant nod, leaned back quietly in my seat and thought: My little show has taken him in completely. It was easy enough to do, of course; fooling the ignorant almost always is. Indeed, if I had used the commonplace English names, bluebird and goldfinch, the usually savvy Boilvin surely would not have raised a whisker. But my display had been so dazzling that he had apparently forgotten entirely my insistence on meeting him in private.

"Then why insist on meeting me in private?" Boilvin said at that very instant, and from his easy tone I couldn't even tell for certain if he had ever been fooled at all.

I sighed, wearily I think, and briefly closed my eyes. When I opened them I looked around to see him staring at me quizzically.

"I'm not here for birds, Mr. Boilvin," I said.

"I know, Mr. Hull," he said.

"Does everyone?" I said.

He smiled and turned slightly pink around the ears. "I overstate, Mr. Hull. I don't *know*, or at least I didn't until you just said that. But I figured as much; I guessed. And that's what they're all doing: fairly busting their brains trying to figure out what you're up to.

"And I congratulate you on that much. You have them guessing, all right. And that's good. They're a ruthless bunch, so they'll come after you once they get it right. But they're not stupid, either, and they don't dare act on guesses, so they won't do anything till they *know*. But then, like I say, watch out."

Boilvin lit up some tobacco in a crude bowl and stem he'd obviously carved for himself. I sipped my ale and wondered how much he really knew.

"So . . . what do you think about Meriwether's death?" I asked, and to my surprise he stared off almost wistfully.

"I knew him very well, sir. He had his quirks, like everybody, I suppose. I mean, the way he loved to dress in those fine suits of his. And those beautiful pistols he had, and that saddle. But he was hard as nails underneath: he led that expedition to the ocean and back, and everyone on it that I ever met worshipped him like a father. Even that one man—that George Sibley, who he flogged for desertion—I met Sibley once and he cried when he talked about how much he loved Meriwether Lewis.

"He was a fighter, Captain Hull. He never lay down to anything or anybody. And if politics wasn't his strong point, well, so be it. And now you ask me what I think about how he died, and I can only tell you that I know in my heart he couldn't have taken his own life. Not then, not ever, not in a million years."

There was an awkward silence while I let his words settle in the tepid air of that rank little room.

"So then he was murdered," I said quietly.

"Well now, I'm not saying—"

"Boilvin, please!" I growled. "Spare me the twists and turns so common to this place. The man died of two gunshots, and if Lewis didn't fire the weapons himself, somebody else did." I took a deep breath and glared at him. "Isn't that right?"

He looked at me with that same wide-eyed expression again, and I asked myself, Is it genuine this time?

"Yes," he said slowly, "that's right."

"So?" I said, being intentionally cryptic.

"So? So what?"

I looked straight into his eyes for a long moment. "So why is everyone here so frightened of what Wilson and I are doing? Are they afraid we'll find something out? Or have we already answered that question?"

He had no reply worth repeating. Only vague, circular ramblings that floated in some undetermined place between dumbness and dissimulation. Also, I felt there were traces of real fear showing up in those otherwise cool blue eyes.

But I kept him there a while longer because there was one other matter on my mind.

"Did you know Brahan?" I asked him after another mug or two and a shot of whiskey besides.

"I'd met him, yes," he said. "Too bad about him."

"Mmm, yes, too bad," I muttered. I was slowly becoming disenchanted with Boilvin, but then almost everybody out here seemed to have that effect on me sooner or later, didn't they?

"He came to see Wilson and me. Said he had papers he wanted us to look at. The way he acted, I was suspicious, so I didn't go. I thought he might be working for someone."

Boilvin looked at me with real amazement tinged with disgust. "Brahan? Who for, for God's sake?"

I shook my head. "You tell me. One of this 'ruthless bunch,' as you call them."

Boilvin's disgust was slowly fading to mere annoyance. He abruptly finished his ale and called for another.

"John Brahan." He said the name with careful slowness, more to himself than to me, then leaned back and laughed. "Brahan was an idiot, too stupid for anybody to—"

He broke off suddenly and stared off. "You say he had papers? For God's sake, did you see them? What was in them?"

I cleared my throat and composed my thoughts. "He said he'd talked to Neelly in Nashville and gone to Grinder's where Lewis died. He said he had notes of his interviews. But I never saw them. I went to his rooms when I heard he was dead, but there were no papers there, nothing."

Boilvin shook his head and laughed again. "Oh goodness, Hull," he said. "Overzealous suspicion isn't limited to their side, now is it?" He paused and looked at me with a mix of sympathy and bemusement. "John Brahan, I'm sorry to have to tell you, Captain Hull, was a rather dull-witted man of complete honesty and sincerity who without the slightest doubt in the world was exactly and precisely whatever and whoever he told you he was."

C H A P T E R

Eight

Am I, I wondered, really in the little outpost of St. Louis at the rustic edge of a new nation? After all, I thought, the country is not yet thirty-five; yet these are intrigues worthy of some ancient race: the Borghias, perhaps, or feuding Arab princes. Indeed, could the court of any potentate be more mysterious or divisive?

"No wonder they drink so much," I said to Wilson in a slightly dreamy voice. Or should I say slightly drunken? After all, I'd had a few by then—of rum, to be exact. And I was hardly what you would call sober; definitely, my friend Wilson would not at that moment have described me in that way.

"Really," Wilson said, archly stretching out the word and pointedly doing the same with those wonderful eyebrows of his.

I laughed quietly. I was in no mood to dispute anything he said, even in jest. For Wilson seemed better today: his color was back and he was eating again.

Besides, I'd had to get a little drunk not so much because of our surroundings but because I'd had to tell him what Boilvin had said about Brahan, and I was worried that such news would devastate him once again. As it turned out, he took it rather well; this time, I decided, he really was on the mend.

"So Brahan was"—Wilson waved his hand in a sort of fluttering motion—"telling the truth?"

I flinched at his words; I hadn't allowed myself to really think of what had happened. "Truth?" I said and asked myself, Do I know what that is anymore?

My hand trembled as I reached for the rum. I closed my fingers around the jug and with some effort brought it to my lips. I took a small sip, put it back, stood up slowly and moved over to the bed.

I lay down and thought, Just what have I done?

Then the room spun around, and I buried my face in the pillow and suddenly knew for certain the real reason I'd gotten drunk and that now it was my turn to feel sick of this place—sick almost to death.

"This just came," Wilson said and tossed a letter on the bed. I picked it up, still half asleep, shook away the mist and looked it over. It was from Dr. Benjamin Rush, Wilson's old friend and colleague at the University of Pennsylvania in Philadelphia. It was, in its way, a terse and angry letter, very much to the point:

> Thomas Jefferson once said: "All will bear in mind this sacred principle, that though the will of the majority is in all cases to prevail, that will, to be rightful, must be reasonable; that the minority possess their equal rights, which equal laws must protect, and to violate which would be oppression . . . We are all democrats—we are all federalists [and] if there be any among us who would wish to dissolve this Union or to change its republican form, let them stand undisturbed as monuments of the safety with which error of opinion may be tolerated where reason is left free to combat it."
>
> Jefferson also said: "I prefer freedom with danger

to slavery with ease . . . I hold it that a little rebellion now and then is a good thing and as necessary in the political world as storms in the physical. This truth should render honest governors so mild in their punishment of rebellion as not to discourage them too much. It is a medicine necessary for the sound health of government."

But now Tom Jefferson says: "Regarding the death of Meriwether Lewis, he was much afflicted and habitually so with hypochondria. This was probably increased by the habit into which he had fallen and the painful reflections that would necessarily produce in a mind like his . . . During his Western years, the constant exertion which that required of all the faculties of his body and mind suspended these distressing affections, but after his establishment at St. Louis in sedentary occupations they returned upon him with redoubled vigor and began seriously to alarm his friends. He was in a paroxysm of one of these when his affairs rendered it necessary for him to go to Washington. [And at Grinder's Stand] at about three o'clock in the night he did the deed which plunged his friends into affliction and deprived his country of one of her most valued citizens."

Well, I suppose I can excuse this, my friend, by saying that nobody's perfect, not even old Tom Jefferson. But can you—can anyone—tell me where in all the world he obtained such nonsense? What "hypochondria"? What "distressing affections"? What "alarm" among his friends? My God, Lewis, as you know best, was always the most agreeable of men, and nothing like what Jefferson suddenly says. He was his usual self all during his Washington years and that way again after he returned from the Pacific Ocean. And no one I know says he was any different while at St. Louis. To me, it makes no sense whatsoever, and I am now more confounded than ever by the mystery of it all and more and more in agreement with you that Lewis was murdered.

"Horrible," I muttered, staring at the letter in disbelief. Jefferson had alluded to it briefly before, seemingly agreeing that Lewis had taken his own life. But this was full-blown discourse and now there could be no mistaking his conclusions: as far as Thomas Jefferson was concerned, Meriwether Lewis had killed himself.

"Horrible, indeed," Wilson murmured.

I sat up and swung my legs over the side of the bed. "Now what?" Wilson said wearily, and I rubbed the tips of my fingers along my forehead and over the lids of my eyes.

"We go on, Alexander," I said with a vehemence in my tone that surprised even me. I looked over at him and laughed.

"No, no, you're right," he said. "That's the only answer to my question."

"Well I want to get to the bottom of this," I said. "It's not fair to Lewis; it's not fair to the country, for so great a man to have so terrible a stigma fouling his good name." I stood up and paced off little circles around the room. "And now, every time we turn around, there's some new twist in the bargain. Nothing's what it seems, nobody says what they mean. Now, even Jefferson . . ."

I trailed off with a miserable shake of my head. "And there's this Brahan, who . . ." I stopped again, this time biting my lower lip to hold back (just barely) the emotion I felt.

"Who died, perhaps in part because of us, because of our suspicion, our neglect," Wilson said.

"Yes," I said very softly.

There was a long, difficult silence while I stood against the far wall by the little window, staring at the floor but in truth seeing nothing but the awful emptiness of my own ghastly shame.

"So we push on, Alexander," I said at last. "We push on no matter what. Understood?"

"At any and all costs," he said with surprising strength in his voice, "regardless of the risk."

And so we'd spoken of it at last—not fear so much for ourselves, but doubts we'd had, each of us about the other. And now that we'd said it the nagging apprehensions simply vanished like the steam off a kettle at full boil.

It had come right after our talk, an invitation to a "smoker" at Government House that evening. It was for both of us, but Wilson, we'd decided, would not go. Not to this one; indeed, not to any of their "functions," unless it was absolutely unavoidable. After all, they obviously disagreed with him profoundly.

"I'll bird-watch more," he said. "I'll be up and gone by six each morning, while you cultivate the little rulers here for all they're worth. And I'll be asleep most nights before you're even back."

I laughed at the way he'd put it: "the little rulers." They certainly are, I thought: in more ways than one.

So there were Nyles Jackson and Henry Phelps, of course, as well as Bates, David Bradford, Colonel Bently, the Frenchman Georges Charbonneau and a handful of others, including the infamous Colonel Thomas Hunt. Notably absent were Will Clark and General Wilkinson; Boilvin was also among the missing.

Hunt, for one, wasted no time getting to the disagreeable heart of things—or what he and perhaps the rest of them were apparently figuring was at the heart of my visit to St. Louis.

"So what do you know about the fur trade?" he asked smoothly enough. I must say that he had a pleasantly ingratiating manner: his voice was soothingly quiet, his smile pleasant, his features regular, his complexion typically flushed around the edges—not at all the man one would expect to have been behind the dastardly scheme to ambush a peace party on its way to Meriwether Lewis.

But then the Indians didn't fall for it, did they? They knew Hunt was a big liar underneath. It's those eyes of his that give him away, I thought: dark and suspicious and even a little angry.

I smiled amiably. "Very little, really. I know the British have it, and we want it. I know Astor's coming in with money of his own."

That last seemed to bring them up short. There were muffled

gasps around the room, and I was suddenly the object of several menacing glances. Was Astor's new venture supposed to be a big secret? I wondered. But that made no sense: it had been well enough known for quite a while now. Perhaps it was simply that my being an outsider meant I wasn't supposed to know anything at all.

"I know your own Missouri Fur's apparently making inroads," I pressed on, and that seemed to strike them like a thunderbolt. Bradford's darkly gloomy features were abruptly torn by the canyonlike maw of his wide-open mouth, and the others didn't do much better at concealing their amazement. Or was it alarm they were so clumsily trying to hide?

"You seem to know your subject well enough," Bently said with a bemused expression. Indeed, he was the only one not especially discomfited by my remarks. Does that mean, I asked myself, that he's the only one here who's not part of the new venture?

Suddenly I realized that my words might have much darker meanings for them than for me, for while I had in fact told them everything I really did know about the fur trade, they of course had no way of knowing that.

"Well, you know what they're saying back East," I said with a slightly pompous edge to my manner. "That fur is St. Louis and St. Louis is fur."

"That's—"

It was Bates, cutting himself short to clear his throat after his voice broke on that one word into a high-pitched whine.

"That's what they're saying back east?" he managed in a somewhat more normal voice, though he was still breathless and obviously agitated.

"I've heard it said, yes, Governor," I lied matter-of-factly. Naturally, I had heard no such thing.

Bates glanced miserably at Bradford and Hunt, then looked nervously around the table while sweat beaded up on that famous lip of his. Then there was a silence so long and awkward that Bates finally cleared his throat again and made a pained gesture for Hunt to move off with him to a more private area.

We had all been sitting in easy chairs around a big oak table over cognac and cigars, but now that was the signal to drift off into less formal little groups. Jackson and Phelps motioned for me to follow them out to the balcony.

"Harry, for God's sake—" Jackson fairly thundered, but Phelps held up a quieting hand.

"Harry, you'll give them all apoplexy if you keep this up," Phelps said with quiet good humor.

I closed my eyes briefly, opened them and affected a pose of what I hoped was something like serene wisdom. "What's your stake in this?" I asked them both in a quiet tone. "What's your part in Missouri Fur?"

"Oh God!" Jackson bellowed.

"Nothing, Harry, really," Phelps insisted. "It's only that we're known to the others as friends of yours, and—"

"And you're becoming an embarrassment, Harry," Jackson cut in.

Phelps opened his mouth and closed it, and, as I recall, I did the same. "But why, Nyles?" I finally managed. "I only answered Hunt's question. I told him what I knew, which is precious little." I shook my head. "What are they so afraid of, anyway? What do they think I *really* know?" I stretched out the word "really" and put a tremolo in my voice besides, and as I spoke, I raised my hands and fluttered my fingers as if I were a ghost of some sort endowed with magic powers. They both laughed loudly, though probably in spite of themselves.

"Glad you're amused, very glad," came the familiar silken voice. We turned to find Colonel Hunt, a forced smile frozen on his lips, standing beside us. He was in turn flanked by Bently, trying to look serious and only partly succeeding, and Bradford, trying to look jovial and succeeding not at all. Standing just behind them was Charbonneau, who seemed to study me with interest.

"Here, try this," Hunt said, handing me a snifter of cognac. "Private stock, marvelous stuff."

I took it with pleasure, swirled it around in the glass and took a sip. I smiled; in truth, I almost moaned with pleasure—it was that good: smooth, delectable, no bite to it at all—only that sensational mellow flavor.

"You like it, you do; I can tell, I can always tell," Hunt said. He beamed a big smile at everybody around, and they all obligingly beamed back—or tried to.

"It is some of the best, monsieur," Charbonneau put in with a predictably knowledgeable air.

Suddenly I felt Hunt's hand pressing firmly on my left elbow and found myself being nudged to one side. Still smiling, he stared at me with a deliciously confidential look. "So, Hull. Tell me. I mean really. What do you know? What do you hear?"

And with that I'd suddenly had enough. I smiled my very best and said playfully, "You tell me, Colonel. What do *you* know? What do *you* hear?"

I laughed out loud, and, laughing with me, he bit, just as I knew he would. "About?" he asked with an engaging tilt of his head and even a lilt in his voice. And that was all I needed.

"About Brahan," I said, a little too loudly—or at least loudly enough so that everyone around could hear. "About his death," I went on. "About his murder."

Watching his sinister smile fade into anger, watching the amused look in his eyes turn to alarm again, was, I thought, much like watching a piece of crockery shatter across a kitchen floor. The pieces might somehow be composed again, but the break itself, and the moment in which it occurred, could never be forgotten or erased.

There was a silence as they all regrouped. Poor Phelps and Jackson looked as though they wished the earth would swallow them up—or swallow me, I couldn't be sure which. Bradford, at least for a moment, looked truly terrified. Only Charbonneau and Bently did not lose their composure.

"Ah yes, Brahan. Sad affair, sad affair," Bently said, his manner and tone so ingenuous that I honestly could not tell if he was sincere or merely mouthing the words to cover the awkward moment and give Hunt in particular a chance to recover. Whatever the case, the effect was the latter.

"Yes, that's right, very sad," Hunt managed. "Tragic end, terrible end, to a fine officer's career."

They all nodded piously and murmured their agreement, until suddenly Henry Phelps said, "Excuse me, Harry, but did you say 'murder'?"

I looked over at him amazed, saw an unmistakable conspiratorial glint in his eyes and realized at once that for whatever reason, Henry Phelps was suddenly on my side.

"Why, yes, I—"

"Murder? Why, that's nonsense," Hunt bristled.

"Outrageous. Ridiculous," Bradford put in.

"Murder? Really? I thought he killed himself." It was Bently, and I thought: Perhaps the genial commander of this little fort really is as imbecilic as he seems.

And then: "Of course he killed himself."

It was a new voice suddenly hissing across the balcony from just inside the door to the main interior room. We all looked around to see Frederick Bates glaring through the open night air. He was glaring at me, of course, and glaring with a look I'd rarely, if ever, seen before.

It was a look of rage, but more: if only for an instant, it was the mad determination of some wild animal that has spotted his prey at last and is poised irrevocably for the kill.

C H A P T E R

Nine

I went bird-watching with Wilson next morning. It was, I decided, the only decent thing to do—all things considered.

Actually, Phelps helped me make up my mind. "Get out of St. Louis for a couple of days," he whispered as I left. In truth, it was more of a hiss than a whisper, and issued rather commandingly at that, I thought.

And then who abruptly slid out of the shadows and right up to us as we stood just inside the open gate to the little fort but Big White, of all people.

"Mmmm," he said, somewhat cryptically, with a nod and a smile, and I took that to mean, Yes, do it, get out of town.

It wasn't, as I think you can tell, too hard to talk me into it.

So we were out and about at the crack of dawn, Wilson and I, watching: we saw a whole flock of magnificent red tanagers heading north; we saw molting pelicans leaving behind their virtual feather bed along the banks of the river; we saw blue jays and finches and crows, of course.

Mercifully, we saw no carnage—no swooping eagles or screeching vultures. Mercifully, we heard no mockingbirds, either.

"This is wonderful," I said. "We should stay out here, camp out a while."

Wilson cocked his head and looked at me through slightly narrowed eyes. "How bad is it?" he said, his tone beyond dry—arid, in fact, like the sands of the legendary deserts of Arabia. "Can we go back next week? Next month? When, Harry? Just tell me. More than a week, we'll need provisions, you know, maybe a pack horse, a sack of flour, a—"

"Oh, shut up," I said with a silly grin and a shake of my head, and to my relief he laughed out loud.

"Seriously, Harry, what happened?"

And naturally I told him all about it.

"So it's bad enough we really do have to stay away a while," he said a bit glumly when I finished.

"Just a couple of days. Phelps is supposed to meet us at noon the day after tomorrow at the south edge of town. He'll tell us if things have settled down a bit—which I'm sure they will have by then."

He stared off, at what I wasn't sure. Had he seen an exotic new bird? Or was he only looking at some faraway void, as people often will, in hopes of discovering something close, something inside himself, something that would answer his most fundamental questions. He breathed deeply, then suddenly raised his gun and fired—even though there was nothing anywhere around that I could see to shoot at.

"Is there any real danger?" he asked, not looking at me as he spoke.

"No, no," I said with a quick, dismissive shake of my head.

"Really?" he said, but with nothing arch about his tone that time, and I knew at once that I'd made a mistake.

Even so, he still didn't look at me. Indeed, he had reloaded as we talked, carefully tamping down the powder, and right after he'd posed his one-word query he once again pointed the weapon at the tops of some nearby trees and fired. Once again it amounted to nothing more that I could see than a wasted round.

"Alexander, look at me, please," I said, and he slowly put aside the gun and faced me directly.

"I'm sorry, that was thoughtless," I said, "but I'm honestly not sure how to answer your question. That is, I don't know the answer, so I was only trying to reassure you." I paused and took a heavy breath. Instead, I thought, I merely sounded facile, even idiotic. "It could be dangerous, yes," I went on, "but that's honestly all I can tell you. And besides you know as much as I do about what's happened and what these people are capable of. So it comes down after all to opinion, and in my opinion we'll be perfectly all right."

As I spoke I realized that now I was staring off, and when I looked back at Wilson I found him smiling amiably.

"Fine, Harry," he said with a nod, his tone pointedly matter-of-fact. "I just wanted you to tell me, that's all."

And I just shook my head and laughed.

Major Henry Phelps was not at the prescribed meeting place at the edge of the tall forest about two hundred yards from the southern border of the village of St. Louis two days later at noon.

It had been part of my plan with Phelps that he might not show up, and it did not especially alarm me except when considering how Wilson might react, especially as I had neglected—chosen, in fact—not to tell him about it.

"It just means that Phelps thinks things have to calm down a little longer," I told him smoothly. And why not, since for once it was the absolute truth.

The plan was that if he didn't show, Wilson and I were simply to go back to the woods and then return to the meeting place at noon two days later, and to keep doing that until Phelps finally was there to greet us.

"But I told him, Alex, that we'd do it once, even twice. But if he's not there the third time—well, that really would make it just about a full week in the wilds and then we're coming back to town regardless."

Unfortunately, that last was not entirely true, except in my own mind, for I had not said anything at all to Phelps of such a stricture.

Two days later Phelps still did not appear. We waited nervously for nearly an hour before finally giving him up, and after that I must admit that Wilson's inevitable worries proved strongly contagious. For two days we skulked about the woods, our eyes fixed firmly on the ground, too preoccupied with earthly troubles—too frightened, really—to do otherwise.

Why is Bates so angry? we asked each other. And what is Hunt's problem? And what's the relationship between Bates and Wilkinson? And who's really behind it all? And how does all that tie in, if indeed it does, with Lewis's death? And with Brahan's?

We chewed it over and over ad nauseam, enlarging and aggravating our worst fears. And when on the third try Major Henry Phelps finally did show up at the edge of town, my heart soared—not just because it meant our concerns might be exaggerated but because I was at last set free from perhaps the most dismal conversations of my life.

"Were you concerned about some papers, Harry?" Phelps asked in a matter-of-fact tone of voice the instant he saw us. He smiled affably, his usual boyish grin—made only more boyish by his wisp of a mustache. He'd grown it to look older, of course, but oddly enough it seemed to have had the opposite effect. And if at age twenty-seven Henry Phelps was the third-youngest major in the army, and a brat besides, he was perhaps the very youngest-*looking* member of the entire goddamned U.S. Army officer corps. And if I was amused by it once in a while, I found myself more and more frequently annoyed. After all, while the rest of us are getting older, I asked myself, why does Henry Phelps get to stay the same, goddammit! Even so, I rather liked him, and also I found him just as bright—brilliant, even—as everybody always said he was.

"Yes, Major Phelps," I said, stretching out his title and his name with a slightly sarcastic tinge, "I was. I am." I stared at him quizzically but he just stared back. "Why?" I asked.

"W-e-e-ll, I'm not sure. There was something, some whisper or other, about this stack of papers in Bates's safe. And you said something the other day about these notes that Brahan supposedly had, so I simply—"

"*I* said something?"

"Yes, Harry, I'm sure you did, I remember—"

"I didn't know you knew Boilvin so well," I put in at once, for I knew full well he was the only person (other than Wilson, of course) whom I'd talked to about Brahan and his so-called documents.

"Boilvin?" Phelps looked genuinely puzzled. "I've met him once or twice. Why?"

"You're saying you didn't hear this from Boilvin, is that right, Henry? Because you didn't hear it from me, I'm sure of that."

Phelps narrowed his eyes thoughtfully. "I could've sworn . . . but if it wasn't you, then . . . ?"

He trailed off and I glared at him, my anger growing. "What is this, Henry?" I suddenly demanded.

He raised his hands in a calming gesture. "Nothing, Harry, don't worry. I'm with you now, I swear. But I know I heard something somewhere about your interest in those papers."

And then like a lightning bolt piercing my mind I suddenly remembered. "Aha," I said out loud, recalling my conversation with the so-called marshal, the one named Clovis who was in Brahan's room the day he died—and of course Clovis could have blabbed to anyone about it.

"All right, Henry," I said, my voice fairly saturated with obvious relief.

"Well?" he insisted. But now it was his turn to be toyed with—and to get annoyed as hell about it, too.

"We'll talk later," I said with a grin. "Shouldn't be seen out here. Should get back to town."

That pulled him up short, for of course I was right; we'd already lingered far too long in this odd spot by the woods.

"So is it safe in town?" I suddenly demanded.

"Safe enough," he answered obligingly, "though Bates has been looking for you, I hear. He's sent you at least three invitations to one thing or another."

I stared at him, but as before he waited for my next question. "What for?" I said at last, as calmly as I could.

Phelps shook his head and smiled. "You won't believe this, Harry," he said, "but what I hear is he wants to apologize."

I looked at him in amazement. "Shut up, Henry," I said.

"No, really, that's what they're saying—that he wants to tell you he's sorry."

"Not because he really is, I presume."

Phelps cocked his head and positively leered at me. "Of course not," he said, "but for some reason you have them all so mystified they're a little intimidated. And they want to stay on your good side."

Wilson, who'd been silent the whole time, suddenly laughed out loud. "What fools," he said, and we both laughed with him. "What snakes is more like it," Phelps said after a moment.

And that, as they say, took the wind out of our sails, and we headed quietly back to the confines of the town.

So: St. Louis is fur and fur is St. Louis.

Is that really what I'd said to Bates and the others that long-ago evening? (In truth, hardly a week had passed.) Remarkable, I thought, laughing quietly to myself, to have come upon so facile a phrase—and with no warning whatever. There was even some truth to it, I decided, and if this sounds immodest, then so be it, for modesty would have been most unbecoming considering that day's developments.

For one thing, there was indeed a small stack of invitations waiting for us at our rooms when we returned. Five were from Bates to gatherings of one sort or another at Government House. One was from Wilkinson to some similar-sounding affair. Another was a slightly sinister note from Boilvin asking me to look for him at Lacey's at my "very earliest opportunity and with utmost discretion." And the last was an even more provoking missive from Georges Charbonneau telling me somewhat cryptically that he'd like to "talk over several matters of importance"—though mentioning no specific time or place for such a discussion.

Besides all that, on leaving our rooms that evening I spotted with no trouble at all a very large, if hastily lettered, banner strung prominently over Tower Street (the old Rue de la Tour) proclaiming . . .

Well, what do *you* think the letters proclaimed?

Of course you may have guessed by now, but at the risk of straining your patience I repeat it one last time. The sign said: ST. LOUIS IS FUR AND FUR IS ST. LOUIS.

As you can imagine, I stood and gaped at the banner for a very long moment. "Oh, wonderful," I said dryly to Phelps, who had come to fetch me for the evening's little dinner. (It was being held in my honor, no less!)

"I thought you'd like it," Phelps replied with a wicked little smile. And we headed quickly up the street.

"So, Captain Hull, you really believe John Brahan may have been murdered, is that right?"

It was Frederick Bates, acting governor of Upper Louisiana, sitting across from me at the large oak table at the enclosed end of the main hall at Government House, speaking in the most solicitous tones.

"You see, Captain, the reports all said he killed himself. The town marshal said it, and my own staff, and the army men. And the possibility of murder had never even occurred to me. And then when I heard you the other night, I thought, well, we have enough problems out here already and now here's this fellow trying to stir up some more. And so I overreacted, I became angry too quickly, no doubt about it. So I wanted to apologize, which I now do"—he nodded dutifully, and I dutifully nodded back—"and also to get your views on the subject. Because naturally I respect your views, and if indeed John Brahan was murdered then I want to find out about it; I want it thoroughly investigated. Isn't that right, Colonel?"

He turned to Bently, who nodded dutifully and smiled. "Most definitely, Governor," he said in his usual bland and amiable tone.

Bates looked around at each of us, specifically, just myself, Bently and Phelps—Bradford, Hunt and other more sinister types having mercifully been banished for the evening.

"Mm-hmm," Phelps murmured agreeably, which I took for a yes.

"Certainly, absolutely," I put in.

"Well then, I think this should be reopened, Colonel," Bates said. "A full and thorough examination of all the evidence, all the circumstances surrounding this man's death. Precisely how he died, of course, and who he knew and talked to before that, and who might have wanted to kill him."

"Yes, Governor, certainly," Bently said. "A thorough probe will be undertaken."

Bates shook his head with convincing exasperation. "How could this have been handled so carelessly in the first place—that's what I'd like to know. But it's the motive I want looked into, don't you see? Anything unusual about where he went, who he saw, what he did, especially in those final days of his life."

I looked around to see just a hint of anxiety flickering across Phelps's face. "But don't forget, we should also keep a lookout for reasons he might indeed have killed himself," Phelps said with wonderful airiness.

And then it struck me, much like a clapper strikes the inside of a bell: Bates was maneuvering me into a deathtrap.

"Oh, of course, of course," the governor said with a sudden rush of brusqueness. "But this murder idea." He paused artfully and slowly turned toward me. "Tell me, Hull, just what are your reasons for believing Brahan was murdered?"

And there it is, I thought: Just that simply the trap has been set and now awaits only my clumsiness to spring it. For if I tell Bates what I saw in Brahan's room that day—the newly cut hole, the dull knife, the absence of any mess—then I give up whatever advantage I have. For above all that was what Bates wanted: to know what I knew. And it occurred to me that I might be giving up much more than simple advantage, for if I alluded to the missing papers then I would have to reveal how I knew of the papers in the first place.

And that would place Wilson and me among the so-called unusual people Brahan saw in his last few days.

Then in truth Bates wouldn't even have to have me killed. He would simply concoct a case against me for Brahan's murder.

Of course, what Bates *really* wanted, even more than to know what I knew, was for me to back down. And from the look on Phelps's face I could see that he understood it all perfectly and felt just as I did—that I had no choice.

"Now, now, Governor, I never said he was murdered. I said he might have been. I was simply raising the possibility." I took a single small sip of whiskey.

"Oh, really," Bates said, stretching out the words with a smile he couldn't quite hide. Indeed, the concerned, even compassionate, demeanor he had so impeccably maintained that evening was rapidly giving way to his more usual unctuous manner. "So you were only 'raising the possibility.' I see, Captain. Obviously I misunderstood you even more fully than I thought, so I apologize once again." He paused and tossed back a healthy swallow of rum—the very first drink of liquor (it suddenly occurred to me) that I'd ever seen him take.

"So then, you . . . don't think he was murdered? Is that right, Captain Hull?"

"I'm not sure, Governor." I hesitated, slowly figuring how I might satisfy him without quite closing the door on the possibility. "So on second thought perhaps it isn't such a good idea to open up a whole new investigation." I smiled silkily. "Not now, at least. Not unless some really startling new evidence comes to light."

"Mmmm," Bates murmured, suddenly eyeing me with disdain. "On second thought, eh?" And I wondered if it hadn't been a mistake in my tactical retreat to have tried to have it both ways. "And what sort of evidence might that be, Captain Hull?"

"I have no idea, Governor," I said at once. For I was becoming as tired of toying with him as I was of being toyed with.

Bates looked as though he were about to say something: he opened his mouth, then quickly closed it, apparently changing his mind. But despite my growing uneasiness I suddenly couldn't resist egging him on a little.

"Yes, Governor?" I said. "You wanted to ask me something?"

"Well, I . . . that is . . ." He stopped, glared at me and cleared his throat. "It's only . . . you seem so interested in the fate of this man, and I was just wondering, did you know him well? Was he a particular friend of yours?"

Almost triumphantly, he beamed a big smile from beneath his sopping upper lip. Unluckily for him, though, it was one question that I had anticipated.

"I served with him under Lewis back in the Whiskey Rebellion," I lied with near-oily smoothness. "I hadn't seen him for years. Then we finally meet up again, and right after that he dies." I shook my head. "It was a shock, I can tell you, Governor, and perhaps the other night I overreacted, as well. So I apologize to you, sir, if I caused you any undue alarm or distress."

Studying the face of the acting governor of the territory of Upper Louisiana, I once again had the sensation of seeing a valuable plate or vase break into a thousand pieces. Had my little speech so entirely shattered his preconceptions about me? I wondered. How confused is he now about my real intentions?

"Well, well . . ." he huffed. "So you don't think . . . that is . . ."

I smiled inside myself and thought: Evidently, very confused indeed.

"Well, of course I accept your apology," he said, his composure returning quickly enough. We exchanged nods once again, there was an awkward silence and then: "Very tired, gentlemen, very tired—so if you'll excuse me . . ."

Bates trailed off, we all stood respectfully as he left the room—and just like that our little gathering was over.

C H A P T E R

Ten

So where do we stand now, Harry?" Wilson asked in his kindly tone. We were back in our rooms on LaGrange Street where evening had turned to dreary, moonless night and I had taken many sips of whiskey, none of them small.

Wilson sat up with me as he always did on such occasions, though come to think of it there had never been an occasion quite like this one before—not in my life, anyway. But he stayed up as usual, snuffing a bit while I got drunk.

"Just a wee bi' west o' the shit house, good Alex," I answered. "Close enough ta' be in it, but nae so close tha' we know it yet for sure."

It was (as you hopefully can tell) my drunken imitation of a Scottish accent, burr and all. In truth, it was the only time that I could properly rattle my *r*'s that way: when I was properly drunk.

Wilson smiled faintly—then, as it sank in, actually laughed out loud. "It can't be that bad, can it, Harry?"

I looked him over lazily, numbly. "What's that, Alex? My

Sco'tish, ya' mean?" I was still attempting a bit of a singsong. "It's pre'ty bad, I'll wager."

Wilson laughed again; in fact, he kept laughing quietly for a minute or two. "Your imitation is fine, as always, Harry. I meant—"

"I *know* what you meant, Alex," I said, my tone suddenly dry and deadly serious.

Wilson looked at me then with the saddest imaginable glaze over his dark, intelligent eyes. And I thought: They are gloomy eyes, Presbyterian eyes. At least some of the time—such as right this minute.

There was a long silence, though not an awkward one—we knew each other too well for that—until finally he looked up with, of all things, a big smile.

"Forgot to tell you, Harry," he said. "Got a new customer today." His tone was positively chirpy—as it usually was when he talked about birds or anything to do with them. In this case, he referred to the upcoming third volume of his ornithological study, which, like the earlier parts, he'd financed largely through subscription sales.

I stared at him, trying to look indifferent but grinning in spite of myself. "Who?" I finally said, asking the question he'd been longing for.

"You'll never guess," he said.

I cocked my head and narrowed my eyes. "Yes?" I offered at last.

"Well . . . Wilkinson," he answered with chirpy pride, and the mere mention of the name sent a chill up my spine.

"Oh?" I said, trying without success to sound calm—even though it wasn't at all clear to me why I felt such a deepening sense of doom. "When did all this happen?"

"He came by this evening while you were out." Wilson looked at me with sudden interest. "Why, Harry? What's wrong?"

I shook my head. "I don't . . . Nothing really." I mulled it over a moment and managed my best smile. "Nothing at all. In fact, it's wonderful. So . . . he came when I was out, did he? What did he say? Did he ask for me?"

"He wondered how you were doing, yes. Said he heard you had a 'set-to,' as he put it, at Government House the other week."

"And then?"

"And then . . . he bought the book. Paid cash on the spot. Two hundred dollars. So for now our money troubles are over. We can use a little of it, anyway, to pay expenses for this trip, at least till we get back to Philadelphia. So . . . we'll be fine, don't you think?"

I tried with all my might not to show the terrible fear I suddenly felt again. I smiled and let a pleasant silence settle in a moment before I pushed ahead.

"So—wonderful, Alex," I said with soothing smoothness. "And what else did the good general have to say? You said he mentioned my 'set-to'? What did he say about it?"

"Well . . . he said he heard it had something to do with you saying Brahan was murdered, and he wondered why in the world you would say such a thing. And I said I hadn't the faintest idea, and that if you said it you must have been drunk or crazy because it was the silliest damn thing I'd ever heard."

And with that I slumped back in my chair, and my heart, which had felt like molten-hot lava ready to burst from my chest, suddenly soared with a feathery feeling of relief that I have never experienced quite the equal of before or since.

"Wonderful, Alex," I moaned happily. "Thank God you didn't tell him."

"Tell him what?" Wilson said a bit grumpily. "You never told me anything about this before, and I still don't know why you said what you said about him being murdered."

I literally gaped at him in amazement. "You mean . . ." I trailed off, realizing at last that I had indeed forgotten to tell him anything about the clues I'd seen in Brahan's room that day.

"Anyway, he invited me to dinner at his house tomorrow night," Wilson interjected lazily. "He asked you too, of course."

"Ah," I said, once again taken by surprise—once again gripped by a feeling of terror that, if kept up long enough, might just break my heart after all.

"I have to get those papers," I snapped with near-demonic intensity to the third-youngest major in the whole damned army.

"Take it easy, Harry," was his answer. And he leaned back in his big easy chair, puffed on his pipe and smiled laconically. "We don't even know for sure if they're the right papers, and we don't know if they're worth anything if they are."

I had an evil desire at that instant to knock the pipe from his mouth and hit him very hard in the face. But of course, as one generally does at such evil moments, I demurred from such drastic recourse.

"But the only way to find out for sure what they are and what they're worth is to get them," I said, my tone not exactly calm but nonetheless noticeably less maniacal than before. "Isn't that right, Henry?"

He puffed away, gazing over at me through the haze of tobacco smoke. "Yes, Harry, that's right," he said.

We were in his rooms at Government House inside old Fort St. Louis with a view of the parade ground below. I stared out over the muddy field, unkempt even as frontier parade grounds go. Surely the Spanish had kept it better than this in the forty-odd years they'd run it, I thought. And what of the French? They'd returned, of course, but only after a fashion. In truth, they'd never really run it at all, for the treaty of 1801 ceding Louisiana from Spain back to France had been secret—so secret, in fact, that the French had never told anybody, not even their own. So the Spanish kept right on running it till the very end when the Americans came in, and then there was that big double ceremony.

Of course! That could very well have been the last time the grounds had been used on a formal occasion, fully six years ago. I recalled Meriwether talking about it with a laugh. He'd been here for it, helped put it together. We'd bought it all from France the year before, and the moment finally came when we took actual control.

But the French didn't even have any troops in the area; there were just Americans and Spaniards. So the Americans were in effect "loaned" to the French, and they came upriver from New Orleans in a little flotilla flying the French flag. And then, under the terms of the agreement, the Spanish troops lowered their flag over the fort and withdrew, and the "French" raised the tricolor. And then the very next day they did it all over again. The "French" lowered their flag, and the Americans raised the stars and stripes and took charge at last.

"Peculiar, don't you think?" Lewis had said with a chuckle. But I suspected he'd secretly enjoyed it, getting to do it twice. He had, after all, always liked a bit of spit and polish in his life. And now here below me was this muddy field looking as though it hadn't been used since.

"You know, those papers could be anywhere," Phelps put in. "I presume they're in his office, hopefully somewhere easy to get to, but they could be in his safe. Or he may have burned them by now. Who knows?"

He puffed on his pipe and leaned back once again in that big chair of his—the only slice of luxury in the otherwise sparsely furnished little suite. I turned away from the window and retook my seat on the edge of his bed.

"Meriwether Lewis didn't kill himself," I said with renewed ferocity. "Neither did Brahan." I frowned and leaned forward. "I can prove it, but I need your help. I need those papers, Henry—please help me get them."

Phelps glanced downward, sighed and seemed to think it over a while. Then at last he put his pipe aside and looked straight at me.

"All right," he said in a whisper so quiet that it might have been uttered by a ghost.

They'd fixed up a little house for Wilkinson inside the fort. There was a living room with several nicely crafted pieces, most notably a sideboard of polished teak, obviously imported, and a handsome armchair that Wilson insisted with utter certainty was genuine Sheraton. Off to one side, the dining area featured an elegant silver service for twelve and one entire wall paneled with darkly varnished pine. A colorful weave known as rag wool or rag carpet covered the floor—a bit primitive but still the handsomest nicety I'd seen in a while.

Wilson and I were ushered in by a Negro servant and stood for a long moment literally gawking at the luxury. Evidently, I decided, somebody feels that the eminent James Wilkinson, one-time general-in-chief of the whole U.S. Army and former governor of this place, requires the amenities of life—even in otherwise rustic St. Louis.

"I cannot wait to see your new book," Wilkinson said jovially over a dry red that I couldn't quite place. "I should have subscribed long ago—to the first two. I told you I saw them; they were just magnificent."

Dinner was served: first, fried catfish, followed by sweet cakes, and then roast beef with baked potatoes. Afterward, the servant passed out little pipes and pouches of tobacco. Wilkinson himself filled our glasses with a lusty port.

"Very nice, General," I said, sipping the wine.

"Mmm," Wilson murmured, eying the glass with thinly veiled distaste. Then I watched astonished as he pulled out his snuff and put a very small dab up each nostril. Indeed, I could not remember ever seeing him do that before in mixed company. After all, it was by his own view a weakness that he preferred to keep private.

"General?" he said, offering him the box and spoon, and Wilkinson, to his credit, reacted with practiced grace—though I could not help noticing the surprise that flashed across his features at first.

"Snuff," Wilkinson said. "It's been years."

He inhaled a very small spoonful, then immediately let forth an enormous sneeze which blew about a third of the finely ground powder out of the box and halfway across the table.

"Oh my," he said nasally, while Wilson stared in frozen-faced horror. "Thank you," the general said with casual good humor and handed back the box.

Wilson quickly closed the cover and put it away. Needless to say, he didn't so much as glance at it again that evening.

Wilkinson leaned back, smiled, took a long, slow sip of port and said: "So what do you think about Brahan, Captain Hull?"

I'd been expecting the question, but to my sad surprise Wilson looked genuinely startled. "I thought birds were our subject for the evening," he said, making no effort to hide his discontent.

"It's all right, Alex," I said, attempting a breezy chuckle along with it. "I'm afraid that's been blown all out of proportion, General. I simply said he *might* have been murdered. I didn't mean to indicate I knew one way or the other, or that I had evidence of some sort. And I certainly didn't mean to cause such a fuss. The best thing for everyone, me especially, is to just forget I ever said it."

I forced another idiotic little laugh, and Wilkinson nodded with his cheerful gray eyes and a really wonderful smile—a meaningful smile.

"I understand you stopped at Grinder's on your way here," he said in the same amiable tone and without the slightest change of expression.

I heard Wilson, sitting beside me, let loose a brief gasp of surprise, and I didn't dare look at him. I felt my own smile lines crack a bit, but I pushed on.

"That's right, sir," I said. "Gloomy little place. Paid our respects to Lewis and continued our journey."

"Ah," Wilkinson said, "that's right. He's buried there." He puffed his pipe. "Grave well tended, I hope."

"No, it was not," Wilson said, too quickly for me to stop him. As you might expect, his voice was much too revealing.

"Alex was upset by its condition," I said, still trying for a lighter tone. "I was, too. It was pretty well overrun."

"I paid that Grinder to put up a fence around it," Wilson growled, "but who knows if he will."

Wilkinson put his glass aside and clasped his hands together in a thoughtful pose. "So he's that sort, eh, Mr. Wilson? Think he'd do that? Think he'd take your money under false pretenses?"

I touched my hand to Wilson's elbow as indiscreetly as I dared, and he kept quiet. But with a quick glance I saw his face roiling with anger, and I knew at last how sick the lies had really made him and that he was finally ready to burst from holding back the truth too long.

"I doubt it," I said with a casual shrug. "I'm sure that even now the fence is up and keeping off the wolves."

Wilkinson smiled appreciatively. "I hear his wife is something," he said with a wink, and I felt my own stomach tie up in knots.

And I suddenly realized what he was doing: behind the smiles and the amiable charm, General James Wilkinson was probing, almost as if at dagger point, not so much for information but for spots of weakness—the tender spot below the heart or a soft place in the imagination. With his iron will revealing just a glimmer of itself behind those smiling eyes, I sensed, as well, that he felt himself on the verge of drawing blood.

"Mmm," I managed, "typical farmer's wife. Nothing special, you ask me."

He pursed his lips and nodded, as if I had just said something fascinating.

"You, uh . . . you don't think Lewis was murdered, do you?" he asked, looking from Wilson to me and back again. And once again I heard a soft, involuntary little noise from Wilson.

I pushed my chair just slightly away from the table and leaned back, the better to keep an eye on my friend. To my horror, I realized his lower lip was quivering.

"Murdered? We never thought that, did we, Alex. We always thought—"

"Killed himself," Wilson cut in, his tone terse but not unreasonable.

Wilkinson unclasped his hands, leaned slowly forward and took a small sip of port. "Hmph," he said. "Somebody thought he was murdered. Was it Brahan, maybe?"

"No idea," I said, quite a bit more quickly and definitively than I should have. But I wanted to be sure I spoke before Wilson blurted something out.

"Hmph," Wilkinson said again. "Because if Meriwether Lewis was murdered, then I for one want to know about it. Because he was too great a man for us to let so terrible a cloud hang over him for the rest of time."

"Terrible, indeed," I said, "if it turned out that—"

"I'm sorry but I'm not well," Wilson said suddenly in much, much too loud a voice. "All this. So unpleasant. Murder idea, stupid. Horrible to rake it all up. Next time, General, we'll talk of birds, all right?"

With that, he rose and bolted from the room, me hot on his trail—though not before I paused just long enough to see Wilkinson's face: To me, he seemed genuinely taken aback, and whether Wilson had intended it or not, his ploy once again had had the perfect impact.

C H A P T E R

Eleven

It had been the closest we'd come yet to revealing our real reason for being here.

"His crafty reputation's certainly deserved," Wilson said as we closed the door to our rooms behind us. "He's had word from Neelly, I suppose," he added, and I must admit being jolted at hearing that almost certain bit of truth revealed so matter-of-factly.

"Or Grinder," I put in.

Or both, I thought. Or maybe even the lovely Betsy had played some role in telling him about our visit to Grinder's Stand.

As I lit the lamps, I realized how deathly pale Wilson was. "Lie down," I said commandingly—a tone I rarely, if ever, used with him. Surprisingly, he obeyed at once.

"You're right; tired out," he said, a slight quiver in his voice. "Sorry, Harry, not doing you much good this trip."

"Not true," I snapped back. "You're here because you believe in what we're doing—that's what's important. That, and . . . you keep me sane."

After all, I wondered, who else could I talk to in this terrible place? Indeed, without him I could see myself quickly drowning in drink and melancholy.

"Besides, I'm the one who made the mistake—my dramatic revelation in public," I said. "It's been one narrow escape after another ever since."

We talked a short while longer till exhaustion caught us both. First Wilson nodded off and then a moment later I was sleeping as soundly as I had in a long time.

"What in hell are you trying to do?" Boilvin shouted angrily the instant I set foot inside Lacey's saloon.

I peered around, blinked my eyes and smiled when I finally spotted him in the dimly lighted room. "Nothing much," I said. "Get a drink. Find out what you wanted. Why?"

He started to answer but I quickly turned away, stepped up to the barman and ordered a beer and a shot of whiskey. I downed the shot in one gulp and took a sip of beer.

"One more," I said, then took the full shot glass and the mug and walked over to where Boilvin was sitting a few feet away.

"You think they'll put up with your shenanigans? You think they won't come after you?" Boilvin downed his whiskey and flagged the barman for another. "You know who you're dealing with? You know what's at stake?" He shook his head miserably. "You're playing with fire, Hull. And when—"

"—you play with fire you get burned," I interjected with a smile, and he glared at me with real fury in his eyes.

"I thought you were Lewis's friend," I said calmly.

"I was. I am. It's only—"

"Only what, Mr. Boilvin. That it's inconvenient to raise doubts about his death? Inconvenient for who? The British, perhaps? Or Missouri Fur? Or maybe even Astor? Is that who's paying you?"

He snorted and shook his head. "You can't go on this way, I tell you. You have to stop, or—"

"Or what?" I said. "Will I meet some violent end? Will I be

another suicide? And if so, how? Perhaps I'll shoot myself—*twice*. Or maybe hang myself in some impossible way."

"Impossible?" he blurted out, his voice just shy of an actual shriek. "What do you—"

He cut himself short, apparently realizing his blunder. The muscles in his neck throbbed, and he even turned slightly pink around the ears as his angry indignation dissolved into embarrassment.

I stared at him evenly, concealing my amazement that my little stab in the dark had proven what I'd suspected for a while now: that Boilvin might have been a friend of mine once upon a time, but no longer. I quickly downed my shot and finished my beer.

"Goodbye, Boilvin," I said and left that place at once.

I heard a strange muffled noise as I approached the doorway to our rooms. I stopped just outside and pressed my ear to the wood, but couldn't quite make it out. Finally, I pushed the door open and stepped inside. There was Wilson sitting on the edge of his bed, his face cast downward, his body shuddering.

"Alex?" I said, and when he raised his head I saw there were tears streaming down his face.

"What is it?" I asked, and after a moment he choked out, "Henry Phelps is dead." And I slumped back against the door and stayed that way for a long while.

They were calling it a riding accident, Wilson told me, and I raced to the scene—a heavily wooded area about two miles north of town. There, a dozen soldiers were either on guard or hovering over the body. Phelps, it seemed, had been out hunting when his horse suddenly bolted. Before he could rein in the speeding animal he was struck in the head and knocked to the ground by a low-hanging branch.

Kneeling beside the body, I pulled back the covering and saw that his forehead had indeed been crushed—as if hit with enormous force by a hard, blunt object. Looking up, I could see the offending branch.

"Terrible, eh, Harry?" came a sad-sounding voice. I looked around and saw Nyles Jackson standing just behind me.

"Terrible, yes," I agreed. I stood and gave him a consoling pat on the shoulder.

A young lieutenant—name of Edmundson, I believe—appeared to be in nominal charge of this unhappy detail. But to my considerable surprise, I realized after a few minutes that the man actually in command was no less than David Bradford, Bates's personal aide, whom I could just make out through the tall trees about thirty yards away.

"Where's the horse?" I called out. And when he didn't answer right off, I asked him again much more loudly.

Slowly, he turned around and seemed to spot me at last. "Hull," he said with a terse nod by way of greeting.

I nodded back, waited a brief moment, then asked him a third time.

"There are men out looking for it now," he finally replied.

"It just kept going, eh?" I said, walking toward him.

He shrugged. "The horse, you mean? It's not anywhere around, so I assume that's what happened." His tone was bored, indifferent.

"I'd like to see that horse," I said, and he looked at me with a bemused expression.

"What for, for God's sake? I told them to shoot it when they find it and leave it where it lay."

"Oh?" I said. "Then why go after it at all?"

Suddenly he stared at me much more closely. Apparently, I finally had his attention. "Well . . . for the saddle, of course, and the rest of the gear."

I nodded with practiced disdain and thought of suggesting that the animal might be examined first to see if there were any hint of what might have frightened it so badly. But I kept it to myself. After all, I thought, silence seems to be my only reliable weapon against these people.

"Mmm," I said enigmatically, or at least hoping it sounded

that way, and that was all I said. Then I turned and walked slowly back toward Jackson.

"I liked Henry a lot, Nyles," I said, doing my best to keep my composure while not looking too cool and detached. "He was a fine officer, very bright. Had a great future."

Jackson nodded, biting his lower lip. "He was my best friend," he said.

"I know."

We shuffled awkwardly for a moment, till finally Jackson said: "I don't get it, Harry. He was riding Longjohns, and she wouldn't do that; she never got spooked."

Longjohns, I thought, and recalled the horse with affection: a speckled gray mare with a gentle disposition that Phelps liked to take out now and then for quiet rides in the woods.

"Longjohns! That's more a boy's name, isn't it, Henry?" I'd told him one time with a laugh. But he'd answered that it fit her because "she's so gray and drab she looks like long underwear," and that in any case it suited her easygoing manner.

Of course any horse can get spooked, I thought, but then again . . . ? "You have a point there, Nyles," I said quietly. And I suddenly wondered, Does he know that Bradford's given the order to shoot her?

I thought it over and once again decided that silence was golden; I would say nothing to either man.

"We'll talk about it later, all right?" I said, and he nodded agreeably. "For now, just do me a small favor, will you, Nyles? Find Wilson at our rooms in LaGrange Street. Just tell him I'll be away all day, and maybe tomorrow, too. Tell him not to worry."

Jackson nodded again. "I'll tell him, Harry," he said.

"And Nyles," I said, "just tell it to Wilson, nobody else. Understand?"

He said he did, we shook hands and I offered him one last word of condolence. Then I mounted my horse, nodded farewell to Bradford and the others and headed back to St. Louis at a meandering pace.

Or at least that was the way I seemed to be heading.

It took me over an hour to circle the long way around and finally
pick up the tracks of the runaway horse and its pursuers. After that,
it took me a full day of riding to catch up with the men who'd
caught up with the horse. Indeed, they were on their way back
toward town when I finally spotted them in early evening just as
the sun was about to set. They were hooting and hollering, and as
I drew close I realized they were all very drunk.

"About three miles back," one of them said with a silly grin
when I asked where she was. And I followed their tracks in reverse
until I found her in a small clearing.

One soldier had drawn a decent enough bead to bring her
down from a distance, but it had been a little high. Then the others
had moved in, ostensibly for the kill, but to my great disgust and
considerable anger, there was this creature riddled with a dozen or
more rounds—all inflicted at close range but with so little thought
that they had not got the job done: Longjohns was still alive.

I stood a moment, shaking my head with real rage as I
watched her thrash about, obviously in terrible pain. I pulled out
my pistol and was about to fire a single shot through the heart when
I realized that the idiots had not taken the saddle after all—that it
was still cinched tightly around the stomach.

I put the weapon aside, bent down and loosened it. "Hmph,"
I muttered when the horse seemed to breathe more easily—*much*
more easily.

What's going on here? I wondered. Carefully, I stepped
around the animal to where I could reach the saddle from the top
and gingerly pulled it back as far as it would go. There was an
instant when she seemed to flare with pain again, then just as
abruptly became more relaxed.

I slid my hand under the saddle blanket and she yelped horribly. I pulled my hand back and there was blood on my fingers.
With one great tug, I yanked the blanket out from under the saddle.
For an instant the horse screeched and jerked about more than ever,
then seemed positively serene with relief.

I pulled the blanket to one side and turned it over. There on the underside was a muslin bag stretched flat, pinned to the blanket and filled with little burs. Thorns from a dozen or more of them were sticking through, and the bag was spotted with blood.

No wonder Bradford wanted that saddle, I thought, then said quietly to myself, "No more pain." I walked around her once again, took position, aimed and fired. She died instantly.

"Longjohns," I murmured, then quickly mounted up and rode off—telltale blanket and its evil attachment in tow.

I camped out for the night and arrived back in town late next afternoon. "Back, are you?" Wilson said a bit tersely before I even got through the door. More and more lately, it seemed to be his way of concealing, or trying to, how frantic he'd been.

"Didn't Nyles come by and—"

Wilson cut me off with a pointed nod in the direction of the window. I looked over and saw Jackson standing there.

"Ah, Nyles," I said amiably, but stopped abruptly when I realized he was glaring at me with genuine anger.

"So Henry was on a mission for you—is that it?" he demanded much too loudly. "Trying to get . . . what? Some papers? And now he's dead, and—"

"Lower your voice," I interrupted in a menacing tone, "and have a seat."

He paused, took a breath and obediently sat down in the hard little chair in the far corner—the same chair Brahan had used that very early morning some three weeks before.

"What do you know about that, Nyles," I asked, "and how did you hear?"

Jackson eyed me suspiciously, and I suppose my own anger showed in my face.

"It's my fault, Harry, I told him," Wilson suddenly put in, and I wheeled around in amazement.

"No, no," Jackson declared at once. "It was Boilvin who told me. He said—"

"Boilvin?"

"Yes, he said Henry was in cahoots with you on some dirty

deal, and all of a sudden he was dead and that you were a nasty man to hook up with. So I came over here looking for you, and Mr. Wilson filled me in a bit more. But I still don't get it, Harry. What papers?"

I stared at him in utter astonishment as he spoke. *"Boilvin?"* I said again. "But how? Who told him?"

Jackson stared back at me as if I had to be the biggest fool in Louisiana. "Well, Henry, I suppose. They were good friends. Henry knew he'd been close to Lewis; he liked Boilvin, talked things over with him—things he wouldn't bother me with. Things like this."

I felt the room swirling around me, and suddenly I wanted it to go faster—so fast it would literally swirl me out of there and off to some distant star far away from the troubles that men so endlessly and ingeniously invent for themselves.

"So . . . what papers, Harry?" Jackson asked again. And I looked at both of them a long moment, wondering how they would take the latest news.

"Well, for one thing . . ." I began, then stopped talking, slowly unfolded the blanket with the deadly burs inside and spread it out on the floor in front of them. "For one thing, Henry Phelps was murdered. This charming little bur holder was pinned to the blanket just like this when I took it off Longjohns yesterday. It's what frightened her, of course."

Wilson stared at it from his seat on the edge of the bed. Jackson stood up, walked over, squatted down and ran his right hand gingerly over the thorns.

"You can still see a bit of dried blood," I said, and he leaned closer.

"Longjohns's blood?" Jackson asked, looking up for an instant as I nodded my answer. "Where is she?"

I opened my mouth and closed it. It hadn't occurred to me that he wouldn't have heard by now.

"Dead, Nyles," I said. "Bradford sent a squad of men after her and told them to shoot her." I paused and looked at him sympathetically. "Sorry, I thought you knew."

"But how did—"

"Bradford told me yesterday morning when we were out in the woods. I started back for town, then changed my mind and went after them," I said, twisting the truth just a little, hoping he'd forget that I'd deceived him as well as the others. But it didn't work.

"You . . . you didn't change your mind. You knew you weren't coming straight back. That's why you had me come here and tell Wilson."

I sat down in the big armchair just off to one side of the room and rubbed my fingers over my eyes and forehead. "Lately, Nyles, every time I open my mouth somebody else gets killed. I just didn't want you to make a fuss. I rode hard after those men; I wanted to stop them—frankly, no matter what horse it was. I wanted it alive to bring back as evidence. But by the time I reached them, it was too late. So all I've got is this business here—this blanket and these burs in a muslin bag. Not worth much, really; not in a court of law."

Jackson shrugged, with disgust it seemed to me, stood up, walked slowly back to his chair and sat down. "Tell me what it's about, Harry," he said evenly.

"But Nyles—"

"Just tell me," he said again.

I leaned back and closed my eyes, suddenly engulfed by a wave of exhaustion. Besides Lewis, there'd been Brahan and Henry Phelps. And now here was Nyles Jackson, bland and good-natured and hardly the brightest fellow around—and now he wants to know everything and who's to say that if I tell him he won't be next.

I could trust him, of course. At least I thought I could, but in truth who could anyone trust with these filthy fur millions hanging in the balance? Look what had happened to Boilvin, for God's sake: once Lewis's good friend—and now coiled like a snake ready to strike at whoever might step between him and his money.

On the other hand, it could certainly be said that what I had done so far wasn't working. It was, I knew, time to do more. Much more.

"We're here to catch a murderer, Nyles," I suddenly blurted out. And Wilson actually flinched, for it was the first time I had said those words out loud to anyone, even to him, since before we'd arrived in this place called St. Louis.

C H A P T E R

Twelve

Notes from Georges Charbonneau kept appearing under our door. He wanted to talk, the notes always said, but never when or where, let alone what about.

"Strange," I remarked, "but just as well. I don't want to see him anyway."

"He even came by while you were away," Wilson had said right after Jackson left. "He wouldn't talk to me, but he said he needs to see you urgently."

"Well, he'll have to try again then, won't he," I said, and that seemed to close the subject.

Meanwhile, at my urging Jackson slipped into Phelps's rooms and searched them thoroughly.

"Nothing, Harry, not a scrap," he told me with downcast eyes when I saw him next evening at Government House.

"Well, we'll try elsewhere then, won't we," I said with a smile. I had a drink or two and left early; truth be told, I was in no mood for any of them.

"I'd like to get that Bates and choke the truth out of him," Wilson said with a snarl when I returned.

I gaped at him, wide-eyed with amazement over so uncharacteristic an outburst.

"Yes, really," he said.

"That's if Bates knows the truth, of course."

He looked around at me with a knowing expression, as if to say, What possible doubts can there be?

"Just keeping an open mind," I said with a knowing smile of my own. Actually, it wasn't too far from a smirk.

"Well, that's all to the good," he said. "Most of the time."

He stopped and let that much of what he thought hang in the air of the warm spring evening.

"And?" I said insistently.

"Not 'and'," he said playfully. "But."

I blinked at him and couldn't help laughing a little. "But . . . ?"

"*But* when dealing with certain matters there comes a time to take a different tack. And this is such a matter, and now is that time—time to close your mind and keep it closed, once and for all."

The knocks on the door, though loud, were not menacing. Somehow, the regular intervals between each rap hinted at someone determined, but not dangerous.

"What time is it?" Wilson murmured, already half asleep.

"Just after ten," I said. I'd been reading, and the lamp by my bed was still lit.

I stood, walked to the door, pulled it open and stared in disbelief. It was the Mandan Indian chief, Big White.

"Uh . . ." I managed with a gulp of surprise.

"Time we smoked the pipe, young Hull," he said, looking at me carefully with those dark, compelling eyes. And we stood that way, looking at each other for a long moment, and I decided there was something else there. It was . . . Ah yes, I finally realized: Patience was what I saw in his eyes.

"All right," I said with a gasp.

He nodded, quite majestically it seemed to me, then turned and walked off down the corridor.

"I'll be very late, Alex, get some rest," I said, as I hastily dressed and went after him.

We didn't go to his house inside the fort. Instead, we went to a little tepee he'd set up at the crest of a hill about a half mile out of town.

"For the summer," he said. "Cooler." Then he pointedly turned, faced me and actually winked. "Also more private," he added.

As we approached the entrance, a young man emerged with silent grace from the surrounding darkness. Big White told him something in Mandan and introduced us.

And I thought: Like father, like son. But then:

"Little Big Deer," Big White's son offered with a surprising smile—not at all like his father's habitually stern expression.

"Harrison Hull," I answered, and then he quickly disappeared back into the blackness.

"Try this," Big White said as we went inside and sat down around a smoldering remnant of a fire. He handed me a handsomely carved pipe about a foot long with several colors painted on the sides.

I looked it over carefully, especially the bowl. "This looks so new," I said amiably.

"It is," he said. "Carved just for you. Did it yesterday and today."

I studied it admiringly, rubbing my fingers along the little carved-out ridges.

"Nice work, huh?" he said.

"Beautiful," I replied. "You do it?"

He shook his head. "My son; he likes making them. For me, it's too much work nowadays. Makes my hands hurt."

I looked from the pipe to him and back again; I was no expert on Indian matters, but I knew it was quite an honor to receive such a gift.

"Thank you, Chief, and thank your son," I said, feeling as though words were inadequate for the occasion.

It had been twenty minutes or more since we'd sat down and begun talking when I suddenly realized the chief's wife, Little Tree, who I remembered from our long-ago evening at the theater in Washington, was asleep on the ground on the other side of the tepee.

She rolled over, blearily looked our way and murmured something in Mandan. Big White answered a bit snappishly, I thought, then turned to me; "I told her it's none of her business, go back to sleep," he said with a slightly pompous outward thrust of his chin. It was, I thought, an all too familiar gesture of men I'd known when speaking about women—or at least about their wives. And in spite of myself I smiled inwardly, comforted in some idiotic way by the notion that men are the same toward women no matter who they are or where they live.

We lit the pipe, and I smoked the strong tobacco and felt a sense of contentment I hadn't felt in a long time—truth be told, not since Philadelphia. Thus lulled and distracted, I had quite forgotten that matters of some import might very well come up that night and was hardly ready for Big White's sudden shift of conversation.

"You don't know anything, do you?" he said in that same even tone and with the same stern expression on his face.

I looked at him with a slightly startled feeling, then quickly found myself even more amazed by my own answer.

"No," I said very calmly and without any sense of injured pride over the matter.

And watching Big White at that moment, I thought, Is there something new at last on those well-chiseled features? Is his mouth open just a little bit with satisfaction and even surprise? Could that by any chance be just a hint of a smile playing over his lips?

"Good," he said. "Good to know that—to know you're ignorant."

"Yes," I said, "it is."

I took a large puff and passed the pipe to him, and then he took a puff, and I knew that in truth mine had been very small indeed.

"You've lost many friends lately," he said, again with no change whatever in his tone of voice.

"Yes, I have," I said.

"One of them you didn't even know was your friend. And now poor Phelps—he was a fine fellow." He paused and took a heavy breath. "But I know that Lewis is the one that brought you here. And that's why I have kept watch. Kept, as you say, *an eye on things.*"

With that, he tugged at the corner of a nearby blanket, leaned forward and pressed his right eye (his eyelid, actually) against the rough material.

"Funny expression," he said, and once again I thought I saw him smiling faintly, and I couldn't help smiling, too.

"Lewis was very great," he went on, "maybe the greatest man I knew. And that's why I'm interested, because he was so good and straight and truthful. And so strong and brave. So when I hear what they say, I know it cannot be true, that there is no way on earth that such a man could take his own life."

He leaned back and took a very, very long puff, and a slight glaze formed over his eyes and then he really did smile for the very first time.

"So there I am in St. Louis, inside that fort," he said, "with nothing much to do. You've seen me there at night, and in the daytime too sometimes. And I hear things. Many things." He paused and sighed with some mysterious inner satisfaction. "Remarkable things, really, but they never mattered, not to me. Because what do I care about the conniving of the British, or the secret plans of the Spanish, or even the feuding among the Americans. After all, Hull, it's the Americans who are to blame for my being away from my people for so long.

"So I never cared about any of it. Never—*until now!* Because now when I hear these terrible things they say about Lewis, I worry. Because no man, Hull, should die under so dark a cloud, especially when it is false. So I worry, and I am angry, too."

He stopped and stared off, and after a few minutes of silence I began to get nervous, because of course I assumed that what he'd said was only the beginning and I wanted to hear it all. But he suddenly seemed so far away that I felt it would be pointless to press him in any way.

So I just sat and waited silently beside him until after nearly an hour he asked me if I would please come back the next night because suddenly he was very tired. And though I felt annoyed and even cheated a little, I didn't show it—or at least I tried not to. I thanked him profusely and told him that I definitely would return. And a moment later, I was on my feet and heading back to town.

Though it was very late, no doubt well past midnight, all the lamps were lit inside my rooming house in LaGrange Street and there was a little crowd outside. Climbing the stairs, I saw the doctor standing in the doorway to my room. Beside him was the town marshal, Clovis, as well as the landlady, Mrs. Evans, in her dowdy homespun as always—even at this mad hour.

As I approached, they all stared at me with a definite look of pity in their eyes. And I recall feeling vaguely annoyed.

"Mr. Hull, your friend's been stabbed," the doctor said, and my annoyance gave way to something like horror. I quickly pushed past them, and there was Wilson with a large dressing over his right side, his face ghostly pale.

"Alex," I said, and pressed my hand over his. Very, very faintly, I felt his hand press back.

"Harry," he whispered feebly. And I told him not to talk.

"Rest, Alex," I said, then slowly pulled my hand away and went back into the hallway.

"I heard a commotion, then a shot," Mrs. Evans informed me with remarkable composure. "Came as quick as I could. Found his pistol right beside him on the floor."

"So it seems like maybe this man, whoever he was—this intruder—was lunging at him with a knife when Mr. Wilson shot him in self-defense," the doctor said. "The man wobbled and missed his target, though still made his mark, then stumbled out here. You can still see the blood leading down the hallway. See it? Going out there toward the back stairs?"

The doctor shook his head. "You can't tell with a wound like this," he said, mercifully without waiting for me to ask the inevitable question, "but with a little luck he can recover and do fine. He'll need to rest, though. Shouldn't get out of bed for at least a week."

I nodded appreciatively and noted in my mind that all that time the marshal hadn't said a word.

"Anybody try to follow the trail?" I said, looking at him.

And he actually looked back at me for a long moment, scratched his head and said, "Follow?" in a completely baffled tone of voice.

"Yes," I said, blinking my eyes with exasperation. "The trail of blood. See here? In the hallway?"

Clovis looked at me and then at the blood spots. "No," he said, scratching his head again. "Little late now, I guess."

And I thought: I would love to kill this man. But instead of course I took a long, deep breath and pushed the evil wish out of my mind.

"Well . . ." I said, fumbling for a way to end the clamor and get rid of them all. "Think you can clear away the crowd?"

"Yep," the marshal responded, for the first time with a little energy in his voice, and began shooing people back into their rooms. Then he headed outside to send those people home, as well. Evidently, I had at last stumbled upon the sort of work he could warm to.

"Give him this," the doctor said, handing me a container of what looked to be the same nasty liquid that he'd prescribed for Wilson once before. "And keep him warm. And keep the shutters closed—no sunlight!"

I listened obediently, then watched as he looked in on Wilson one more time. "Let him sleep," he whispered as he glanced at the dressing on the wound. Then he turned, walked quickly out, and a moment later was gone.

I sat with Wilson a few minutes, listening to him breathe and watching him lie there pale and still. Then, when the noise outside finally died down, I lit a lamp, went out into the corridor and, walking very softly, followed the faint trail. It led out the rear door and down the back stairs, all right, then pretty much vanished in the dusty alleyway. I walked up and down it anyway for the length of that block, looking for who knows what, but saw nothing of interest and after a few minutes returned to the room.

I made sure the shutters were tightly closed so no morning sunshine would burst in. And I checked to see that Wilson was well covered with two of the usual blankets and a quilt that the landlady had kindly let him use.

Then I went to bed, but if I slept a wink I don't remember. All I recall was my friend's steady breathing all night long.

They found Nicholas Boilvin's body two streets away at first light that morning. Jolted awake by the commotion, I raced down to look: it was him all right, with a gunshot wound to the stomach and looking as though he'd bled to death.

The marshal came running up right behind me, and I started to tell him what I knew. Then I suddenly remembered my new rule and didn't say a word. Besides, sooner or later even he might be able to make the connection, I thought, and then Wilson and I would be in more danger than ever.

I hurried back to the room—I was nervous about leaving him alone, even briefly. Shivering in the predawn chill, I bathed, dressed, ate breakfast and asked Mrs. Evans to watch him as closely as she could for an hour or so. Then I went straight to Government House and requested an immediate appointment with General William Clark. After just a few minutes he came out with a big smile and a booming voice.

"So you have those samples for me, eh, Hull?" he said. "Old Wilson's been after me to subscribe to his new volume. I told him I might if he could let me see a sample drawing or two. Come in, come in."

He put his arm on my shoulder, ushered me into his office and firmly closed the door. Instantly, he slid away his friendly hand and abruptly took his seat behind his big desk.

"What is it, Hull?" he said, his smile gone. Indeed, his headful of reddish hair, normally a boost to his usually convivial demeanor, was no help at all now, and his tone was so abruptly quiet and to the point that it filled me with sinister forebodings.

"Wilson's been attacked, General," I managed after a moment. "Stabbed in—"

"Christ," he put in angrily and pounded his fist once very hard on the desktop.

"You two have really stirred things up," he went on. He stared off, seemingly deep in thought, then finally brought his gaze back to me. "Why are you here, Captain Hull? And get right to it mister. I've heard so many stories my head is swimming. Just tell me. Now!"

"Sir!" I said snappily, gulping air and struggling very hard to keep what little was left of my composure. "Sir, we believe that Meriwether Lewis was murdered."

He looked at me suddenly with new interest—as though I might be more than a buzzing mosquito he was about to swat down. "Yes, I'd heard about that," he said quietly, a bit of real surprise showing on his face. "Among so many others—and that one was dismissed as nonsense." He shook his head, apparently lost in thought again. "Though I'd suspected as much all along," he murmured, so sadly and softly that it seemed to be meant more for himself than for me.

Then he looked me up and down with an impatient glare. "I told you when you first came here to ask me for help if you needed it. My God, don't you think if Meriwether Lewis was murdered that I'd want to know—want to help if I can." He shook his head angrily. "Don't you understand? Christ, of course you don't. Don't you see what you've done? God, they're all so filled with suspicion, and the stories they've been spreading—at least the ones they've been feeding me.

"Don't you get it? It's all about the damned fur trade, and that's what they've thought all along—or as I say that's what they've been telling me they thought: that you and Wilson were here spying for some competitor, or worse yet that you had your own syndicate, that you wanted it all for yourselves."

He paused again and took a heavy breath. And suddenly I had the overwhelming desire to laugh out loud.

"So Alexander Wilson is the latest victim, eh?" he said, again more to himself than to me. "A great man, Wilson. Hope he's all right. How is he anyway, Hull?"

I gulped again, caught off guard at the sudden opportunity to speak at last. "He was stabbed in the right side, sir," I managed in a calm enough tone. "The doctor says he should recover. He was resting fine when I left him a short while ago."

"Good, good," Clark said, and drummed his fingers on the desk. I waited for him to ask if I knew who might have done it, but the question never came—at least not quite in the way I expected.

"So you think Lewis was killed, eh?" He stared at me intently. "Any proof? Any idea who's responsible?"

"Nothing firm yet, General, but I—"

"Good God," he shouted. "Two men dead besides Lewis, and that's all you can tell me—that you still have nothing firm? Do you know Henry Phelps was one of the . . . Well, yes of course you do. Sorry, Hull."

I hesitated a moment to make fairly certain he was finished. Then: "Three, sir," I said, and he looked at me quizzically. *"Three* more men, sir. Wilson shot the man who tried to kill him, and—"

"Good for old Wilson," he put in heartily.

"—and they found Nicholas Boilvin's body this morning, sir, in an alley two blocks away. Dead of a gunshot wound to the stomach."

Clark opened and closed his mouth, and turned unmistakably pale. "Boilvin?" he said in a disbelieving tone—much the way I no doubt had said it the day before. "But I thought he was Lewis's friend."

"So did everyone, sir. So did I. So did Henry Phelps."

Clark looked at me through wide-open eyes. "Ah, I see," he said, apparently grasping in an instant what it had taken me weeks to figure out. On the other hand, of course, poor Phelps had never caught on.

"Slippery customer, that Boilvin," Clark said sadly, then tap-tap-tapped his fingers again. "So why didn't you come to me sooner, eh, Hull? What took you so long?"

He looked at me carefully—studied me, really. And I knew

that he wasn't just asking the question to hear himself talk. He wanted an answer!

After thinking it over a moment, I decided to tell him the truth once again. I cleared my throat, braced myself for the inevitable thunder ahead and said: "Because we'd heard that you were a silent partner in Missouri Fur, and we decided that anybody connected with that was suspect."

He leaned back in his chair and for a brief instant looked very old and tired. "I can understand that," he said softly, his tone almost wistful. And I breathed a truly exquisite sigh of relief.

He seemed to mull it over awhile, then almost smiled. "Silent, eh? That's a laugh," he said with a weary shake of his head.

He stared off and then there was a silence that lasted a long time—long enough in truth for me to watch the morning sun begin to peek over the outer wall of the fort and shine glaringly into an east-facing window. Slowly, the light crept over the sill and down across the hard wood floor. Soon, I knew, it would beam right into the general's eyes.

But then, at that very instant, long before the light could reach him, the door to the office swung open and an old Negro man in a soiled servant's coat stepped inside. Silently, he walked to the window, very quietly pulled closed the big double shutters on either side and even dropped the wooden bar lock in place—lest a breeze off the river or something else unexpected push them open again. Then he left just the way he'd come—all but invisibly, and as far as I could tell Clark never noticed what he'd done, or for that matter that he'd even been there at all.

"So what do you want, Hull, what brings you here now?" Clark said at last, struggling it seemed to get a little energy back into his tone and bearing.

"General, I would like you to put Mr. Wilson under twenty-four-hour guard for as long as he lies bedridden and helpless. Then, as soon as he's well enough, I'd like you to provide an armed escort to take him home to Philadelphia."

Clark pursed his lips, nodded and shook his head, somehow all at the same time. "Is that all, Captain?" he asked dryly, and I told him very softly that it was.

"The guard," he said with a more emphatic shake of his head, "is a hard one, Hull. Too conspicuous, could draw too much attention, make things worse instead of better. And then there's the problem of how to pick the right men for it, men we can trust."

He leaned back in his chair again and rubbed his fingers through his bushy eyebrows. "Do the best you can without that one, Hull, and I'll arrange to have someone I know—someone *not* with Missouri Fur—look in now and then." He smiled faintly. "Why I'll even drop in myself once or twice, if *that's* all right?"

He stopped, and I nodded with a smile and said: "And the escort, sir?"

"That's more feasible, yes. That I will arrange." He paused again and seemed to mull it over. "When did they say he can go? Two weeks or so, I suppose?" I nodded my answer. "Let's see, I'm starting upriver soon; due in Pittsburgh in ten weeks. I'll have to leave here myself in three."

I watched him as he stared thoughtfully across the room.

"And if he's not ready by then?" I asked.

He nodded slowly and looked straight at me. "Yes, I see what you mean. Naturally, I should be here myself to make sure it gets done—and done right, with the right men and so on." He shook his head, and suddenly the weariness was in his eyes again. "Well then, I'll delay my trip until he's ready, that's all. That all right with you, young Captain Hull?" He rubbed his hands, as if with considerable satisfaction. "So it's settled then, and—Well, wait a minute! yes, by God, that's what I'll do. I might as well, since I'm going to wait for him anyway. I'll just take him with me as far as Pittsburgh when I go. After that it'll be simple enough to arrange the rest."

He looked at me closely again and beamed his famous smile. "Now is *that* all right with you, Captain?"

I smiled back at him and gulped away a tear or two—or tried to. "Yes, General Clark, that's fine with me," I finally managed.

And then right there in his office, with the time still not quite nine in the morning, he brought out the whiskey and we each had one and shook hands on the deal.

"Maybe I should get out of this fur business, after all, eh?" he offered quite suddenly after downing his drink. "All that money;

makes men crazy. That's the way it is when boom times are coming and everybody's trying to get in at the start. Canals and roads abuilding. Steamboats coming soon. And who knows how much silver, even gold, is out there." With a grand sweep of his arm, he gestured vaguely west, then downed his second whiskey and poured us each another. "A whole new country to build, Hull, and so much money to make, so many opportunities."

He looked at me pointedly, then shook his head. And I wondered, Am I a lost cause in his eyes? But it turned out he had some others in mind: "When I think about the Indians . . ." he said. "Who knows how long they've been here, and yet . . . It's funny, Hull, everybody thinks Meriwether and I were such experts on them. But truth be told the more I meet them the surer I am that I don't understand them at all."

We had another round apiece, and he told me it was good to see me again but now he had lots to do. And I thanked him profusely for his time and his help. A few minutes later I said my goodbyes and was gone.

Thirteen

W e'll use an old pipe of mine tonight," Big White said as he saw me coming up the trail.

"I'm honored," I said.

After sitting all day with Wilson, I'd left our rooms right at sunset and arrived just as darkness fell. Earlier, I'd actually toyed with the idea of bringing some whiskey along—maybe get the chief drunk, I thought, get him to spill it all out a little faster. But then I'd found myself wondering just what sort of man I'd become anyway to think of such a thing, and I dispensed with the notion right then and there.

"No moon again tonight," the chief said, and then we went inside and took our seats. "Little Big Deer joins us tonight," he added with a faint smile at his son, a young man who I took to be in his early twenties. "Little Tree does not," he said with a bit of a scowl.

Indeed, she was nowhere in sight and I thought: The mysterious ways of the Indian at work, or just a domestic squabble of some sort?

"You were—" I was actually about to remind him where he'd left off the night before, remind him that he was "worried about accusations that Lewis had committed suicide." But I suddenly realized how idiotic that would be, talking to this venerable chief as if he were some white man who'd been interrupted by an urgent dispatch or an unexpected upset of some sort.

What's wrong with me today, anyway? I asked myself, having all these silly thoughts. Maybe it's that whiskey from this morning still affecting my mind. Just let the man take his time, do it in his own way.

Then he said: "I was saying yesterday, Hull, how angry I am about these falsehoods that Lewis had taken his own life. Do you remember?"

I looked at him numbly. "Yes," I said and suddenly thought, Why am I always giving this man one-word answers and then feeling as though I'd said something terribly wise?

And then he said: "Do you know Georges Charbonneau?" And I felt for an instant as if the earth itself might open up and swallow me whole.

"I know him," I said.

"He's been trying to talk to you for some time, I believe. He had something he wanted to tell you, isn't that right?"

"Yes," I said.

And while I thought that over, he lit the pipe at last and after a while passed it to me. I drew on it deeply until I felt a pleasant sensation in my chest and a bit of lightness in my head, as well. Then I passed it to Little Big Deer, who took three positively enormous puffs.

"Do you like my pipe?" he asked with a smile. But before I could answer, Big White spoke sharply to him in Mandan.

"My father says that was very rude," he said, "to ask that without you offering it first."

"No, no, my fault," I insisted. "I should have told you myself as soon as I returned here tonight. And yes, I love your pipe. It's a fine pipe and an honorable gift."

Tonight, though, using that other pipe—that old pipe of Big White's—the outside world somehow seemed ever more distant. We passed the pipe around our little circle many more times before the chief finally resumed revealing what he knew.

"Charbonneau wanted to talk to you because he wanted money," Big White said.

"And just why did he think I would—"

"I believe he believed he had something you wanted. Those papers everybody's been after."

"Everybody?" I said.

"Almost," Little Big Deer answered with a smile. "Phelps wanted them because you and Wilson wanted them. Phelps told this to Boilvin and Boilvin told this to Charbonneau and—"

"Boilvin was wonderful," Big White interrupted, "at what he did. He told a different story to each different person, and no one ever knew what he really thought. The more he thought of the person, the bigger the lie he told. I think he was the most honest with you, Hull."

There was a brief silence while they apparently waited for me to reply, but not surprisingly I didn't feel as though I had anything worthwhile to add. Besides, I was wondering what Boilvin had told Henry Phelps to get him to lie to me that time about hardly knowing him at all.

"So Boilvin told this to Charbonneau," Little Big Deer resumed, "maybe because he was drunk or maybe because Charbonneau even had Boilvin fooled a little. Anyway, Charbonneau decided he wanted them, and he told this to me."

"To you?"

"He thought if he told me about them that I would want them. He said they were worth 'big wampum.' He wanted me to steal them."

I found myself staring at him with wide-eyed amazement. "But you told him no," I said.

"But I told him yes," Little Big Deer answered. "And then I told my father."

"And then I convened a council and told them," Big White put in.

"Convened a council?" I said with a skeptical smile. After all, as everybody knew the two men sitting with me at that moment were the only Mandans within hundreds of miles—aside from the absent Little Tree, of course.

"They are here in our hearts," Big White whispered.

"And our heads," Little Big Deer added.

"We smoked the big pipe," the old chief went on, pointing to a reedy-looking black affair in the center of the tepee that must have been ten feet long. One end of it lay across the ground in a far corner, while the nearer end was set in a bowl right in the middle—right where the fire would have been in chillier weather.

"We smoked the strong weed," Big White said. "The council came. They told us what to do."

Little Big Deer smiled again. "And then I told him no," he said.

"Charbonneau?"

"He was angry, but there was nothing he could do."

"And then?"

"And then he got the papers anyhow," Little Big Deer said. "Took them himself probably."

"They all thought Phelps did it," Big White said, "because that's what Boilvin told them."

"And now Phelps is dead."

"Yes," they both said very softly.

"Do you know—"

"No," they both said, not softly at all.

I looked at the two of them, an obviously doubtful expression on my face.

"We're telling you only the truth tonight, Hull," Big White said, "and we don't know who arranged for the murder of Phelps."

"We know in our hearts, of course," Little Big Deer put in. "So do you."

"But not in the way the white man wants to know these things," Big White said with a certain disdain in his voice. "Excluding you, of course."

I looked at them both with what must have been a certain

weariness in my face, because Big White immediately picked up the pipe and handed it to me.

I gratefully took it and fired up, then realized: He had let me light *his* pipe. "Thank you, my friend," I said, and he smiled knowingly.

"So Charbonneau has the papers now?" I said a few minutes later, when I'd somehow collected my thoughts.

"He wanted to sell them to you," Big White answered. "But now . . ."

He trailed off, and I stared at him impatiently. "Now *what?*" I suddenly demanded. Indeed, it was probably the first direct question I had asked him all evening.

"He's gone," the chief replied obligingly. "Up the Missouri, into the wilderness beyond."

I stared at him wildly, any remnant of Indian serenity abruptly vanquished by this all too worldly development.

"What the hell for?" I said, my voice nearly a shriek by then. But both men simply shook their heads.

" 'Why' we can never tell you," Big White said.

"Not about the white man," Little Big Deer added with a soft little laugh.

"Now, 'where' I think we can help with," the chief put in. "Quite far, actually. Four moons, maybe more."

"Arikara country," I suddenly offered. And they both nodded appreciatively.

"Of course," I said.

After all, where better to head with potentially damaging documents than to a tribe still furious with the American government over the death of their chief?

"The British will be there, as well," Big White added sagely, and I nodded emphatically.

"No doubt, but he only left yesterday, isn't that right?" I said, having received my latest note from Charbonneau just two days before.

"Of course," they both said with big smiles.

Big White fired the pipe again, and we passed it around till it seemed the whole inside of the tepee was enveloped in a thick haze of sweet, pungent smoke.

"So how do you know all this?" I said, looking from one to the other. "How do you find out?"

They smiled and looked at each other, then at me, then at each other again.

"We listen," the chief said. "We listen a lot."

"Nothing else to do around here," Little Big Deer added.

"But doesn't anyone ever notice? Don't they ever see you . . . lurking around?"

Big White looked at me quizzically. "Lurking?" he said, and his son said something in Mandan that I imagine explained it far better than I might have in English.

"Ah," Big White said, then looked straight at me. "Do you ever know when I'm there?" he asked me, and I shook my head. "That's right: never. Not unless I want you to."

Father and son exchanged glances again, and I could only smile with admiration.

"Little Big Deer—that's still a young man's name," Big White went on. "A few months from now, he gets his real name, his manhood name. We called a council and we all decided: Great Shadow. That will be his name from now on."

Little Big Deer smiled proudly and I congratulated him on so fine a choice.

"My son, he tells me I also should change my name, but of course I'm too old for that now," the chief said.

"I told him if I'm going to be Great Shadow because of our life here, then he should change his name," Little Big Deer said with a laugh. "Gray Ghost—that's what it should be, don't you think, Mr. Hull?"

I smiled. "Great Shadow and Gray Ghost—they're perfect," I agreed.

And then like some imposing grandfather clock gone too long on its own we began to wind down: a few more puffs on the pipe, a little more talk of less and less significance.

"I have no words to thank you," I finally said when it really was time to go.

"It's for Lewis," Big White said sternly. "And Wilson—another great man."

"I understand," I said.

"And for you, too," I thought I heard Little Big Deer murmur, but so softly I couldn't be sure—though when I turned around to face him he quickly looked away and turned just slightly pink with embarrassment around the ears.

"Goodbye," I said at last.

And then in a moment I was walking back to St. Louis again.

Wilson became feverish the next day, but the doctor said that was to be expected. We piled the blankets on and even lit a fire in the little wood stove in the middle of the room, but still he shivered, it seemed to me, like a naked man in a snowdrift.

Even so I knew I had to leave—if not that very day, the next day at the latest.

So all day long I sat beside him consoling myself, or trying to, that it would be what he wanted—to go after the man who might hold the long-sought key to the riddle of our friend's death.

Even so, by nightfall I sat there telling him over and over again in a soft whisper, which of course he could not hear, that that was why I had to leave him at this terrible time. I told him and told him until tears streamed down my face, and I hated myself for the weakness of it.

They say old John Adams used to weep every time he heard a good speech in the Senate. Of course I knew all about him and even met him once, and believe me he was as snobby and snooty and nasty a man—frankly, as big a fool and a lover of kings—as anyone I ever heard of who came to fame or fortune in this country. And the idea is, I suppose, that if that s.o.b. could cry, then any man has a right to. But I didn't like it, not for myself, anyway.

So as always I bit my lower lip and held back the tears as best I could. I sat beside my dearest friend and told him again and again that I had to leave him just like that—lying there in what very well might be his deathbed. Because after all I had to catch up with Georges Charbonneau, not only before he reached the Arikaras, but before someone else around this cesspool of suspicion figured out just what had happened and got to him first.

So the next morning I packed my gear and saddled my horse. I ate a big breakfast and paid Mrs. Evans extra (a *lot* extra!) to watch over my friend. Finally I met one last time, very briefly, with William Clark and told him where I was going and why. Clark repeated his promise that he'd take Wilson with him when the time came, and he gave me a map of the Missouri River valley that had been drawn by no less a team of mapmakers than the famous explorers Lewis and Clark.

And then just like that I headed out into the wild country of the American West.

C H A P T E R

Fourteen

Charbonneau was no horseman—I knew that much, and he was something of a player, besides. He liked his whiskey and his women, and I knew he'd take his time and stop when he wanted to. And he'd travel by boat: first, the brief few miles up the Mississippi to St. Charles and then west along the wide Missouri—the Big Muddy, as everybody was already calling it by then.

I headed out on horseback over the gently rolling hills that gradually leveled off into flatlands—the famous North American prairie I'd heard so much about. The thick forest slowly gave way to scattered trees—willow and cottonwood in the lowlands and walnut and oak on higher ground. In daylight the late spring sun pounded down, but at night the star-filled sky was like a black, twinkling dome.

I pushed my horse hard, and just five days out of St. Louis I reached La Charrette, a sleepy little village of about a hundred on the banks of the Missouri. I had a drink in what passed for the local tavern—actually, the living room of some man's house. And after regaling the patrons with tales of big-city life, I learned from my host that "a big canoe just come through from St. Louis day before yesterday." And I knew that I'd missed him, that I was still two days behind. In five days of fast riding, I'd picked up only a day.

So, I thought, maybe Charbonneau understands more about the trouble he's in than I gave him credit for. Maybe he wants to put some distance between himself and the scene of his little theft before he slows down the pace.

I'd been so certain that he would stop here, but maybe my thinking was out of date—harking back to the days of Lewis and Clark when little La Charrette was the last white outpost on the river. But that was changing now; little way stations and towns were springing up everywhere.

I studied Clark's map and found Fort Mackay, also known as old Fort Orleans, at the junction of the Manitou about one hundred fifty miles further west. It had long been abandoned at the time of the expedition, but now it was supposed to be a struggling little outpost of fifty or sixty whites.

With hard riding I could make it in a week, maybe less. And I knew I'd beat him there because I knew how tough the river was along that stretch. I knew because Will Clark had told me so.

The slopes gentled out more and more, the trees grew scarcer and the sun hotter. But in just six days I reached Fort Mackay, a settlement of just five houses scattered along the bluff above the river just outside the walls of the old fort. One family invited me in, and when the children went out to play and his wife wasn't looking, the man of the house offered me a shot of whiskey, which I gratefully accepted.

"Good to know you fellas are startin' to come out this far," the man said. And right then his wife came back in.

"Sure is," she added, "there's plenty we can use. Yarn and a new spinning wheel and . . ."

She threw up her hands with a smile, and I realized that somehow or other—maybe just from wishful thinking—they had mistaken me for a traveling man or peddler. "Why, uh . . . yes, got plenty," I said. "All coming by boat, up from St. Louis. My, uh, partner's bringing it. You haven't seen anything like that, have you? Boatload of stuff coming through here the last few days?"

They both shook their heads emphatically. "Must be a month since the last white men come up Big Muddy," the woman said.

"You got somethin' to fix a wheel?" the man asked. "Broken wheel for a wagon?"

"I think so."

"And how about that yarn. We need some clothes around here, and—"

"Got store-bought dresses," I said with my best smile, and her eyes bulged so wide open that I thought they might pop right out of her head. After that, she actually wobbled a little and had to sit down for a while and fan herself.

"Been so long," she kept saying, while her husband just stood there numbly and dumbly—not sure whether to be happy I was there or embarrassed at being caught in the act of trapping his wife and family in a place that probably was as close to the middle of nowhere as anyone could get.

They obligingly offered me lodging for a night or two—for surely my "goods" would be along by then. I knew they'd want to be paid in merchandise later on, so I offered them cash instead— "just in case," as I put it. But of course they turned it down—they had no use in those parts for money of any sort.

I spent the next two days cultivating them and everybody else in town. I regaled them with tales of famous and important people I supposedly had "sold." I talked of parties in the capital, described luxurious drawing rooms in Philadelphia and even told of the President's House in Washington City, which, I said, I had visited once. I was, all in all, the exotic peddler with goods on the way from far off St. Louis and points east.

About noontime on the third day, there was a loud report of gunfire and then somebody ran through the village shouting that the "big canoe" was here at last. And I thought, What a surprise is in store for poor Charbonneau!

It was another hour till the boat actually came around the bend and slid ashore on a convenient little strip of sand. The happy residents raced down to meet it, while I waited with my host and toasted the grand occasion.

The happy villagers swept Charbonneau and his boatman up the little bluff and into the house where I'd been staying, until there they were right in front of me, Charbonneau looking absolutely bewildered—until he saw me.

"Hull?" he said.

"Of course, who did you expect?" I replied with a smile. "So—everything all right? You have the goods?"

"Goods?" he said.

I looked at him with an astonished expression on my face, and Charbonneau just stared back. And finally I said, "My friends, I'm ruined," and sank back into the nearest chair.

Charbonneau was a squat bull of a fellow and he put up quite a struggle, but the villagers bound him hand and foot, trussed him up like a pig for roasting and locked him in a nearby shed.

"The thief," I moaned. "The swine."

"We searched the boat, sir," one of the neighbors agreeably reported. "Nothing there but food and traveling gear. Except this box of papers."

The man—he lived right next door—handed me the box, and I pried it open and peeked inside. My heart pounded: even that brief glance told me I'd stumbled on to a veritable treasure—well beyond what I'd expected.

"Hmph," I said. "Contracts; legal documents. Perhaps something can be salvaged, my friends. Let me have some time alone with Monsieur Charbonneau."

"What about this one?" they asked, dragging in the hapless boatman.

I eyed him carefully: he looked as dumb as they come, but you never could tell—I'd learned that much. For all I knew he'd race back to St. Louis and get help.

"Better keep him around a while," I said, "while I talk with my so-called partner."

Carrying the newfound papers safely with me, I went to the shed and found him still securely bound.

"Hull—"

"Shut up," I said, and he obediently stopped talking at once.

I lit a lamp on the far side of the shed, sat down beside it and began to sift through the documents.

"The British will pay thousands for those, Hull," he said. "We can split it, you and I. I'm not greedy; it's more than enough."

"Shut up," I repeated. "I'll kill you if you say another word."

And with that he stopped again, and the first thing I read was a series of notes between Bates and Wilkinson written approximately one year earlier, from May to August of 1809:

May 8
My Dear Wilkinson: Do we have a plan yet? No, we don't. But suspicions are growing, and we must get one soon.

Bates

And three weeks later, on May 29:

Wilkinson: Our "friend" grows suspicious. We must decide on a course of action.

Bates

Then, on June 17:

Wilkinson: Our real friends grow anxious. Our "friend" grows more suspicious by the day. What do you propose? We must do something soon, or risk losing everything.

Bates

One week later:

Bates: I've spoken with our real friends, and they seem quite solicitous and very much at ease. I assured them that our plan with them is entirely intact, and they assured me that they are not the least concerned. As for our "friend," as you call him, I am arranging a solution—though it may take a while. Please don't worry so much; everything will be fine.

Wilkinson

And in mid-July:

Wilkinson: Our "friend" is now beset by troubles of his own. But he may try to resolve them by traveling all the way to Washington City. That of course may give him an ideal opportunity to report on certain other matters of which he seems to be increasingly aware. We must act soon, or all will be lost!

Bates

Finally, on August 4:

My Dear Bates: Please allow this letter to introduce to you the distinguished James Neelly, major of the Tennessee Militia. Major Neelly is recommended most enthusiastically by the most highly placed and distinguished friends that we have. And I in turn commend him to you as the ideal man to carry out even the most difficult and strenuous assignments. He is, I might add, from this moment forward under your direct personal command and awaits only your orders to carry out his duties to the letter—whatever they are.

Your devoted friend,
James Wilkinson

I read that last one through twice more, then put it aside with the rest. Slowly, I stood up, pulled out my sharpest hunting knife, walked over to Charbonneau and pressed the tip of the blade very lightly against his throat.

"Our 'real friends,' " I said. "They're . . . who?"

148

"The men in Missouri Fur," he answered.

"Clark?"

"No, not Clark!" he said. "The rest of them: the bankers, the money men."

"And the one Bates calls his 'friend', with quotation marks around it?"

"Lewis, naturally."

"Very good," I said. "Very helpful," and I pulled the blade away—gave him a minute to relax a little. But of course he just started up again.

"Hull, I swear to you. There's so much money to be made. The British want these letters. They'll try to ruin Missouri Fur with them, or stir up the Indians, or bring down the whole American government if they can. Or all three. They don't care, really, just so they get the fur trade and all the money. It's all in place and promised, Hull. That man Dickson set it up for me—the one Bates likes so much, the one he has to all his parties, the fool."

I closed my eyes and rubbed the tips of my fingers over my forehead. Of course I recalled Robert Dickson, the big redheaded Scotsman whom I never trusted.

"Shut up, Charbonneau," I said, and put the blade back on his throat. Carefully, I slid it from one side of his neck to the other. "Ear to ear," I said, "if you don't shut your mouth."

And I thought, Why is it I feel more than ever like weeping?

"Who are these 'highly-placed and distinguished friends'?" I asked. And then it was Charbonneau who briefly closed his eyes from the sheer, deadening enervation of it all.

"I don't . . . you know as well as I do," he whispered, and I pressed the blade a little harder.

"Burr," he said at once. "At least, I imagine that's who."

Of course, I thought: Aaron Burr. He and Wilkinson have been friends for years. "Who else?" I demanded. "Just tell me!"

He blinked again. "I . . . I'll never say that name," he insisted to my amazement in a tone that I can only describe as unchangeable and adamantine. And I thought, There is only one man in the country who can command such deference in a situation such as this, even from Charbonneau. And I was suddenly afraid of the name, as well; I am, in truth, afraid to write it now.

I pulled the blade away, slowly walked to the far side of the room and returned to the papers. Next came Brahan's notes of his interview with Betsy Grinder. For the sake of brevity and clarity, I have eliminated his rather lengthy introductory explanation, as well as numerous asides and digressions, and present only what I consider to be the heart of their conversation:

A short time after Meriwether Lewis and his two servants arrived at Grinder's Stand, Mrs. Grinder says three other men rode up and called for lodgings. She says Mister Lewis immediately drew his pistols and challenged them to fight a duel, and that the other men quickly withdrew and rode off to the next lodging house several miles away. After supper Mrs. Grinder says she realized that Lewis was mentally deranged and asked his servants to take his pistols from him. But the servants replied that he had no powder, and that if he did any violence it would be only to himself. She says right after that all three men retired to bed in the guest cabin.

Mrs. Grinder says about three hours before daylight she heard three gunshots from the guest cabin and someone fall. Soon after, Lewis knocked at her door and asked for water, but she says she was afraid to open up and didn't give him any. She says she looked through a crack in the wall and saw Lewis crawling across the road on his hands and knees.

She says that after daylight the two servants appeared and apparently they had not slept in the guest cabin but in the stable instead. One servant had Lewis's fine clothes on and his gold watch in his pocket, and claimed that Lewis had given them to him. She says she told them what happened and asked them to search for Lewis. They found him after a while across the road wearing an old and tattered suit of clothes and brought him back to the house, still alive.

She says at one point he begged her to look at his wounds, but then right after that grabbed a knife and tried to cut his own throat. She says despite Lewis's objections, she sent for a doctor, but one never came, and he died around ten that morning. She says she sent someone to look for Major Neelly and that after he arrived he and the servants took possession of Lewis's belongings and buried the remains.

I read it through twice more, wide-eyed and open-mouthed throughout, and I thought:

Lewis challenging three men to a duel?

Lewis crawling off across the road?

Lewis's servant wearing his clothes and carrying his watch?

Lewis asking her to check his wounds one minute, then trying to slit his own throat the next?

Lewis demanding that Betsy Grinder *not* send for a doctor?

Betsy Grinder sending someone "to look for Major Neelly"?

And of course the most remarkable statement of all: Lewis getting off not two shots but three—and still not getting the job done.

So this was yet another version—her third of what happened that night, and even Brahan had scrawled across the bottom of the page: "This seems so different from what she told Neelly—doesn't it?"

Thus, I sat there on the floor of that little shed in tiny Fort Mackay, very much in the middle of nowhere, and held my head in my hands. I was speechless—or I would have been if there had been anybody around to properly talk to about any of it.

I fished around inside the box to see if I'd missed anything, and sure enough tucked in a corner were two small sheets of paper rolled up and neatly tied with a piece of string. I slid off the wrapping and examined them. One was an invoice dated August 19, 1809, showing a payment of $1,000 to James Neelly, Major, Tennessee Militia. The other, also an invoice, was a frayed and faded little slip written in Spanish but easy enough to translate. It was dated January 31, 1802, and noted a payment of $3,500 from the Government of Spain to one James Wilkinson. At the time of the payment, as I well knew, Wilkinson had been commanding general of the Army of the United States. Apparently at that same time—as the rumors had so long insisted—he was also a spy for the Spanish government.

So Bates had been holding on to a bit of ammunition even against his own closest associate, I thought wearily. But of course how foolish of me to be surprised by such a revelation.

And then: "Mister Hull, you all right?" a voice came quite abruptly from somewhere outside, and I must have jumped a foot. But it was only my host and his neighbors checking up, for I had been in there with Charbonneau quite a long time.

"Yes, just fine, thanks," I yelled back, but they banged on the door anyway.

"Really, I'm all right," I said, opening up to let them see for themselves. "I'm almost done here; I'll be down to the house in a few minutes."

They peered inside, saw their "prisoner" still firmly trussed up, smiled and withdrew. I closed the door behind them, waited until they were well out of earshot, then turned to the Frenchman.

"Don't come back to St. Louis," I said with quiet menace in my voice. "Keep going upriver. Go see your friends the Arikaras and the British, but you'll have to do it without your precious papers. Just tell them what happened; they'll believe you; oh yes, they will."

I laughed wickedly—I couldn't help it, I felt a bit deranged myself by then. Then I quickly packed up the papers and left.

"My friends, I thank you for your help and I'll do my best with these important documents to retrieve my goods and salvage my fortune and reputation," I told the amiable settlers of Fort Mackay.

I added that I would prefer no charges against Charbonneau or the boatman, but that if they wanted to hold them a few more days—"if only to give me a chance to get back to the safety of St. Louis"—then I would be much obliged. Not surprisingly, they agreed enthusiastically to do just that. They even supplied me with fresh provisions, including a small jug of whiskey, for the return trip, and I happily accepted.

The next morning the whole village turned out, solemnly wished me luck, and waved and cheered as I rode back the same way I had come.

C H A P T E R

Fifteen

I heard the mockingbird that day.

I heard it sing its own sweet song—nobody else's: "Ta-ta-tweet-tweet, ta-ta-tweet-tweet-thwait; ta-ta-tweet-tweet, ta-ta-tweet-tweet-thwait."

I looked for it everywhere out there on the trail, but only heard it over and over again.

It was a sad song, and of course you recall the legend. And when I arrived back in St. Louis nine days later, the landlady Mrs. Evans handed me three letters. Two had come overseas and up the Mississippi, all the way from Bucks County, Pennsylvania. One had been mailed thirty-seven days before, the other sixty-two. I thanked the landlady for her trouble, went quietly into my old room, sat down in the little chair by the window and opened the more recent one first. It said:

> Beloved Friend and Neighbor, It is with deep sorrow
> and regret that I inform you of the death by natural

causes of your father, Morgan Hull, during the night-time hours of April 29, 1810. This wonderful and vigorous man had become ill some weeks after your departure on your western journey. He lingered for some time, but despite everything the doctors did, he slowly lost strength and finally expired in his sleep. I know the sadness this news will bring you, and I extend to you my most heartfelt condolences and the loving best wishes of your family in this time of trial.

It was signed by a longtime family friend and neighbor, Benjamin Randolph.

Without stopping to think, I tore open the earlier letter, which was from my mother:

Beloved Son, I pray and trust this letter finds you well in your expedition to the West. I can only guess at my age of the hardships of the untamed wilderness, but I have not a scintilla of doubt that your strength, which I have seen in both your character and physique all your life, will carry you through.

I have some news which is important and also may be considered bad, depending on your disposition at the moment. Within days of your departure, your longtime betrothed Letitia Greenleaf announced her engagement to another man. And in rather hasty fashion, if you ask my opinion, they have already been married. The man's name is Albert Chauncey, of the Harrisburg Chaunceys, whom you may (or may not) remember. (They lived down the road from us for several years when you were a young boy.) Thus a chapter in your life has come to a close, a chapter which I long suspected you would have closed much sooner but for lack of resolution.

On a purely happy note, both your sisters have become engaged and even Edward (I'm sorry, I do not mean to be cruel by saying "even," but I know you understand) is, so I have heard, on the verge of asking for a woman's hand. I have also heard that the woman and her family are favorably inclined, or will be if your brother ever does actually ask her.

Thus it has not been quiet here in your absence, though I think all in all it has been a happy time. Again, may God be with you throughout all the trials of your journey, and your father, who is sitting beside me now, asks me to extend his love and best wishes.

As always, I remain, with fond affection, Your Mother.

I leaned forward in the little chair, put my face into my hands and fought against it. But what a strange and remarkable mixture of news to get all at once, and I felt the tears trickling down, much as the past flooded over me. The home I'd known, the friends and family. So many memories, sweet and sad.

Letitia Greenleaf, I recalled with a slight smile: And in my heart I said goodbye and wished her well with a truly powerful feeling of relief—as though a great stone had been lifted off me.

Dour Edward—even he had captured a mate somehow, or apparently was about to. Poor Edward. Bates's gloomy secretary, Bradford, had always reminded me of him a little. But how unfair that is to Edward, I thought, because pompous as he could be he never had, so far as I could tell, a single mean-spirited thought in his head or bone in his body.

My lovely sisters Ellen and Laura, whom I held so dear. They liked to laugh—that was their secret. They liked having fun. And sitting there in that sad little room a thousand miles from everyone I loved, I heard their laughter in my mind, felt it wash over me like the sweet song of the mockingbird, and I saw their pretty faces laughing in a thousand candlelit evenings around our dinner table of long ago. And knowing that by the time I returned they would be gone to homes and families of their own, knowing that with my father gone, as well, our family would never be as I'd known and loved it for so long, I felt a pain inside me so deep and terrible that it has never quite left me, even to this day.

And if you're wondering why I have waited so long to tell

you a little more about who I am and where I came from, it's because I was, strangely enough, embarrassed by the circumstances of my family. You see, we were in truth very rich. The simple Bucks County farm which I mentioned earlier was in fact a grand manor house situated on a huge estate. And even that candlelit drawing room in Philadelphia where Alexander Wilson and I shared our thoughts one long-ago evening and made our momentous decision to head west belonged not to a "wealthy friend," as I said before, but to me.

So we were rich, and I did not want to be judged—or *mis*judged—on that count. And in the matter of the death of Meriwether Lewis in particular, I didn't want anyone to think I was merely some spoiled young man on a lark. I wanted to be taken seriously, for once—though that's unfair, of course, because I have been many times. But Charbonneau didn't, and neither did Bates or Boilvin or any of that crowd. They toyed with me, perhaps because they thought I was toying with them. Maybe it's my somewhat light and superficial manner that misleads people, I thought; maybe I should be more like Edward, after all. Maybe then I wouldn't have to make the extra effort, which always seems to be required, simply to be taken as a man of substance.

I don't mind revealing all this now because so much has changed since my father died. He was a wonderful, good-humored, kindly man whom I loved dearly. (In fact, Will Clark always reminded me a little of him.) But after he died, it turned out we weren't so rich after all, except in land. And in the years since we've had to sell off nearly all of it—even including the Philadelphia house with that lovely drawing room—to pay off back taxes and other debts. So since we really weren't so rich in the first place, and since we aren't at all anymore, I'm no longer embarrassed by it and don't mind talking about it in the least.

The third letter I received that day was from Alexander Wilson. I'd missed him by nearly a week, but Mrs. Evans assured me that he had looked much better, and that indeed General Clark had taken him along on his trip up the Mississippi and Ohio rivers on his way to Pittsburgh.

"He was fine, sir, really," she said in her most kindly tone, and having saved it for last, I read the letter he'd left with the landlady. "My Dear Harrison," it began,

> By the time you get this I will be well on my way home, which I must admit is probably the best thing. I still feel weak from the wound, of course, but I am improving every day and hope to be fully recovered by the time I reach Philadelphia. General Clark has told me much of what you've learned since you and I last talked, and hopefully you will learn much more on your journey. I wish you everything in the way of luck and good fortune that I can in fulfilling our mission. It is worthwhile; it is for the best. And believe me, believe me, believe me, you not only did the right thing but the only thing you could have done by leaving when you did. Give it no further thought, for I hold you in the highest esteem and look forward eagerly to seeing you back home in Philadelphia at the earliest possible moment. With all my very best wishes, I remain your devoted friend, Alexander Wilson.

Now that was a letter I read so many times that the paper itself began to fray at the edges, and I finally put it away for safekeeping because for obvious reasons it meant a great deal.

So Wilson was gone, and I was on my own. And it took me a little while to get used to the idea. But when I did a couple of days later—after finishing a brief little bender of whiskey and rum—I knew exactly what to do.

The letters, receipts and the rest of the papers I'd found were fascinating stuff, of course, but they would do me no good on their own—not here in St. Louis with this filthy crowd.

So I looked up Nyles Jackson and told him farewell—and that was pretty much all I told him. And then I packed up my gear, saddled my horse, told my landlady goodbye and headed out once again, only this time my direction was due east.

C H A P T E R

Sixteen

James Neelly's mother's farm sat in a little arroyo nine miles north by northeast of Nashville, Tennessee. It was typical of those parts: forty or so acres of unexpected slopes, gullies, boulders and tree stumps. But the house was among the more imposing I'd seen, built of nicely crafted timbers with, from the look of it, four or five rooms inside, a handsome gabled roof, an actual brick chimney (with smoke puffing out) and a fresh coat of bright white paint.

A few hundred feet to the west was a well-situated bluff covered by thick woods from which one could clandestinely look down and see everything going on at that house and the land around it. I made my camp on that bluff about fifty yards inside the woods, and for one week when I wasn't sleeping I watched. I awoke at four every morning, set myself up behind a big tree, and from before sunrise till after sunset each day I kept my eyes riveted on that arroyo.

From what I could tell old Mrs. Neelly lived alone on the place much of the time, though of course she had servants and farmhands—slaves, more than likely; after all, this was Tennessee. There were three Negro men working the fields, a middle-aged black woman housemaid, and a young Negro girl of no more than twelve or thirteen who seemed to do odd jobs and run errands that everyone else was too busy to bother with.

Mrs. Neelly herself looked to be well past fifty with a pleasant head of gray hair and a wrinkled, smiling face that once might have been handsome—and in a way still was. (I say this from having met her briefly at close range once before—the time Wilson and I went looking for Neelly just after we'd stayed at the Grinders.)

All week long it was strictly routine: cooking, cleaning, tending, planting, milking, fixing—the whole long list of chores that somehow never quite seemed to get finished on any farm I'd ever seen.

Finally, on the morning of the eighth day, riding up from the south at an ambling pace, presumably on his way from Nashville, came a man who fit the description I'd been given. He was in his early thirties, of medium height and build, with regular features and generally speaking a not unpleasant face. Most distinctive about him, as I'd been told more than once, was his full head of sandy-brown hair and prominent sandy-brown mutton chops—which in turn seemed to complement his light tan complexion.

It was him, all right; I was sure of it. For if all that wasn't enough, what he had strapped around his waist was proof positive for me: it was a pair of pistols, distinctive even from that distance, pistols with ivory handles, colorful trim and shiny plated barrels that gleamed magnificently in the bright morning sun. Even at that distance I knew those pistols: they had belonged to Meriwether Lewis. And the man wearing them was undoubtedly Major James Neelly of Tennessee.

So I waited. My plan had been to wait for him to leave again, since from what I'd heard he never seemed to stay very long—no more than a few days at a time. And I would follow him till the right time and place and confront him at last. But then came an unexpected turn of events: the very next morning two of the Negro men packed up the carriage, a short time later Mrs. Neelly kissed her son goodbye and then she, the housemaid and all three of the men crowded aboard and left.

Only James Neelly stayed behind—though at that precise moment I could not account for the whereabouts of the young Negro girl.

Naturally, I reevaluated my plan. The mother would surely not be back for at least several days, not after all that packing up. But maybe Neelly was expecting some others, even as soon as this afternoon. Maybe I should ride in right now in a casual manner; after all, I thought, he doesn't know me.

On the other hand he was obviously a man who was careful, if not suspicious, with plenty to hide and perhaps others after him besides me. I took a good look around that farm, noted the long stretches of open ground around the house in all directions and finally made my decision: I would wait until dark.

I kept a close watch all day; I didn't want Neelly slipping off to parts unknown—not after all this time and effort. Finally, about a half-hour after sunset, when only the faintest hint of light still shone in the evening sky, I quietly rode down.

I circled the long way around and came in the way he had, from the main road to the south. As I neared the house, I even unlaced the sheath to my dagger and got ready either to dismount in a flash or take off out of there—just in case I met sudden gunfire or was attacked in some other way. But all was quiet as I approached, and I left the horse right there in front, in the open, tied to a tree no more than twenty yards away.

I walked right up to the front door as quietly as I could, but still saw no sign of life. The door was slightly ajar, and I pushed it open just a little farther and even stepped partway inside. And then at last I heard noises, groaning of some sort and human breathing.

There were enough lamps lighted to see the room easily, so I walked the rest of the way inside, still being deathly quiet; as I stepped in, the groans and breathing grew slightly louder. There was no one in the front, so I crept softly to my left toward what looked like a rear room of some sort. But it turned out to be a passageway leading to the kitchen, albeit a rustic one—and meanwhile the noises nearly disappeared.

I came back through the front room and headed toward my right, and the noises grew again. Now it sounded like soft crying, while the breathing got louder and louder. I drew my knife and headed quietly toward the sounds. I walked past the door to one bedroom and the sounds got louder still. Finally, I reached it—the room where the sounds were obviously coming from—and peered inside.

A lone oil lamp flickered faintly on the bureau at the far side, but after a moment it was enough light to see by—though in a way I've always been sorry that it was.

Now let me pause just briefly at this point to note that we are not children here, and I for one have no wish to pretend as though I have lived my life in some pristine pure fashion. To the contrary, I consider myself a worldly man who "knows life," as they say, and is not easily shocked.

But what I saw that evening in the bedroom of that pleasant farmhouse in the hills outside Nashville, Tennessee, must of necessity be reported with some tact and even delicacy, if that's possible. So in as spare and factual a manner as I can I will simply tell you what I saw. I will spare you my outrage. I will let you take that for granted, as you should, and as I in turn will presume you'll share once I finish this part of the story.

The young Negro girl whom I mentioned before, and whom I had not seen all that day, was lying on her back in the center of the bed. Her wrists were tied above her head to the bedposts. There were tears in her eyes and on her face. She was crying and perspiring heavily. She was naked.

Lying face down on top of her was James Neelly, also naked, also short of breath and covered with perspiration because he was exerting himself in a very strenuous way. Specifically at that moment he was very plainly on the verge of impregnating the young black girl who lay beneath him. Incidentally, he was not crying. From what I could see he was enjoying himself.

I stood frozen in the doorway for a long moment. I suppose I reacted that way in part because of sheer astonishment. I was also, as I say, outraged and repelled, but I can't deny I had other feelings. Do I want to risk allowing this girl to see me? I asked myself. Is there some crucial person she might tell? Could she be on some-one's payroll in this far-flung conspiracy?

That is how deeply the madness of it all had touched me by then—that I could watch what I was watching and worry about anything else.

And then the child looked over and saw me standing there. She made no fuss, no new sounds or gestures of any sort. She merely looked at me with wide-eyed misery—as if hoping against hope that she might be rescued from this nightmare after all. She is, I thought, begging me with her eyes.

And finally I moved swiftly and silently across the room, and as I had done with Charbonneau before him I pressed the sharp blade of my dagger against James Neelly's neck and said in a voice so filled with pure, wicked determination that it frightened even me, "Stop now, or I'll kill you."

He stopped, of course—I had apparently reached him just before actual insertion. Then with my left hand I took firm hold of James Neelly's sandy-brown hair and with the knife still at his throat I pulled him slowly, easily down the length of the bed and off it. He fell with a thud to the floor and sat there naked with his legs awkwardly beneath him. His jaw trembled and his eyes were full of terror. I almost smiled.

The girl was crying much more steadily now, but not with any new sense of shock or fear. To me it was simply as if she at last felt free to let out what she'd been holding back, or trying to. Probably, I thought, she'd simply been afraid to reveal the true extent of her unhappiness with what Neelly was trying to do.

"It's all right, child," I said, comforting her as best I could, though wishing to God that my mother or sisters or even someone like Letitia were here to care for her properly.

I untied her wrists and pulled the bedding up to cover her. "Rest here if you like," I said. "Sleep if you want to."

And to my surprise she looked as though she actually took me at my word. She nodded faintly and closed her eyes, though I doubted she would really sleep.

"Go into the front room," I ordered Neelly. "No, no, don't

get up," I added quickly as he started to stand. "Hands and knees," I told him. "Crawl."

And that's what he did—crawled on his hands and knees out of the room, down the short hallway and into the front part of the house. On the way I grabbed a nightshirt for him, and I also grabbed those famous pistols that were on a hook on the wall beside the bed.

"Get into this," I told him once we'd arrived in the front room and tossed him the gown.

"Just stay right there on the floor," I warned him again.

"But how can I—"

"You'll figure it out."

And of course he managed to squirm easily enough into the garment even while sitting on the wooden floor.

"You do this often with little slave girls?" I said, trying my best to keep an even tone of voice.

He glared at me with an angry, appraising look. "You're Hull, aren't you," he said, and as he spoke I carefully loaded both pistols. "I heard about you, traveling all over, making wild accusations."

"Don't change the subject," I said evenly, and fired a shot that lodged in the floor about five inches from the top of his head.

"You crazy—"

"Shut up," I yelled, and fired another shot that grazed his left shoulder.

"On your stomach," I snapped, "hands down at your sides." And he quickly turned over.

I stood, pulled a chair up close to him and slid the blade of the dagger softly along the back of his neck. "Really, I've heard about men like you," I said, "and I'm curious: what's the thrill here, what's the attraction of fucking a helpless child?"

Once again there was no answer. But what answer could there be? And I didn't have time to dwell on it, did I? Truth be told I didn't want to, because every time I did it was all I could do to keep from putting a bullet in his head.

"No ideas on the subject? No reason for doing what you do?" I shook my head with disgust while he lay on the floor facedown at my feet. A tiny trickle of blood dripped out of the little wound on his shoulder.

"So I've been making wild accusations, eh?" I said. "What a funny thing to say, because I've certainly never accused you of a damn thing."

And it was true in a way, because I couldn't recall his name even coming up in conversation, except briefly with Brahan. Unless of course he'd heard something from the Grinders.

"So you've heard from Bates, eh?" I said, taking a stab in the dark. "I did, many times, while I was in St. Louis; we became good friends, he and I; had dinner with him twice a week or more. Yessir, I was very popular with the governor and his friends."

"Hah! They hate your guts," he said, and I thought: Hah! Now we're getting somewhere.

"Really?" I said. "They seemed friendly enough. Bates was always telling me—"

"Bates thinks you're a fool. They all do."

I clucked my tongue and sighed loudly. "Well, it just shows you can't ever tell about people," I said, wondering just how gullible Neelly really was and how long I could keep him going this way.

"Now Wilkinson—there's a prince of a man. Why he had me to dinner right in his *house,* for God's sake, so you can't tell me he doesn't think that I'm—"

"What do you want, Hull?" he interrupted, and I knew that that part of our little game was over.

"I want to kill you," I said. "Very badly. But first I want to know some things. And if you behave yourself and tell me those things, then maybe I won't kill you, but if you don't, then—*don't move,"* I suddenly shouted, for at that instant I had begun to sense a certain tensing of his body, as if he were about to try something.

I pressed the blade as hard as I dared along his neck, then slid it around underneath and along his throat. "Don't move!" I repeated, drawing out the words, and he lay perfectly still.

"Relax!" I ordered, and slowly I could feel him uncoiling.

"So what do you want?" he repeated, his tone suddenly weary, even resigned.

"Who paid you to murder Meriwether Lewis?" I asked in a quiet voice.

He stared at me with wide-eyed amazement. *"That's* what you want?" he said with a loud, nervous laugh. "That's *crazy*, Hull. Lewis killed himself. Believe me, I was there."

"You were—"

"Well . . . nearby. I'd been with him for weeks. I know how he was acting. He suicided, that's definite. There's no other possibility."

I let all that settle in the warm evening air for a long few minutes while I smiled to myself and held my dagger at the back of his neck.

"What did you think I wanted?" I finally asked him.

"Hmm?"

"You sounded surprised when I asked you about Lewis. What did you think I was after?"

He snorted—a sound intended to deride, I suppose, and I even thought I could see the corners of his mouth turn up in a faint smile.

"The fur trade, of course," he said. "That's what they all think in St. Louis. In fact that's all they *ever* think about in St. Louis. And that's what they think about you—that in some very strange, clumsy way you're trying to wedge your way into it."

"Ah," I said, "how funny. No wonder they think I'm a fool."

I actually chuckled then, and he chuckled, too.

And then I said: "You're a filthy goddamn liar!" in a mad, demonic voice. And at that very same instant I grabbed him by the hair with my left hand, pulled his head up and very quickly with the dagger in my right sliced off just the very tip of his nose.

Blood began to drip out steadily—and then a little more than steadily—and as he realized what had happened, Neelly began to shriek.

"Who paid you to murder Meriwether Lewis?" I asked again, ignoring his screams. Very carefully, I moved the blade along the bridge of his nose.

"Bates," he said at once, and I thought, Well, now we're finally getting to it.

"And who set it up?"

"What . . . ? Oh, uh . . . Wilkinson. He sent me to him. Wilkinson and . . . that other man. I . . . won't say that name."

By then blood was really spurting out, and I stood up, walked into the kitchen, found some rags and brought them back.

"You're bleeding a lot, better turn over," I said. He rolled over on his back, and I handed him the rags. "Better hold those over it," I said, and he patted them down over the spot where the tip of his nose used to be.

"There's a potion that helps," he said, "in the bedroom on the bureau. In a little vial. Something the Chickasaws use."

I eyed him suspiciously. "Just keep patting with those rags," I told him, but to be honest they weren't doing much good.

"Really, there is," he pleaded. "Right there in the bedroom. Please, if you could just—"

"No," I said coldly.

He kept pressing the rags but the blood, though slowing a bit, kept coming.

"All right, it's right there," he groaned at last, "on the table by the sofa."

And indeed there was a small container of some sort of herbal mix sitting right there in the front room.

"So damned smart, aren't you," I said, handing him the vial. "Better sit up to do that," I added, as he was about to pour it all on at once.

He actually thanked me for that tiny touch of mercy, then slowly raised himself to a sitting position, poured a few drops onto an unbloodied part of one of the rags, and dabbed it on. Thankfully (mostly for my sake!), the bleeding gradually slowed to a tiny drip, drip, drip, and then finally stopped altogether.

"Can you get up?" I asked him, and he nodded and very slowly pushed himself up to a standing position.

"Better lie down on the couch," I said, and he went over and made himself comfortable.

I let him rest quietly a few minutes, then said: "Tell me what happened, how you met Lewis in the first place and what happened that night."

And without much more in the way of prompting, this is what James Neelly told me as we sat in the front room of his mother's farmhouse in Tennessee about the mysterious death of Meriwether Lewis:

"Bates paid me in early August of last year, but it was clear to all of us—me, him and Wilkinson—that I should take my time and handle it the best way I saw fit.

"And, quite rightly I think, I decided that Lewis's trip to Washington, which was by then common knowledge, would provide the best opportunity.

"When it became clear pretty much when Lewis would leave and what route he would take, I took a boat ahead of him and decided to wait at Natchez. My plan was to board the boat there and travel with him by river and sea, awaiting my chance to effect some 'mishap.' I waited at Natchez two weeks until finally there was the boat carrying the distinguished man himself. But lo and behold, he had contracted a malarial fever and had been near delirium, or so I was told, for several days and was forced to disembark.

"A few days later, I learned that he was improving but had changed his plans and would now complete the journey by land. He would travel by horseback along the Natchez Trace to Nashville.

"Now of course it's always easy enough for me to find an excuse to go to Nashville, so I made one up and told Russell, that lush of a commander at that little fort, that I was available. And of course he hospitably introduced me to Lewis.

"I told him as I was going that way in any case that I would be happy to accompany him. I reminded him that while a recurrence of the malaria was unlikely on the overland route it was still a rugged journey, he was still weakened from his illness and that I would be happy to go along just to look after things and make sure he remained in good health.

"A week or so later we departed, and I kept thinking all along what a stroke of good fortune his illness was for me because with the patches of slightly strange behavior he still was showing from time to time it would be no problem convincing the world that the man had become deranged and taken his own life.

"After two weeks of hard riding, we were within a few miles of Grinder's Stand, and that was when I let two of the horses escape. I suggested to Lewis that he ride on ahead and stop at the first lodging house he could find, and that I would catch up with him later, probably the next morning, after I recaptured the animals. Naturally I knew exactly where Grinder's was and would have no trouble finding it after dark.

"My plan was to slip into the stand after midnight and that's exactly what I did. But something unexpected happened. You see, I didn't actually shoot Lewis. Peter Grinder did. I—"

"You don't expect me to believe that," I cut in at once with a silky smile.

He shook his head and laughed. "Look, I don't care what you believe. You can't prove a damn thing anyway, not against me, so I don't—"

"I have the invoice," I said quietly.

"The . . . what?"

"Bates's invoice. From his files. It shows a payment of one thousand dollars from him to you on the ninth of August of last year. I also have several letters between Bates and Wilkinson that describe their 'arrangement' and fit perfectly with what you just said."

I watched as he opened and closed his eyes several times, seemingly deep in thought. "What idiots," he muttered, "to save that stuff." Then: "An invoice! How could . . . ? No, no, no. You're joking with me, right, Hull? Nobody could be that stupid."

I smiled and shook my head. "The invoice," I said.

He sighed and stared off for quite a long while. Finally, speaking slowly and carefully, he said, "So what you're saying is—"

"What I'm saying," I said very quickly and bluntly, "is that you can testify against them and save yourself."

He nodded slowly, as if he were giving the idea serious consideration. Then, a moment later, he abruptly dismissed it. "No, Hull, sorry. It won't work. I won't do it."

I glared at him, stood up and walked over to him with the knife showing plainly in my right hand. "Why not?" I insisted.

The muscles in his neck throbbed and the composure he'd slowly regained during the telling of his tale swiftly vanished. Fear was in his eyes again.

"Because *I* didn't kill him, Hull," he said, his voice quivering. "You've got to believe me. I was going to; I admit that; I admit everything else. But Grinder did it, I swear."

He paused, waiting for me, I suppose. "Go on," I said.

"I tell you, I caught him in the act," he said. "I had slipped into the stand long after midnight. I had my pistol out, loaded and ready to fire. One clean shot through the temple, I thought. Everyone would call it suicide. So there I was, sneaking up. My God, I'd been there so often I even knew which was the guest cabin. And just as I reached for the door, there was a gunshot. And before I could move or think, there was another. Then I pushed inside, and there was Peter Grinder standing over him.

"Well, if all that came as quite a surprise, even more amazing was that Lewis *wasn't dead!* I mean, his forehead was torn open and you could see his—"

"I know that part," I cut in with a scowl.

"—brain."

"Go on, goddammit!"

"Well, there was that wound and another in his chest, and the man was still alive! And talking!"

"Talking?"

"Asking for water. Asking me to check his wounds."

"Go ahead."

"Well, first I told Grinder to drop his weapon, which he did. And I told him to sit down, which he also did. Then I took a look at Lewis, and as I say the more I looked at the wounds the more astounded I was that he was still breathing.

"At first I played hard with Grinder, telling him I was arresting him and that I would have him charged with attempted murder. But he's not entirely the blockhead he looks. He was very suspicious and grew quite bold in his conversation.

" 'And just what brings you here in the dead of night with a drawn and loaded pistol in your hand?' he asked me more than once.

"Well, we talked a while, and I decided that with so much at stake for our St. Louis friends it would probably be best to smooth it all over. So I explained how Lewis had been ill recently, and how this would fit in with my suicide idea. Anyway, we decided to compromise: we would divide Lewis's cash between us, he would keep Lewis's horse, and I would take the pistols."

I looked at him at that point with what must have been particular disgust because he stopped and stared back at me.

"I had to do it that way," he said. "I had to make it look like I'd wanted to rob him myself. He already assumed that that's why I was there, and I certainly couldn't tell him otherwise. And if I hadn't taken something he would have become even more suspicious."

He lay back quietly, and after a minute I told him to go on.

"Well, then Grinder started getting nervous. He wasn't much of a talker, he said, and what if there was an inquiry. He didn't know if he'd be up to it. I kept trying to reassure him, but nothing worked, until finally he got the idea of bringing his wife into it. He could trust her completely, he insisted. And that would be the best thing because then she could say he wasn't even home at the time, and of course she'd insist that I was nowhere around, either. I was camped out for the night, so the story would go, after trying to round up those stray horses.

"So we woke up Betsy Grinder and explained it to her. And explained it to her. And explained it to her. She's not a stupid woman; I think she just played dumb because she didn't want to get involved, and she hoped we'd forget about her and try something else. Also, I suspect she plays dumb a lot for her husband's benefit. But in any case Grinder insisted, and she went along—mostly out of fear, I think. You ask me, that woman was more afraid of him than any wife of any husband I've ever seen.

"Even so she made it difficult. She kept insisting that there were two gunshots, and I kept telling her, No, that won't work, because we're saying it was suicide. But she absolutely would not back away from that idea, so finally I figured I'd just take a chance and hope nobody would notice. And amazingly enough nobody did. Until you came along."

"Me and a friend of mine," I put in softly.

He murmured something that sounded like, "Yes, I know, I heard," then took a breath and cleared his throat. "Well, the three of us had this very long and involved conversation, and we finally got the story straight. And then Grinder and I went back out to the guest room, and what do you think? *Lewis was gone!* Our 'suicide' had gotten up and walked away—or crawled, I imagine.

"We looked all around the stand for him, especially by the well, of course, because he'd been begging for water. But we couldn't find him anywhere.

"Well, we were all pretty frantic, and at dawn we looked again but still couldn't find him. And then a couple of hours later a postman whose name I forget—"

"Smith," I put in, recalling my conversation with the man at one of Grinder's neighbors'.

Neelly looked up at me with a brief flash of alarm, then shrugged it off and continued.

"So this 'Smith' came riding in and said there was a body by the road. We thanked him, trying to act normal, which is to say shocked under the circumstances. And Grinder ran up there and of course it was Lewis, or his body, I should say. He was dead at last, though still warm. It had taken him hours to expire—even after crawling hundreds of yards with two rounds in him, one of them in his head!"

He stopped and lay back quietly on the couch, patting rags on his nose and looking as wound down as an old clock.

"And his clothes?" I asked. "What happened to them?"

"His . . . oh, yes. When we found him he was dressed in old rags, and we didn't know what to think till we realized that his servant, Pernia, had his fine suit on. Well, Pernia hinted at suspicions of his own, and he also complained that Lewis owed him back wages—which may or may not have been true—so we let him keep the damn suit just to shut him up."

Neelly breathed heavily for a minute or two after that, not saying a word, just resting while I waited. I knew what was coming next, and finally he said in as genuine a voice as he no doubt could manage:

"It's the truth, Hull. You've got to believe me. Meriwether Lewis was murdered by Peter Grinder."

I nodded at him with a nasty smile and sat down in an easy chair a few feet away. " 'Hull, I don't care what you believe,' " I said, mimicking his bravado of a little while earlier. I shook my head. "Let's say I believe you, so what?" I went on. "There's still attempted murder, and let's see, what else? How about, conspiring against a government official? I'm sure there is such a charge. So I still imagine you'll want to save yourself, if only from prison."

I stood, walked back to the couch and stood over him again. "Of course, Peter Grinder will be charged, too. I think we should ride over there and talk to him tomorrow. Don't you think? Well, what's the matter, you don't look too happy about that. Even if we don't see him, the authorities will, because when I turn you in, you'll naturally want to tell them who the real murderer is, isn't that right? So I think we should be the ones to see him first."

"Well, uh . . ."

"What, Neelly? Don't you want to go see your old partner in crime? Why not? Is it because you're lying, and he'll call you a liar to your face? Isn't that it, Neelly? Isn't that the reason?"

I paused and he looked up at me with as sad and tired a face as I could ever remember seeing on a man. "I don't want to go there because there's no point to it," he said, "because there's nobody there to tell us anything. Because Peter Grinder is dead.

"And just in case you're interested, Peter Grinder is dead because I killed him."

"He kept . . . coming here," Neelly said. "He kept asking for more. I told him I had nothing to give. But he persisted. He kept hinting darkly at other motives, which, believe me, were absurd. He was just fishing, hoping to cash in somehow.

"Anyway, I didn't mind it so much for myself, but I warned him a few times not to disturb my mother. But he did anyway, more than once. So the last time he came, I followed him at a distance and when he was no more than half a mile from the stand, I circled around, rode right up to him and slit his throat ear to ear before he ever knew what hit him. I took his purse—he had a few coins—just to make it look good, like he'd just been puttering here and there, doing some nearby errands and met up with some murderous bandit." He paused and looked at me oddly. "There are plenty of them around, you know, along the Natchez Trace."

I pulled up one of the small wooden chairs next to the sofa, sat down right beside him, smiled and flashed my knife.

"You're in trouble, Neelly," I said. "No Grinder, no witness; no one else to pin the murder on." I glared at him and pressed the blade to his throat again. "I want Bates and Wilkinson," I said. "I want them to pay for killing my friend."

As I'd done with Charbonneau, I slid the tip of the blade the width of his neck. "Ear to ear," I said. "And by the way, I believe you. Even you wouldn't be dumb enough to try and blame the murder everyone thinks you did on a man you really did murder."

Neelly rolled over on his left side facing the back of the sofa and away from me. He had, he seemed to be telling me, nothing more to say. Meantime, as we talked I had reloaded the pistols; I had also given some thought to what I would do next.

"Get up, get some clothes on," I said, and ordered him into the bedroom at gunpoint so he could dress.

Then I set him up at a little table in the front room with pen, ink and paper.

"Write out a bill of sale," I said, and he looked at me through narrowed eyes.

"Sale?" he said.

"For the child," I said. "I'll buy her from you, take her with me."

He opened his mouth and closed it, then stared at me in angry disbelief. "You're mad," he said in half-whispered contempt.

"Yes," I said, "I am."

In truth, however, it was the only solution I'd been able to devise. After all, I wasn't about to leave her there, but on the other hand I couldn't just take her, either. Indeed, in Tennessee I could be arrested and even hanged for the theft of such valuable property.

In fact even when we reached the North there was the slight possibility that I would be arrested and sent back for prosecution. So, I decided, I would do it legally: I would simply buy her and take her with me.

"What's her name?" I said, and he looked at me numbly. "The little girl, what's her name!"

"Tilly," he answered.

I mulled it over a moment. "All right, put in that I paid you a hundred dollars—"

"Christ, she's worth twice that!"

I glared at him with what must have been an expression of such rage that he quickly looked away and went on writing. But he had a point: I wanted everything about this to look right and proper. Trouble was two hundred dollars was every penny I had.

"All right, a hundred thirty," I said, after quickly figuring what I needed for the rest of the trip home. Yes, you see, I really did intend to pay him because I didn't want any trouble later on—any accusations that I had forced this out of him and then never actually given him the money.

"One hundred thirty dollars," he said, slowly sounding out the words as he wrote in the new figure.

"Just say that you hereby sell to me, Harrison Hull, one Negro slave, name of Tilly, a female of . . . Then describe her: age, height, weight, whatever else." I looked at him with an evil smirk. "You know all that, right?"

He blinked and sighed quietly with what I took to be exasperation, but as before it was all the answer he gave.

For myself, I had never actually seen a paper of that sort, so I was guessing at how it was supposed to be written. After all, I asked myself, just how do you "transfer title" of an actual person from one "owner" to another?

He finished in a few minutes and handed it over, and it seemed fine to me: he'd explained who he was and who I was and where we each lived. And he'd given a full enough description of the girl: shape of eyes, skin pigmentation, size of nose, scar on right shoulder and a lot of other things. I read it through quietly—

although inside myself I felt like screaming when I saw the age he'd written. According to him, she was just eleven.

"And now your confession," I said.

I rustled around, supposedly making sure he had enough ink and paper—though in fact I was just giving him a moment to let it sink in.

"Confession?" he said, just as I'd expected him to.

"Write it all down, just like you told me," I said. "Then sign it."

Neelly sat at the little table, pen in hand, perfectly still for a long few moments. I knew what he was thinking, of course—that he couldn't do it because it would amount to signing his life away. Also, I decided, he was trying to figure a way out. I figured that because it was the only sensible thing for him to do, and also because of the way he kept sneaking glances at me—as if he were measuring the distance between us, or maybe thinking of where there might be a knife or other weapon concealed nearby.

"I've told you everything, Hull," he said. "For God's sake, why do I have to write it down? And it'll take so long—all night, probably."

"We have time," I said in a positively jaunty tone, much as one might tell a friend over dinner not to worry about lingering too long over that third brandy.

"Here, start like this," I said. "That you write these words of your own free will and without coercion from anyone—something like that. Then, as I say, just get on with it."

The evil on my part about what happened next was that in a way I lured him into it. Or did I? I've never been altogether sure. Because I did want that confession; I needed it badly for obvious reasons. So what I did, or may have done, certainly ran counter to that need. But somewhere deep within me I knew somehow he'd never write it, and perhaps what I was doing was simply enticing the inevitable.

In any case I stood there a few feet from him with one of the pistols dangling loosely in my right hand. And I knew well enough that he was still greedily eyeing that gun and estimating just how far away it was and how long it would take him to get there.

He had even written a little bit—mostly that business about the confession being free and uncoerced. And then he made his move at last, a kind of lunging pounce at the gun itself. He even had it for an instant, held it in his hands, though he never really aimed it. Indeed, he never even got his finger on the trigger.

You see, what Neelly didn't know was that I had concealed a dagger up my right sleeve. It wasn't the large hunting knife I'd been using all evening, but a smaller though also quite deadly weapon, something meant more for whittling or even peeling potatoes in a pinch. And as Neelly swarmed all over that pistol, I pulled my hand away and let the weapon fall into his grasp. Then I slid the dagger down, firmly gripped the handle and plunged the blade into the back of his neck. Then, with an added touch of cruelty I'd never known within myself before, I pulled out the blade, pulled back his head with my left hand, pushed the blade into his throat and indeed moved it in such a way that it cut him very deeply from one ear to the other.

Needless to say, the blood gushed out and Neelly gasped horribly, then sank to the floor and died.

And all I had then were the letters I'd come with and his story in my mind.

C H A P T E R

Seventeen

I cleaned up and buried James Neelly far behind the house in a deep grave. Then as dawn broke and Tilly stirred in her bed, I gently woke her up and told her we were leaving.

She didn't want to at first. I begged and cajoled and pleaded, but she wouldn't budge. I suppose she assumed . . . Well, you can guess what she assumed. So finally I said what I hated to say most: "Mister Neelly had to leave, so he sold you. You belong to me now."

I even showed her the paper he'd written, though of course she couldn't read. But she finally was convinced. It was, after all, an idea she could understand.

While she bathed and dressed, I went out to the barn, found an extra horse for her and saddled him up. And in an hour we were ready.

She asked were we coming back and did she need warm clothes, and I told her no, we were not and yes, she did. And a few minutes later, after she'd added a blanket and a heavy coat to her pack, we were off: the grown white man in his tailored suit leading the way on his handsome steed, and the young Negro girl in her shabby homespun bringing up the rear on her broken-down farm horse.

We were quite a sight. We picked up the main road east out of Nashville and drew snickers, leers, winks and even a hoot now and then every step of the way. And at every stop we made people suddenly wanted to talk. Nobody dared ask me directly, of course, just what I was doing with this black child out on the road, and not once did I have occasion to show them my "bill of sale." They were just curious, that's all; they only wanted to know who we were, why we were there and no doubt everything else about us—though of course they lacked the nerve to ask us outright.

I decided I knew what the problem was. Clearly, dressing "up" hadn't worked; it just looked too . . . strange. So the next day I changed from Beau Brummel to buckskin and things calmed down considerably. Now I looked more like a hired man transporting a Negro slave from one place to another. That was not so strange.

We still got occasional nosy looks of course, and a hard eye from one or two marshals, but nothing like before. Even so, after three or four days the stares got on my nerves, so we broke due north on a rough-looking trail that seemed like it might go a ways. It was hard traveling, all right, with rotting timbers littering the ground, steep hills, dozens of creeks and streams to cross, blinding fog in the morning and stinking swamps. But the trail stretched out and for three weeks we didn't see another living soul, and that more than made up for the difficult ride.

At night we camped under the stars, and the first night Tilly, who hadn't said more than a word or two at a time on the whole trip so far, pulled down the front of her dress and bared her little bosom for me to see.

"You want me?" she asked, her voice as always oddly lifeless. And I thought: I will take this child to my mother's house in Bucks County and she will live there with us for as long as she wants. And she will go to school and learn to read and write and everything else people are supposed to learn. And someday maybe she'll learn what she's worth.

"No," I said gently.

"You don't like me?" she said.

"Very, very much," I said, "but not for that. Not in that way."

"But it's what Massa Neelly says I'm for," she said, crying softly.

"Mister Neelly—" I said, my voice angry. I almost said, "Mister Neelly's dead!" I almost spit that out—I wanted to very much, but I wasn't quite sure how she'd take it so I took a calming breath and started over.

"Mister Neelly's gone away," I said. "He won't be back, not for a long time."

She was weeping now, the tears pouring down. "Then why you buy me?" she demanded.

I put my hands over my face, shook my head helplessly and wondered what in the world I could tell this child that would somehow ease her misery.

"Because I love you," I dared at last, in a very soft and solemn voice.

But she just stared at me with more fear and confusion than ever in her eyes, then lay down on the little pallet I'd made for her a few feet away and cried herself to sleep.

Those eerie morning fogs began to ease a little, and the cotton-wood and willow trees gave way to oaks and maples, and I knew we were in Pennsylvania. Home! I thought, or almost.

We rode due north a bit longer, then hooked up with a trail I knew headed to the main east–west pike. We found a little village called Elmsburg with a freshly painted inn that had a suite with a little servants' room right next door.

"Harrison Hull of Bucks County," I told the innkeeper, a paunchy little man named Jarvis, "and this is our maid's daughter. She's been with my cousins in Pittsburgh."

I told him to bring up the biggest supper he had for both of

us, put Tilly in her little private quarters and had dinner brought in.
It was a generous bowl of stew that smelled wholesome enough,
and I told her to eat every bite.

I went to my own room, pushed my plate to one side, lit a
lamp, pulled out pen and paper and wrote:

> I, Harrison Jacob Hull, of Bucks County, Pennsylvania,
> do hereby release and remit from a state of slavery to the
> status of free woman and resident of Pennsylvania,
> United States of America, the child known heretofore
> as the slave Tilly and now and always hereafter known
> as the free woman Tilly Hull. I do make, write and
> hereafter sign this document in full possession of my
> faculties and entirely of my own free will, without coer-
> cion of any sort. Harrison Hull, Bucks County, Penn-
> sylvania, USA.

I sent for the innkeeper and asked if there was a lawyer in the town
who might read over a document and witness it for me.

"I'm the lawyer 'round here," he said with a growl, his eyes
impatient. "Cost you five dollars, though."

Embarrassed, I stammered a bit. "Well, I, uh . . . I'm afraid
I wasn't quite truthful before," I said, "about the child."

He glowered up at me, his impatience growing, but just then
Tilly banged happily into the room. "That was good, massa," she
said with a smile, "but I's still hungry. You got—" Then she
noticed the innkeeper and stopped dead in her tracks. "Oh," she
said, and stood there as if frozen stiff.

The scowling landlord surveyed this scene doubtfully. "Finished it all, eh?" he suddenly demanded. "Bring your plate, child,
let me see."

She scampered out and back in again in the space of an instant
and held up the empty dish. "Here, take his," he said, pointing to
my untouched plateful. She started to take it, then drew back and
looked at me.

"It's all right, go ahead," I said.

She grabbed it, left the room and closed the door behind her, and the innkeeper stared at me as if trying to decide how big a scoundrel I really was.

"Strange goings on," he said, scratching his head. "Let me see your document."

"Ah," I said, for it had actually slipped my mind—I was that rattled by what had just happened—and I handed it over with growing reluctance. After all, I wondered, what can you really tell about people, even those you've known for years? And here I was trusting this stranger, and how in the world could I tell what he might think of such a delicate matter?

"Well," he said, his eyes widening, apparently reading it over and over. "Well, I see." He sat down on the edge of the bed and scratched his head again. "Never seen one of these before. Quite a paper you got here, Mister, uh . . . Hull."

He stared down at it for another long moment. "Got another one shows she's yours?" he said, and I fished out the bill of sale and gave it to him.

He read that one at a glance, said, "Yep" and handed it back, then said, "Tilly, come in here," in a booming voice.

Tilly came in slowly that time, and when the innkeeper motioned for her to sit down beside him she eyed him with her usual suspicion.

"Can you read?" he asked her, then said, "Course you can't," before she could even reply on her own. "It's all right, I'll read it to you. It says that Harrison Hull, this man here . . ."

And then he read it slowly and carefully word for word. "It means you're free," he said at the end. "It means you don't belong to anyone anymore."

There was a moment when she stared at him with wide-eyed confusion, but then, very slowly, she began to smile. Naturally, the growling innkeeper Jarvis had no time for that. Very suddenly he stood, walked over and gave me back the paper. "It's legal, it's fine," he said. "Just sign it, and I'll witness."

We finished up and then he left, then came back a minute later. "Just want to shake your hand, Hull," he said, and I gladly obliged.

"Your money," I said, suddenly remembering the fee, but he just scowled again and shook his head.

"Best of luck to you, sir," he added, then walked out again, that time for good.

A few minutes later, there was a knock on the door. It was the houseboy carrying another heaping plate of stew.

I thanked him with a smile and devoured it on the spot.

I told her very gently that she could come with me if she wanted and stay with my mother and sisters and me at our house in Bucks County. I explained she didn't have to because she wasn't a slave anymore, but if she did we would feed her and take care of her and send her to school. I handed her the paper that set her free.

"You'll learn to read," I said, "and you won't have to . . . do those things anymore and no one will hurt you."

She nodded attentively as I spoke, seemingly taking it all in. "So I don't have to go?" she said. "I can stay here?"

"That's right," I answered, "but I'd worry about you. You won't have any money or any place to stay. I wish you'd come home with me, just for a little while, see how you like it."

She nodded again. "Food like here?" she said, and I smiled happily.

"Better," I said.

"All right," she said, "I'll come."

And we left first thing next morning on the final phase of our long journey.

My thoughts turned to Betsy Grinder as we rode east through the Allegheny hills. She was a widow now—rid of that beast, and I wondered, What's she doing with herself? Is she still there, at Grinder's Stand?

And then I asked myself: Just what has she been up to all along? As things turned out, she'd been telling me the truth: almost certainly, her husband was the murderer.

I thought it over a long time, and then I finally hit on an idea:

maybe, just maybe, she'd been sending signals. Idiotic, unintelligible signals. But in her own strange way, perhaps she'd been trying to tell the world: Look, this doesn't make sense. Just listen to what I'm saying. Isn't it . . . peculiar? Something's amiss here. Take a second glance at how this man Lewis really died.

But nobody did. Until . . .

A two-shot suicide, I thought with a shake of my head. Or was it three? I asked myself with a smile, recalling what she'd told Brahan.

I actually laughed out loud, then looked around to see little Tilly shake her head and roll her eyes with amazed amusement at my strange behavior. Is she feeling freer? I asked myself. Well, maybe just a bit braver, I thought, though that's a kind of freedom, isn't it?

Our house, once so grandly gay, was gray and gloomy now: my mother deep in mourning, both my sisters' weddings postponed.

Had dour Edward's spirit won out after all? I wondered.

But that wasn't it. That was silly. In point of fact, Edward seemed to have relaxed considerably since my last trip home. Had father put some kind of pressure on him that I'd never understood? I suddenly wondered.

Whatever the reason, I actually caught my brother smiling now and then. He was hardly a bundle of joy, you understand, but that grating, pompous edge seemed to have vanished from his demeanor, and I actually didn't mind being around him once in a while.

It was my mother who had changed. All in black, rarely out of her room, it was as if she were slowly withdrawing from . . . well, from everything.

Strange, I thought, the unexpected ways in which people react to unexpected events. Edward, who I'd thought would never change, had come out of his prickly shell, while Mother, who had always seemed to be quite an independent woman, had gone into one of her own.

As for my sisters . . . Well, the childish pranks and giddy

laughter were gone for good, I'm afraid—although that was no doubt inevitable. Still, I hated to see them forced to grow up with such brutal abruptness.

Old Morgan Hull, you died too soon, I thought.

As for Tilly, they welcomed her nicely enough—once they got over the initial shock. But my mother in particular simply lacked the energy or interest to give her the special care I'd wanted so badly for her. So after a short while, Tilly seemed to simply disappear among the other servants in the back of the house.

And I thought, This will not do. But I bided my time; I would get to it later.

"Thank God you're home and well," I told old Wilson.

We were at his new lodgings on the top floor of his sister's husband's house—a handsomely furnished little suite far more commodious than his old rooming house had been.

"You, too, my friend," he said.

And that was when it happened. I won't dwell on it, but that was when I finally broke down and unleashed the tears I'd held back so long.

My grief was set off oddly enough from pleasure—from seeing Wilson again. But of course my father's death and the sad condition of my family and all the terrible things I'd seen and heard since the last time I'd set eyes on this grand, good friend of mine played their parts, as well.

"I understand," he said and patted me on the shoulder—for him a veritable outpouring of emotion.

When I'd gone on awhile, much too long, really, he quietly slipped out of the room, and I thought it was from embarrassment or even impatience. But to my amazement he came back a moment later with a bottle of rum and a glass—just one glass, of course.

"My brother-in-law keeps quite a liquor cabinet," he said, "or so I'm told."

I nodded, and he poured it for me—the first time he'd ever done that. I drank it down and then had another, and after a few minutes my little fit subsided.

"So tell me everything," Wilson said, trying to sound enthusiastic but with a distinct undertone of dread in his voice.

"Well, it's a long, sad story," I said, and then obliged him with all the details.

"So then, you do think Boilvin killed Phelps and Brahan?" Wilson said when I'd finished at last.

The story had taken hours to tell, and needless to say, by the time it was over I had had several more sizeable swallows. By then we had moved downstairs to the front parlor where Wilson's sister, Emma, had joined us. They had both looked alternately shocked and angry as I spoke. Indeed, toward the end they had seemed for a while on the verge of tears.

"Quite likely," I answered, though just possibly, I thought, he hadn't, and I had let the real murderer slip through my fingers.

There was a pause while Wilson and his sister sipped their tea, and I nursed yet another demon glassful.

"Harrison," Emma Wilson Logan finally said in the slightly punctilious tone one might expect from the sister of Alexander Wilson.

She stopped, and I said, "Yes, Emma?" in the kindest voice I could manage.

"This . . . little girl," she went on, "this black child you spoke of. Will she be all right? That is, I know your family's suffered a loss, and I just thought . . . What I mean is, if she's in any way a burden . . ."

Emma Logan looked over at me as she always had, as if she were somehow looking down her nose—though I'd realized long ago that it was entirely unintentional.

". . . that is, if she's too much trouble, she could . . . well, she could stay here. With us."

Her suggestion caught me quite by surprise, and I stared at her with what I imagine was a very wide and appreciative smile. Indeed, of all the surprising things people had told me lately, that was the first in a long time that I would readily describe as pleasant.

"Why thank you, Emma," I said, "for your kind suggestion."

And I thought, That's an idea that just might work out for the best in the long run.

"Your husband, Dr. Logan, he would . . ." I trailed off with a fluttery wave of my hands.

"He'd love it," she answered at once with a definite snap to her tone. And I suddenly recalled that after nine years of marriage they were childless.

"Well, we'll see, Emma," I said. "I'll let you know."

And then we each quietly sipped our drinks.

Alexander Wilson wrote to Thomas Jefferson at what was by then his address of permanent retirement—the elegant house called Monticello in Albemarle County, Virginia. He explained everything in meticulous detail. He even reproduced with great care and astonishing accuracy the handwritten letters between Bates and Wilkinson, as well as the two famous invoices to Wilkinson and Neelly—though at the last minute we agreed not to send the invoices. We should hold something back, we decided, for a later time.

All in all, when he was finished, we sent off a packet of material that was thirty-four pages long.

And then we waited. And waited.

And waited.

When no reply was forthcoming, Wilson wrote again, much more briefly of course, calling Jefferson's attention to "my voluminous correspondence of last summer regarding the tragic death of Meriwether Lewis."

He wrote again, more than once, then finally wrote at some length to Madison, as well.

Still there was no reply. And all the while Wilson withered. Slowly, almost daily it seemed, he grew thinner and paler and sadder and weaker, until at last it was hard for me to look at him without wincing a little.

"Why don't they answer?" he'd say.

And of course I had no answer of my own to give him.

Meanwhile, I tended to family matters. My sisters finally did get married in early spring, and then that June, to everyone's great pleasure, so did Edward. It left my mother more alone than ever of course. She had never really regained her old self, her old liveliness, and now she seemed to wither in her own way; she had, almost overnight, become an old lady.

I also kept an eye on Tilly, who was treated kindly enough and given the necessities, but retained within her voice and eyes that awful lifelessness which so unnerved me. So finally I raised the question, and my mother simply smiled faintly and said that would be fine. And a few weeks later, Tilly Hull, once enslaved to one James Neelly of Tennessee, moved into a fine town house in the big city, where she was fed, dressed, pampered and schooled—just as any child deserves to be—and eventually became Tilly Hull Wilson Logan, free American of Philadelphia, Pennsylvania.

C H A P T E R

Eighteen

W hy don't they answer?'' Wilson asked me again and again.

And I'd smile, or try to, and tell him, Don't worry, just be patient, they will.

And all the while I somehow knew they never would, and my impatience turned to anger, which in turn became a rage inside myself that at times I felt I would not be able to control.

So why *don't* they answer, goddammit? I asked myself a thousand times. And after a while I began to get the idea that just maybe the worst of all conceivable possibilities lay behind their seeming lack of interest. It was something Boilvin had hinted at. And maybe Big White, too. Something that made me shudder just to think about, something I didn't even want to say out loud or put in writing. It was in much the same way that so many people, myself included, wouldn't say the name of that third man who'd apparently been in the scheme with Wilkinson and Bates. Indeed, it had been said that that same third man had been on the edge of that business with Wilkinson and Burr. It wasn't Adams, or Jefferson, or Madison, of course, but a well-known man, a man who might one day be . . .

Well, never mind that now. The point is that what I thought might be happening was almost as dreadfully unthinkable as that—although I couldn't help thinking about it anyway because I was too deep in it by then to do otherwise. And what my thinking told me was, as everybody knew, that Jefferson hated Burr, that Jefferson knew that Wilkinson had the goods on Burr, and that that was what Jefferson wanted, above all. Wilkinson had even testified against Burr at his trial, though it had done no good: Burr had been acquitted. But even so there were favors to repay, rewards to be given out.

So is that what's going on here? I asked myself. Is it simply that nobody—most particularly, neither Jefferson nor his toady Madison—will do anything that might hurt the man who'd once been commanding general of the U.S. Army *and* a Spanish spy—both at the same time? Were Burr's crimes so much worse than that? I wondered.

And my old friend wrote and wrote. And somehow I couldn't quite bring myself to tell him why I thought they wouldn't answer. After all, he was old and sick and it wasn't as if I *knew* the reason. That was one thing I felt certain that I'd never be able to prove.

Still, I wanted Wilkinson. I wanted justice. I wanted Bates, as well.

But Wilson wanted more: he wanted back the good name of Meriwether Lewis. But truth be told, by then I had pretty much decided that that was beyond our grasp for good.

The months slipped away, we sold our ancient family home, and my old mother moved in with my sister Ellen and her new husband on their farm not far away.

I visited with them, and with my sister Laura and her new husband, and also with Letitia Greenleaf Chauncey, and her husband, Albert, "of the Harrisburg Chaunceys," at their very splendid new town house on Old Chestnut Street. Oddly enough I did remember Albert: he was still the same slightly prissy, flat-faced, crashing bore of a fellow that he'd been at the age of seven when he was the only boy around who actually liked a particular swine of a science tutor who had for a time been the scourge of the neighborhood.

And then autumn came and word leaked out. It hit us like a thunderclap: All that summer—the just-ended summer of 1811, to be exact—a secret court-martial had been underway in Washington. The defendant before the tribunal had been General James Wilkinson. The charge: espionage.

As you might imagine, it was hard to find out just what had happened and why, but from what little I learned it seemed that Wilkinson had produced his own logs of transactions with the Spanish from several years ago. They were, he angrily insisted, records of tobacco sales between him and his Spanish friends. And in the absence of any authentic documents to the contrary, that wily man had prevailed yet again. He'd been acquitted. He was scot-free.

I remember thinking how even well-intended human actions can have the most unexpected results. Take secrets, for instance: the government had kept theirs, and Wilson and I had kept ours, and the result had been the acquittal of a guilty man—not to speak of the undoing of my most fervent desire.

It was two weeks before I could bring myself to tell Wilson about it. Predictably enough, he retired to his sickbed almost without a word. It was seventeen days till he was up and about again.

And then the leaves fell from the trees, and before we knew it it was the dead of winter.

"What can we do, Harry?" Wilson said angrily one February afternoon as snow piled up outside his parlor window.

There was vigor in his voice and even a healthy glow in his cheeks for a change—the cold weather seemed to agree with him, but I had no ideas to cheer him up.

"I don't know, Alex," I said with a weary shake of my head, "but I will do something, I promise you that." I just didn't know what, or where, or when, or how. Other than that, I thought, my plan is excellent.

And then, four months later, fighting exploded across America, and all bets were off. The War of 1812 had begun.

The United States had no standing army to speak of and a navy of only five serviceable frigates, a fraction of the British fleet. Under Madison and his war secretary, William Eustis (the man who had so riled Meriwether Lewis in the first place), the entire War Department lay in the hands of a sleepy little corps of clerks who knew no more about the military than the clerks in, say, the counting room of a distillery.

Yet when war was declared on the eighteenth day of June, 1812, it was *not* the British who declared it.

"Whether the United States shall continue passive under these progressive usurpations and accumulating wrongs by Great Britain," Madison had told the Congress a few days before, "or, opposing force to force in defense of their national rights, shall commit a just cause into the hands of the Almighty Disposer of Events is a solemn question which *must* now be considered by the legislative department of the Government."

Thus the unexpected had once again intervened, and the results that time would be remarkable indeed.

I traveled to Washington at once, presented myself at War Department headquarters and asked for an assignment. As you might imagine, the place was in an uproar. Little Madison himself was there, taking personal charge, and actually I was more impressed with him than I had been: his demeanor was steady, firm and assured. Also, he'd finally fired Eustis, just a few days before, and named the energetic John Armstrong in his place. But it was hardly enough to make up for America's astonishing lack of preparation. Indeed, after languishing nearly two weeks in a nearby rooming house I was politely told to return home and await further orders. In other words, in the chaos of the moment they could not figure out what, if anything, I should do.

It was late September when orders reached me at last: Go north, they said, in a hurry and join the command of Brigadier General William Hull (no relation) who was stationed at Detroit and preparing an offensive against British troops across the Canadian border.

I thought, It's nearly winter, and they're planning a battle in Canada. But I packed my heavy coats and cape, said my goodbyes all around, and got underway with all possible speed.

Early snowstorms and other foul weather slowed my travel. One horse came up lame, and another one died. A key bridge was out. And a massive Indian uprising, led by the legendary Tecumseh, blocked all travel through northern Ohio for more than a week.

Even so, I arrived in Detroit on November 9—not bad time even in ideal conditions. Still, I was too late, and in a way lucky at that, for Hull's little campaign was already over and what a fiasco it had been. He'd prepared poorly and provisioned his men hardly at all. He'd vacillated daily in his overall plan. And when the time came to fight at last, he'd attacked when he shouldn't have and stood fast when he should have attacked. The result was that he'd lost scores of men to a slightly smaller British force.

I spent a hard winter helping our scattered forces regroup. We commandeered fresh supplies, constructed thousands of huts, set up a hospital and even tried to train the men a little. But morale was low, the winter harsh, the officers themselves undisciplined and, to put it politely, self-serving. All in all, to me the chances for a successful American land offensive in that sector of the war seemed dismal indeed.

Fresh orders arrived at last in the spring, and my first reaction on reading them was dread. But the more I thought it over the more my heart soared at the prospect. I was ordered east (and even a little more north, if that were possible!) to Plattsburgh and then on to Sackets Harbor, where I would join the newly named commander of the entire northern district, one Major General James Wilkinson.

I would, the orders said, be one of his principal subordinates. To my astonishment I was even promoted to major.

Staring at the paper wide-eyed, I wondered: Am I being set up in some truly diabolical way? Is this the finish to my career? Or is it even, as was surely possible in battle, a sentence of death?

But that's absurd, I reasoned. Wilkinson surely had enough other things to worry about. So maybe, after all this time, he'd decided that it really was just birds we'd been after that long-ago spring in St. Louis.

Also, the more I thought it over the more I thought what a remarkable opportunity it could be. I'd kept all the documents with me, and just perhaps the right moment would arise when I could give James Wilkinson the surprise of his life.

A fifteen-gun salute announced Wilkinson's arrival at Sackets Harbor,★ at the far northeastern corner of Lake Ontario, on August 25, 1813. From the time his orders had been issued, it had taken him five months and fifteen days to get there. I and most of the other officers, as well as the men, had been there for weeks. It was not, to put it mildly, an auspicious beginning.

"Hello, Hull," he said with a big smile the moment I saw him. We were in a makeshift little office he'd set up inside crumbling old Fort George.

"Glad you're here," he said, shooing a half-dozen others, officers and all, out of the room. "You're the only one I can trust," he whispered. "Rest of these puppies not worth a damn. Drunkards. Mama's boys. Spoiled brats and nincompoops."

I studied him as he spoke, and he was different, all right. His face was thin and lined, his voice tired—much of his old robustness gone.

"Been sick," he said, watching me watching him, and I thought: He still doesn't miss much, does he?

"Here, give me a hand," he said, and I walked over to him, puzzled. "Come on," he snapped, holding his arm out. And then I realized that he was waiting for me to help him up—that he couldn't walk on his own anymore.

"You all right, sir?" I said, as I hoisted him to a standing position.

"I will be," he said. "This'll pass."

★See Great Lakes Theater of War Map, p. ix.

With him pointing the way and me propping him up, we slowly walked out of the room into the hallway, then turned left a few paces to the next office down. Wilkinson banged on the door, then pushed it open. My eyes widened as I saw who was seated behind a little table on the far side of the room:

"John, this is Harrison Hull, my adjutant," Wilkinson boomed. "Major Hull, meet the secretary of war, John Armstrong."

"Mister Secretary," I said with a respectful little bow. He quickly stood, came around the table and shook my hand.

"Glad to meet you, Hull," he said, then turned to Wilkinson. "How you feeling, General? Any better?"

"Oh yes, yes," Wilkinson said, some of the old smoothness still there.

"Good, we need you, and soon," Armstrong said with a smile. "You too, Hull."

We shook hands all around one more time and withdrew. Then I took Wilkinson back to his office, requested permission to return next morning, then left to go search out quarters for myself.

Well, you can imagine the lift all that gave to my spirits. Wilkinson ailing, but nonetheless there for serious business, or so it seemed. And Armstrong himself on the scene! What a novelty that was! And I thought: Maybe they really mean it, after all. Maybe this really will turn out to be a hell of a fight!

But the boost was an illusion, so short-lived that I would wonder later on if what I'd seen that first day in Sackets Harbor had been real or imaginary. Detroit, it turned out, would be merely prelude to the unthinkable.

They argued about everything, from how many socks to order to how many bandages to buy to whom to put in charge of supplies and who would construct the hospital. And on it went and nothing got done.

I knew there were literally tons of medicine stockpiled at Plattsburgh just fifteen miles away, but I saw no one devising any way they could be brought here to Sackets Harbor, let alone join an army on the move. I saw desperately needed boots disappearing by the thousands to thieves and deserters. I saw cask after cask of port, meant to warm the men on cold-weather marches, being drunk dry by lazy and conniving officers.

And naturally they couldn't agree about the big things, either. For instance, should we march straight to Montreal, about two hundred miles up the St. Lawrence River, or attack nearby Kingston first—a British stronghold that would obviously be a danger to our rear if we went past it? And should we simply evacuate old Fort George, or leave a skeleton crew behind, or rebuild it—make it strong enough to repel a British assault?

On and on it went until after a few days I finally realized there was something truly unnatural about their disputes:

I couldn't tell which man wanted what.

First, it seemed, Armstrong insisted that Kingston be first. "Otherwise, be at your rear all the way, General," he said more than once.

"They won't budge, I tell you, too scared of being out-flanked," Wilkinson shot back. "They'll stay right there and look after this area while we dash upriver."

"Dammit, you just want the easy glory," Armstrong growled. "Sure, it's fine for you, but think of the men, think of the igno-miny, when you get caught in a pincer."

With that, the esteemed secretary of war melodramatically meshed the fingers of both hands into one, then clapped his palms together with a loud snap.

"Front and back, front and back!" he shouted as he did so.

They finished soon after for the day and resumed next morn-ing. And then I listened in amazement, for it was as if the previous day's conversation had never taken place.

"I think this march straight to Montreal could be an ill-conceived business, John," Wilkinson said, shifting uncomfortably in his chair. "A very, very risky proposition, Mister Secretary."

Armstrong nodded thoughtfully, not an iota of surprise show-ing on his features. (I cannot imagine what I looked like at that moment, though thinking back on it, I can only believe that my face must have been positively paralyzed with astonishment at Wilkinson's turnabout.)

"Well, that's a well-taken point, General, but we don't want to get bogged down, now do we?" Armstrong said, his tone and manner as sincere as anyone's I'd ever heard in my life.

"Bogged down, bogged down," Wilkinson wailed, suddenly adamantly in favor of what he'd fought against so hard the day before. "Why, we'll clean up that Kingston show of theirs in three days at the most, then be in Montreal before the leaves turn brown."

"Well, Kingston's pretty well fortified, General, I wouldn't be so sure," Armstrong went on.

As the days and the arguments dragged on, I began to understand the game: they were jockeying for position, sliding back and forth so often and so intricately that no one who'd heard them could ever be sure just who said what. And that was fine with them because no matter what was finally decided each could blame the other in case of failure.

And I realized that this was pretty much business as usual in the U.S. Army, and that nothing much would ever really get accomplished—not with leadership like that. And even realizing all that I did, I still could not imagine the magnitude of what lay ahead.

The leaves had long since turned and fallen, wintry squalls were up on Lake Ontario and there were even patches of swirling snow by the time the campaign got underway at last. It was the sixteenth of October, 1813.

The first destination was Grenadier Island, just eighteen miles upstream. But in that short distance, high winds and incompetent crewmen piled scores of our boats ashore, and there was a virtual calamity with supplies: Of 340,000 rations that had been loaded without any system or organization, 138,000 were "lost." Of course with no one in charge of them except the contractor's agent, it wasn't hard to figure that, strange as it sounds, the higher the "losses" the bigger the profits.

I also watched medical officers search in vain for medicine

and other supplies that had been stored in the same careless way. And I saw the heavy rains drench and ruin tons of gunpowder and even some weapons, as well.

And as I say, all that in just the first eighteen miles!

It was another two weeks, the first of November to be exact, before we finally left the little island for the second hop—a distance of thirty miles to French Creek. Meanwhile, Wilkinson wrote Armstrong requesting that the army under the command of General Wade Hampton near Lake Champlain join him near the junction of the Grand and St. Lawrence rivers.

Armstrong had firmly pledged Hampton's full cooperation, but the request was futile nonetheless. For no help was forthcoming, and it soon became known that Hampton, after losing a minor skirmish at a place called Spears, had in fact resigned his command in despair.

Meanwhile, by now the British could certainly tell where we were going: that we had indeed bypassed Kingston and were heading for Montreal. The only solution to our troubles was to move quickly. But once again, snow, wind, hail, and Wilkinson's indecisiveness kept us six days at French Creek—though when we moved at last we slipped past the fortified town of Prescott without a hitch, with only skeleton crews on the boats and most of the men—*with* the powder!—marching by land on the American side. It was indeed the high point of the campaign, flawlessly staged by a bright and energetic young colonel named Winfield Scott.

We languished again while Wilkinson tried to collect himself. But sick and worn out, he became alarmed too late—and then almost to the point of desperation over increased British movements both ahead of us and to our rear.

"They're . . . they're all around us, Harry," he said at one point in a shockingly dazed and feeble voice.

"You're ill, sir," I dared. "You're sure you don't . . ." But I trailed off, not quite courageous enough to finish the suggestion that he might want to relinquish his command.

Finally, however, bedridden entirely, he turned over temporary command to a General George Lewis, who the next day finally gave the drenched and freezing troops orders to march on. It was November 11, and we were halfway to Montreal.

But suddenly the half-dazed Wilkinson rose from his sickbed, resumed command and canceled Lewis's orders. It was a fatal mistake. As thousands of men milled about in cold that was measured at twenty-three degrees below zero, British gunboats coming up from neglected Kingston emerged from the morning mist and opened fire. At the same time, British troops moved in by land from the opposite direction.

The American force on hand at the time and involved in the subsequent battle numbered nearly twenty-five hundred. The British troops totaled just eight hundred. Even so, it was the long-feared "front and back" pincer that Armstrong had so disingenuously warned of in his debates with Wilkinson.

The battle went back and forth along a wedge of land about a mile long and half a mile wide for about four hours. With only a vague notion of the specific mission and being none too clear about where to find or even fire at the British lines, the Americans floundered about in rain-washed gullies frequently confused by changing and conflicting orders.

"What should we do, goddammit!" one frustrated major finally screamed right in Wilkinson's face, and two other officers quickly chimed in. Wilkinson, pale, lying on his stretcher in the driving snow, stared at them emptily for five or six of the longest minutes of my life.

"Get them . . . get them out," he finally managed, and the officers who'd waited around to hear that feeble excuse for an order just rolled their eyes and shook their heads and wandered off.

In the thick of the battle, I saw one brave young lieutenant rush forward with two six-pounders. But he was killed almost instantly by well-disciplined British fire and his artillery pieces were captured soon afterward.

At another point, a squad of cavalrymen formed up in a gully and charged the British line. But more than half their number were cut down in minutes, and the rest wisely retreated to safer ground.

It was all over by noontime, the greatest military defeat in the short history of the republic. More than one hundred Americans had been killed, nearly three hundred wounded and another three hundred taken prisoner.

The British counted their total casualties at fewer than fifty. They had crushed an American force more than three times the size of their own.

Wilkinson promptly called a war council—his third so far of the ill-fated campaign. With the troops demoralized, supplies dwindling and no help on the way from Hampton's army, Wilkinson's officers were by then eager to accept his recommendation: Call it off, abandon the march.

The general picked a place called French Mills, about twenty miles downriver, as our winter headquarters. It was a gloomy spot of six or seven houses in a deep, almost impenetrable forest of hemlock and pine. The general had picked it because reports said there was a blockhouse suitable for housing the sick and wounded, but it was smaller than believed. Only about a hundred fifty of nearly two thousand ill and injured men could fit inside.

Construction began on new huts, but the work went slowly. The temperature dropped to a consistent thirty below and men were dying at the rate of a dozen a day. Corrupt officers appropriated the dead men's pay for themselves and confiscated rations for sale at personal profit.

Two weeks after we arrived at French Mills, the men were put on half rations, and some regiments went for days without bread. I tested the flour myself when it finally arrived and found it was mixed with plaster of Paris.

Reports from Plattsburgh twenty-five miles away said the quartermaster corp had simply collapsed—gone to pieces. So I rode over there one day and found that indeed while men at French Mills were starving by the thousands supplies at Plattsburgh were literally piled in the streets, slowing ebbing in the wind and snow.

By then nearly all hospital stores had been lost or stolen. What medical supplies we were able to get came all the way from Albany—a distance of two hundred fifty miles. Pneumonia, diarrhea, dysentery and typhus were commonplace. The death rate grew even higher and morale plummeted to the point that Wilkinson banned the playing of funeral dirges in the camps.

And then there were desertions: officers gave every possible excuse for getting leave, then, when denied, simply left anyway. Soldiers faced with punishment deserted and went home. Others, fed by rumors that they would be welcomed to the British service with a raise in pay and a bonus to boot, fled north to Canada.

And all through that winter, there was no help from Wilkinson or Armstrong or anyone else. Certainly not from little Madison!

Wilkinson maintained his personal headquarters in a large white frame house in a village called Malone, a pleasant few miles from the ghastly disintegration at French Mills, where he dreamed of new offensives and struggled to shift blame.

"They should hang him," Wilkinson railed in private about General Hampton's abrupt resignation of command. And he wrote acidly to Armstrong:

> I will not charge this man with traitorous designs, but I apprehend that in any other government, a military officer who just defeated the object of a campaign by disobedience of orders and then furloughed all the officers of the division he commanded on a national frontier in the vicinity of an enemy would incur heavy penalties.

True enough, I thought, as far as it goes. But what about you? I asked myself. I see your crimes; where's your punishment?

In early January he produced his boldest scheme yet to recoup his reputation. If he could simply collect enough supplies and winter equipment, if the health of his troops improved, if the weather turned better and the state militia would cooperate, and if the enemy would help by remaining conveniently immovable, he would, as he put it, "strike a blow at the British that would reach to the bone."

He described the plan in some detail: Two columns of two thousand men each from Plattsburgh and nearby Chateaugay would converge on British-held St. Pierre, then march on together to capture St. Philippe, L'Acadie and St. Johns. At the same time the force at French Mills would cross the St. Lawrence and seize Cornwall.

He waxed enthusiastic for hours about the plan, ignoring his own long list of "ifs" and adding that it would in any case be for the best to keep the men from eating what he called "the bread of idleness."

There was of course an obvious enough retort to that, but once again I held back. I was still waiting, still biding my time.

Three days later, when somebody brought up the plan again at a routine staff gathering, Wilkinson's eyes glazed over and he numbly shook his head.

"Harebrained," he muttered, his voice suddenly more exhausted than ever. And with that the embarrassed officers drifted slowly out of the room.

But he soon came up with another plan: he would simply "reach out," as he put it, and take Prescott and Kingston with seventy-five hundred men from the force of eight thousand at French Mills. Just how he would do that with so many sick and disabled was not explained. Indeed his own official report in mid-January said less than forty-five hundred men at French Mills were fit for duty.

Needless to say, Armstrong didn't think much of Wilkinson's schemes. Around the first of February, orders arrived to abandon French Mills. The army would be split, with two thousand going to Sackets Harbor and the rest to Plattsburgh under Wilkinson. In addition, about four hundred fifty of the sickest men would be taken in relays by sleigh to Burlington, where at last they would receive the care and comfort of a real hospital.

Even then the scheming didn't stop. In late March, with winter on the wane and his health improving, Wilkinson conjured up one last gasp of a plan. About thirty miles away, just across the border at a place called Lacolle Mill, was a small contingent of British troops ready to block any possible advance by the Americans through the Champlain Valley.

It looked easy enough to take, and even this "small cup" victory, as he described it, might satisfy the administration and keep his enemies at bay. Indeed, a full-scale investigation of his failures that winter seemed more than likely. Also, he insisted, it would give the troops valuable training and pave the way for a larger offensive during the summer ahead.

On March 27, 1814, fully four thousand American troops, accompanied by eleven pieces of artillery, marched out of Plattsburgh. Two days later, within sight of the town and having met no resistance, the order was given: Attack Lacolle Mill.

Only six hundred British troops lay in wait, though they were well protected by a two-foot-high stone wall around the mill. The Americans advanced to within a hundred fifty yards and opened fire. The British fired back, more effectively, of course, because of their protection.

Artillery was ordered up to breach the wall, but only twelve-pounders got into the fight. The heavier guns had got stuck on the road, and somehow nobody seemed able to pry them loose and bring them forward.

The Americans contented themselves with firing from the edges of a nearby clearing and shooting at openings in the mill from various spots along the adjacent Lacolle River.

By evening the attack simply petered out. Disturbed by growing signs of bad weather and the stubborn resistance of the British, Wilkinson ordered a retreat. Four days later, the entire army was safely back in Plattsburgh. For Wilkinson, it was the final humiliation.

"They'll fire me now, Harry," he told me that evening over numerous glasses of port.

"I know," I said. "You deserve it."

He looked at me and blinked, as if wondering if he'd heard right. "Yes, that's what I said, you deserve it," I told him again.

"Now listen, young Major Hull—"

"You're a terrible general," I went on, pulling my chair right alongside him, "and a terrible man. You should be shot."

I pulled out the copies Wilson had made of the notes between Bates and Wilkinson and handed them over. He read them with an uninterested glare and handed them back. "This is nothing; it's meaningless," he said. "These notes were about something else, I can't even remember what right now, but—"

"Yes, I heard you were good at inventing alternative reasons to fit the evidence and justify your actions," I said, and he scowled furiously. He knew that I was referring to his secret court-martial, and naturally it annoyed him that I knew so much about something that I wasn't supposed to know about at all.

"They should have had this at your trial," I said, and handed him my copy of the Spanish invoice.

"This is a forgery," he said at once, spotting the obvious difference, because of course the real invoice was more than ten years old.

"It's a copy, they're all copies," I said. "The originals are in a safe place back in Philadelphia."

"Copy?" he said, looking it over.

"Yes, made by a friend of mine."

"Ah, Wilson, of course," he said, and actually smiled admiringly at the painstaking penmanship. He read the invoice carefully, and the smile faded. He stared off a long, silent few moments—long enough for me to pour myself another glass and drink it down.

"What do you want, Hull?" he finally asked in his smoothly defiant way; indeed, he almost recaptured his manner of old.

"Justice," I said, and he laughed out loud.

"My friend is dead, actually a couple of friends," I said, ignoring his silly laughter. "And that means, for justice to be served, you should die, too."

I opened my coat and slowly pulled out a beautiful, custom-made pistol with an ivory handle and a shiny barrel. He watched it carefully; in truth, for a long moment, he couldn't take his eyes off it.

"That pistol, isn't it—"

"Meriwether Lewis's, yes," I answered. "Neelly gave it to me. He told me everything. I have his confession."

Wilkinson stared at me and the beautiful pistol with wide eyes and the muscles throbbing in his throat. And I thought, At last he looks like any other frightened man. But it didn't last long.

"You . . . you're bluffing," he said, his composure quickly returning. "Neelly's dead. They found his body at his mother's farm. So . . . you killed him?"

"In self-defense."

"But who'll believe that? You have the pistols, and that's proof you were there."

"That's right," I said. *"I* have the pistols. *I* have the Spanish invoice. You have nothing."

"They've already tried me—"

"For espionage, yes," I put in, "but I'll publish that invoice in every newspaper in the country. And don't forget, I also have Neelly's confession, and it meshes perfectly with your letters to Bates. Believe me, I'll see you're charged with murder, and it'll be worth it, even if I pay by facing a firing squad myself. Just imagine: you're a hated man already—a foreign spy and a failed general, and you'll go on trial for murdering one of America's greatest heroes. Think what it'll be like, General. Even if they free you again, will life be worth living?"

By then, I had that near-demonic sound in my voice again, and Wilkinson stared at me with gloomy resignation. "So that's what you want," he murmured very softly, then narrowed his eyes and studied me carefully.

"I . . . I'll leave the army," he said. "I'll . . . disappear. I swear it."

I was running a step behind him at that point, and it took me a moment to realize what he meant when he'd said something about that being what I wanted. And thinking back over what I'd said I could understand why he took it the way he did.

"Will life be worth living?" I'd unthinkingly asked him.

And in that evil moment I did not disabuse him of the notion. However accidentally I had stated it in the first place, I let the lie stand undiluted.

But then I did even more: "Getting out of the army is good," I said with a nasty smile, "as far as it goes." I looked around the office where his headquarters had been the last two months. "Nice collection, General," I said, nodding at the caseful of weapons behind his desk. Then I started to leave the room. "Think it over, General," I said, turning back as I reached the doorway. Then I pulled the door closed behind me, walked out of there and was gone.

Nine days later, on April 12, 1814, orders came through by fast rider from Washington that James Wilkinson was relieved of duty as commanding general of the 9th District of the Army of the United States. But Wilkinson hadn't waited. Sometime between the time I'd left him about eight-thirty that night and when his orderly found him about six the next morning, Major General James Wilkinson had loaded a prize pistol of his own, raised it to his right temple and pulled the trigger. He left no note, and so far as I could determine he was not widely mourned.

C H A P T E R

Nineteen

The mockingbird sang so many times that spring.

So many men, I thought, given up to the dogs of war. By the most ancient standard, Wilkinson deserved to go with them on that count alone.

But perhaps there was an element of punishment all around. Perhaps it was for my benefit that that songbird sang its sad song one more time. For when I rode back into Philadelphia in early May, with British frigates off the mouth of the Delaware, a battle raging in Chesapeake Bay and the capital itself in imminent danger, somehow the last thing I expected was that my best friend in the world would have met his end, as well.

The greatest ornithologist in America, Alexander Wilson, had in fact died on April 12, the very day of Wilkinson's posthumous recall. The cause of Wilson's death was dysentery, which in the misery of the moment gave me a tearful laugh.

"A soldier's disease!" I shouted, for having seen so many hundreds of cases in the previous months, that was how I'd come to think of it—though of course it was an illness that could strike anyone anytime.

I retired to the woods of Bucks County after that. I slept under the stars and put all worldly matters out of my mind. Or tried to: I saw one big-horned owl swoop off with a squirrel, and another one high above me with what looked like a wolf cub dangling from its powerful beak. But I also saw a bright and beautiful red tanager, a softly sweet goldfinch, several kinds of jays, dozens of bluebirds, and a black-throated bunting. I also saw that peculiar creature known as the mockingbird: Indeed, there it was one especially bright morning just a few yards in front of me, chirping away, sounding at that moment exactly like a robin.

I had told everyone I'd be away a week, but when that was up I saw no reason to hurry back, so I extended it another and then beyond that, until after a while I began to lose track. In truth, I might have stayed out all summer except one fine afternoon my brother Edward and a couple of other men came huffing out of the woods and into my campsite.

"Edward!" I shouted happily.

"Harry!" he growled. "Been looking for you two days. Started to worry. Also, this came."

He handed me a letter that looked quite official in its bearing, though with no hint of the sender on the outside. I looked quizzically at Edward, but he just shrugged, and finally I tore it open and read the brief note.

"Who's it from, Harry?" Edward asked amiably, and I pulled him to one side and whispered the answer, but he just scoffed with disbelief. So I covered up the body of the note, because it said to keep it secret, and held it so he could see only the famous signature across the bottom of the page.

James Madison, it said, and Edward smiled—still an event of relative rarity—and asked some impish question about whether it was all right for me to be seen heading back to town with the lowly likes of him.

"Seriously, Harry, what's it all about?" he asked (he'd finally stopped calling me Harrison, by the way), but I told him I didn't know, which I honestly didn't, though the message had given a tiny hint or two.

So I rode back into Philadelphia, packed up my best Beau Brummels, said my goodbyes again (though there were fewer of them that time) and headed dutifully south to Washington City.

The President's House had been "fancied up" quite a bit since last I'd been there. There was a new chandelier or two, and the East Room had been fixed up like a regular palace ballroom. It made you rather happy, or maybe it made you sick, depending on your disposition toward matters of that sort—that is, whether you thought the president of our little democracy should live in such palatial surroundings.

Well, they sat me down in the president's office, which was really not much different from the way old Tom Jefferson had had it, and then James and Dolley Madison came in a few minutes later, and . . . Well, they really were quite pleasant in their own way.

"I took the liberty of showing your friend Wilson's letter to Mrs. Madison here," Madison began, "and she agrees that your friend was a careful and thoughtful man. And we both extend our condolences upon his death."

"I've had the pleasure of seeing his books on birds," Dolley Madison put in, "and I thought they were as beautiful as any work of art that I could imagine."

Madison cleared his throat and Mrs. Madison stopped talking.

"And then when I explained to my wife the extent to which you were Wilson's collaborator, most especially with regard to the letter and the documents he sent me, she agreed with me that you also must be a man of some worth and intelligence."

"You see we both—"

They both spoke at once, and then Madison, the one who was president, cleared his throat again. And then the other one, his wife, stopped talking again—though that time not before turning just a little pink with embarrassment.

"We agreed," James Madison said, "that we need someone of special intelligence and abilities—"

"Someone like you," Dolley Madison put in, her famous irrepressibility showing full force. And by then I was laughing out loud; I couldn't help it.

"Just like you, yes," James Madison resumed, "in the West right now."

Now as of this writing, I am still bound by a pledge of secrecy that prevents me from revealing any more specifics of our conversation, so all that will have to wait for another time.

Suffice it to say it was an assignment that definitely piqued my interest, and with my own considerable amount of unfinished business in the region, I jumped at the chance to return.

"The West would be ideal for me," I said.

"We thought it might be," Dolley Madison replied with a grand smile. Then she rang a bell, and a servant came in and poured a touch of dry sherry all around.

"Winfield Scott speaks well of you," she said. "Says you were one of the few who kept his head during the recent, uh . . . setbacks in the North."

I looked at the president, hoping I suppose for some hint, some guidance, but he just smiled blandly.

"Scott's a good man, excellent officer," I said.

"A protégé of Mr. Andrew Jackson's, I believe," she added.

"Oh really," I said, as matter-of-factly as I could, for until that moment I'd had no idea that the two were even acquainted.

"Man with a future," the president suddenly put in, and I was almost startled to hear the sound of his voice after so long an interval—perhaps twenty minutes or more.

"Jackson?" I said, though I knew that was who he meant.

"Of course," he said with a dismissive shrug. "Man has that air about him. He'll go far with a little luck. Be good for the country, too." He cleared his throat and sipped his sherry. "He's not perfect, of course."

"He certainly isn't," Mrs. Madison put in with an indulgent smile.

"Self-educated man," Madison resumed. "Bit of a drinker, a roughneck. Maybe has some regrets; you know, a friendship or two he shouldn't have made, maybe some other things. But that's all in the past now. Best to let things lie."

"Sleeping dogs and all that," Dolley Madison said with a beguiling little flutter in her voice.

"So finish up what you have to out there in whatever way you choose," the president went on, "and get on with what I've told you to do, of course. But as for Jackson . . ."

Madison trailed off, once again with only a faint smile and a shrug to guide me, but it was all I needed. I pointedly finished my sherry with a gulp, and Mrs. Madison rang the bell again and the servant returned and poured me another. And I drank that off, too, more quickly than good manners generally allow.

For suddenly I couldn't help myself. Suddenly I felt like a tiny child in the grip of powerful forces: I was being used by them, of course, but the scheme was so elegant that I wasn't sure I cared.

We're choosing you because you're the best man for the job, they were telling me. But we also know you have other matters to deal with in that same part of the country, and perhaps with some of the same people who may be responsible for our new (and still secret) problem. So go ahead, deal with them both—first one, then the other, or both at the same time, we don't care. Just do it in whatever manner you see fit, with one exception: leave that man alone.

Ah, the easy beginning of our chat—passing along Winfield Scott's little compliment (if he ever really said it!). Then edging their way to Jackson, and then very gently acknowledging my own affairs. To me the elegance came from the boldness of it: picking me of all people to send back there. Most men, most leaders, would have handled it just the opposite. "Send anybody but Hull," they would have insisted.

But pointedly keeping me out of the West might, in the long run, have raised my suspicions and made things far worse. To have grasped that, to have seen beyond the usual speck of ground in front of them, was impressive, to say the least.

"All right," I said very quietly, then felt an immediate sense of dread and a sudden rush of questions in my mind.

What do they know that I don't? I asked myself. What evidence might I stumble upon to make me regret my connivance in their handsome little plot? What secret proof is there against that unnamed and unnameable third man in the scheme to hire Neelly? Or is there some new link between him and Aaron Burr? And if there is none, why go to such lengths to protect him?

"I'll do what you wish, I'll deal with everything just the way you want," I heard myself adding quickly, as if I were afraid something might come up at the last minute to change my mind.

"There's nothing else I can't do—no other restrictions, is that right?" I went on, my tone suddenly carping.

"None," they both said very calmly.

"Good," I said, "very good. Then in that case as far as I'm concerned that other man is not connected with this in any way. He is completely and entirely immune."

They both smiled warmly and sipped their sherry. And just in case it still isn't clear enough for you, and since in all fairness I must record it here anyway, though at considerable risk, I tell you now that, hard though it may be to accept and believe, the unnamed other man was Andrew Jackson.

C H A P T E R

Twenty

St. Louis was on a war footing. Or perhaps I should say: St. Louis believed it was.

Ragged squads of men marched the dusty streets with sticks instead of muskets. So-called officers scampered to and fro, shouting orders. Mostly, they were cronies of Bates's, political hacks who by comparison gave the northern command which had been so catastrophic a positively Napoleonic air.

But march they did. And march, and march.

And faint. Fainted every afternoon by the score. It was July in St. Louis, after all, and it was hot.

Bates himself still languished after all that time in the job of "acting" governor. But word was he'd gotten used to it, which came as no surprise: I'd always felt he was a man of rodentlike adaptability.

I slipped quietly into town. And that time I made sure I wasn't spotted. I grew a beard the last two weeks on the trail, dressed in buckskin and rode in looking like an out-of-season trapper. And hanging around some likely places those first few days, from what I could tell the secret had been kept. Other than America's lovely First Couple, the only person alive who knew where I was was Alexander Wilson's sister, Emma Logan.

The town had about doubled in size in the three years since I'd left and there were now about thirty stores and houses built of brick. But it was amazing how small the place still was and how much you could learn just by keeping your ears open.

For instance, after a few drinks at the bar at Lacey's (yes, Lacey's had expanded and put in a handsomely crafted, solid oak stand-up bar stretching out fully twenty-two feet, seven and one-half inches—a fact proudly proclaimed by a sign dangling from the ceiling), I found that Will Clark had been called north to Ohio to mop up after William Henry Harrison's latest victory. Big White and his family had finally been taken safely back to their people, the Mandans. Nyles Jackson was a full colonel (it turned out later to be his rank in the militia, not the regular army) in "acting" charge of the Fort St. Louis garrison. And David Bradford was now "acting" territorial secretary—in other words, the same job Bates had once held under Lewis, though word was Bradford's actual duties hadn't changed much.

And then my fourth day in town, my second visit to Lacey's, Georges Charbonneau walked in. And I thought, Now there's a fellow I want to see.

I watched him from down the bar: At five foot five, he was the same muscular stub of a man—with enormous, powerful-looking arms and that big head to make him look even shorter. He wore the same type of checked woolen shirt he'd always worn, and which Frenchmen for whatever reason seemed to favor. And he drank the same cheap liquor and smoked the same foul-smelling tobacco in a pipe he'd obviously whittled himself.

I hung back in the shadows as he drank three quick whiskeys, then nursed a fourth while drumming his fingers on the bar and glancing around with growing impatience. By the time he'd finished that one and was halfway through the next, he looked fed up and about to leave when a man walked in and caught his eye. Then the two of them moved together into a back corner, where the light was too dim to see and their little table was too far from the rest to get close to—at least not without tipping my hand.

I hadn't caught the new man's face, but his clothes were even more drab than Charbonneau's—a hunter's cap pulled well down over his forehead, a plain gray shirt and high boots. And from what I could tell their conversation was serious, even solemn.

They talked nearly an hour, but I made sure I was in the right place to see them without being seen myself. And as I'd expected, when they finally finished they didn't leave together. Charbonneau returned to the bar, while the other man ducked out a side entrance. But I was ready for him, and for one instant as he stepped through the doorway into the blinding summer sunshine, I could see his face quite clearly: It was David Bradford, and I realized that his drab clothing had obviously been meant as a disguise of sorts.

I was nearly seduced by the moment: I wanted to follow Bradford then and there, but it was nowhere near time for so daring a move. Instead, I lingered quietly in the bar while Charbonneau, to my surprise, began drinking heavily. While I nursed one fresh one, he downed five—and that was over and above what he'd had before.

Just what did Bradford say to him? I wondered. And my mouth watered over what the Frenchman might blurt out later, if I handled it right. Trouble was he was already staggering and slurring his words, and after two or three more he stumbled out into the noontime sunlight.

I followed him to the near edge of town, the south end, to be exact, just two streets away, where he walked into a ramshackle shed. I crept alongside, peered through a crack in the wall and saw him, drunk as he was, gathering up his gear and saddling a horse. I dashed back for my own and tied him nearby. A few minutes later, Charbonneau mounted up and rode off at a slow gait into the woods, all the time sipping whiskey from a flask while I followed at a safe distance.

About two miles out, he rode into a well-used clearing with the ashes of a dead fire in the center and even a few provisions scattered about. He climbed off his horse, stumbling to his knees as he hit the ground, then somehow got up, managed to spread a blanket, flopped down and, from what I could tell, was out cold in an instant.

"Hello, Charbonneau," I said, sitting a few feet away and holding a pistol that was aimed at his heart.

He was still confused and groggy, struggling to come out of the inevitable gloam of two or three dozen shots of whiskey.

"Huh?" he said, squinting through the mid-afternoon light. "Who . . . ? Hull?"

He jerked around, grabbing for his knife, I suppose, but I had quietly taken that, his musket and anything else that might be dangerous, and hidden them behind some rocks about a hundred feet away.

He studied me a moment, saw the gun and slowly grasped what had happened. "Hello, Hull," he said calmly and even managed a sappy smile. "Heard you were coming."

"Oh?" I said, though it was hardly a surprise, and then of course he sat there staring at me dumbly, until finally I said, "All right, go ahead, tell me how." And then he actually smiled again.

"Well, from what I heard," he said, "Armstrong sent Bates a letter. It said 'a special agent of the President' was on his way, and to give him 'your full cooperation.' Something like that."

"And they guessed it was me?"

"It said something about the agent 'being familiar with your fine work in Louisiana.' They figured you were the likely man, yes."

I shook my head and told myself I should've known the secret wouldn't be kept. Then, with a smile of my own, I said, "So is that what Bradford told you this morning?"

"Huh? When?" Charbonneau squinted at me with a little shake of his head. "God, was that today?"

"At Lacey's, remember?"

"Lacey's. Right. You were . . . Jesus, you were there?"

"Is that what he told you?"

"Yes, right."

"What else?"

"Well, that . . . That was it, really. Just that I shouldn't be surprised if you showed up soon and that I might want to leave town for a while."

And I thought: Was that really all they talked about for nearly an hour? But for the moment I let it pass.

"Bradford in the habit of bringing messages to the likes of you?" I said. "The acting secretary of the territory bringing information to a foreign spy?"

"That's a lie!" he said with predictable indignation, and I laughed out loud.

"He know you stole those papers?"

"Course not," he said, his tone suddenly sheepish, the brief touch of bravado gone in a flash.

"He know you were trying to make a deal with the British?"

"No," he said with a funny little whine.

He'd been propped up on one elbow, staring over at me, watching me—or maybe watching the pistol in my hand—with considerable interest. Abruptly, he lay back and held his hands over his eyes.

"Too much whiskey makes you wise," he said with a quiet moan and a little laugh, and I vaguely recalled the sardonic joke—an epithet used by little children in the streets of Philadelphia and other towns.

"He know you're a murderer? He know you killed Phelps and Brahan?"

Slowly, Charbonneau lifted himself to his elbow again. "What makes you think that?" he said, though with nothing like his earlier indignation. He even looked at me in the oddest way—almost leering with a devilish little smirk.

"I think we should get him out here," I said.

"Who?"

"Bradford. We'll—"

"Bradford! What for?" He stared at me with wide-eyed amazement.

"We'll talk it over, get it all out in the open, get things settled once and for all."

Charbonneau took a heavy, calming breath, but it didn't seem to help. The muscles in his neck throbbed, and he blinked nervously. "You're crazy, Hull," he said, slowly drawing out the words.

"Yep," I said with a big grin, and he just sat there quietly, as if thinking it over. Then, sneering:

"How you plan to do that, Hull? How you plan to get Bradford out here?"

"I won't," I answered. "You will. Same way you always do: you'll write him a note."

Charbonneau took a big gulp of air, then opened his mouth and closed it several times.

"Here, write it," I said, handing him pen, ink and paper that I'd taken from his saddlebag. And while he wrote his, I quickly scribbled a note of my own.

"Let me see," I said a few minutes later, and took the paper from him. It said: "Come at once, the usual place," over his initial.

"Hmm," I said, thinking it over. "What's the 'usual place'? Isn't that Lacey's? What's the difference between here and there?"

He glared up at me, for the first time a touch of real anger showing on his face.

"Do it again," I ordered, "and not 'at once.' Later on tonight." And this time he wrote: "Come after dark, outside town."

"Better," I said, after glancing it over. "It better be better," I warned with as much authority in my voice as I could manage—considering that of course I'd just been guessing all along about whatever secret signals they might use between them.

The next part was tricky, for even among frontier types Charbonneau was unusually resourceful, and I had to take every possible precaution.

"Roll over on your stomach," I told him, "and put your hands behind you."

Then, putting the pistol aside and holding my knife between my teeth, I quickly tied his hands. Then I put the knife down and bound his feet as well, then ran the rope from his hands to his feet. I had to threaten him with the knife against his throat to get him to bend his knees and raise his feet as far as they would go, but he finally brought them up enough so I could pull the rope tight.

"Goddammit!" he shouted with a yelp, but he was a sturdy man who looked as able to get pain as give it, and I ignored his complaint.

I tied his horse up a good distance away and double-checked to make sure there was nothing in his pockets or nearby that he could use to escape. Then I dragged him to a distance of about five feet from a big tree, tied a noose around his neck and ran that rope around the tree trunk. Then I ran another line about twenty feet from around his neck to the next nearest tree. Now he was caught in the middle, I thought, and could easily choke himself to death if he tried too hard to move.

"Back soon," I told him, then mounted up and hurried to town.

I left my horse on the outskirts and walked in, gave a dollar to a boy on the street and told him to take Charbonneau's note to Government House. Then I walked around for about twenty minutes, found another boy and gave him a dollar with the note that I had written.

And that was it, except suddenly I felt like a whiskey, so I bought a pint and took it with me, sipping it lightly on the short ride back. The whole business hadn't taken two hours, but sure enough when I returned, the Frenchman had somehow broken loose: The ropes were lying in a heap, and he was nowhere to be seen.

I dismounted at once and crept carefully into the campsite. And then I heard a horse whinny, and then an instant later Charbonneau jumped out from behind a tree and was on me.

He had the strength of a bull, but I had my knife, and lucky for me he had found his horse but not his weapons. I slashed him on the arm and managed, just barely, to squirm out of his grasp. Naturally, he lunged straight for my knife hand and squeezed my wrist until my fingers were nearly numb.

"Charbonneau, stop!" I said. "You're not—no point to this."

But he only growled more fiercely and squeezed more tightly than ever. "Stop!" I told him one more time, but to no avail. And then with my right hand about to give way, I reached with my left down into my boot, pulled out my smaller knife—the whittling one—and drove it with all my strength into his stomach.

It took a moment—or at least it seemed that way to me—but finally that deadly grip of his relaxed, his whole body went limp, and I pushed him off me and slid away. Still, I eyed him fearfully a few more minutes before being sure at last that the life had gone out of him for good.

I took off his old shirt, tore off a strip and tied it around him like a dressing of sorts over the wound. Then I put a fresh shirt on him, carried him over toward the center of the clearing, laid him down carefully and propped his head on a blanket roll. Later on, I would even put his pipe in his mouth.

I made sure my horse was tied up well away from there and my gear was nowhere in sight. Then I brought his stuff, horse and all, into the clearing, spread everything out so it looked more or less natural and got a fire going. I even stepped back a few feet to the edge of the clearing to see for myself, and in the flickering light it looked as if Charbonneau were indeed relaxing by the fire, having an evening smoke.

It looks all right, I thought. More or less. Almost.

And then I thought, No, I cannot do this. I cannot dwell on the grotesque reality of what I've done.

Not now, anyway.

Later, I thought. Later I will think.

And weep.

I waited. Darkness fell. And a few minutes later I thought I heard a very faint rustling out there in the trees. And I smiled. That's right, I thought. That's what I should hear. And then about an hour after that, I heard more noise, very faint at first, then slowly, slowly louder. And finally a man rode out of the woods and right into the clearing.

"What is it, Charbonneau?" the man said gruffly. "What is it now?"

He dismounted a few feet away, dropped the reins of the horse in the dirt and glanced around with growing annoyance. And in the light I could see it was David Bradford, looming up. For indeed he was as tall as Charbonneau had been short, a six-foot-four-inch figure towering in the darkness of the woods like some mythical monster of old.

"Too hot for this, isn't it, Charbonneau?" Bradford said, walking to the fire. "So what is it, damn it?"

"Charbonneau's resting right now," I said, coming up behind him.

"Don't move, I have a gun," I said as he started to turn around.

He stopped at once, and I poked him in the middle of his back with the barrel. "Over there," I said, getting him around to the other side of the fire and then a few feet beyond. After all, he didn't have to know my little secret about Charbonneau. Not quite yet, anyway.

"Sit down," I insisted, and he dropped to the ground with his back to the fire—and the body—just as I'd wanted. Slowly, I came around in front of him.

"Hull?" he said, just as Charbonneau had a few hours before. "We heard you were coming," he added. And with that the similarity gave me an eerie sensation.

"Shut up," I said, suddenly feeling a bit queasy. Thank God I bought that whiskey, I thought, then took it out of my pocket and drank a long swallow.

"Drink?" I said to Bradford, but he declined with an unctuous twist of his head.

"What is this, dammit," he suddenly insisted after a moment of polite silence.

"Charbonneau's not feeling well," I said, my state of mind growing more lurid by the minute. "He had something to tell you, but now he's asked me to tell you instead."

I paused, took another large swallow, stared off and wondered, Just how ghastly is this going to get before it's finally over?

"And?" Bradford demanded. Clearly, I thought, the man is losing patience.

"Shut up, Bradford," I said again, waving the gun and fiercely drawing out the words. Somehow this is not going quite the way

I intended, I thought. But it *is* going, I decided, and it will have to do.

"All the documents I have, all the evidence—none of it seems to mean much," I said with an exaggerated shrug. "Even so, people keep dying along the way. First Neelly, then Wilkinson, now . . ."

I trailed off, gesturing vaguely at the dead man on the other side of the fire, but Bradford just stared at me with a quizzical squint.

"Why'd they kill Lewis, anyway?" I asked. "What'd they think he was trying to do?"

Bradford looked over at me with a wicked little smile, and I fired a load that whistled past his left ear.

"Oh God, no," he shrieked. He put his hand up to his ear, felt around and pulled it away again. When he saw nothing, no blood, no sign of injury, he felt around again more slowly, then gradually heaved a sigh of relief.

"Why?" I said again, and this time he answered at once:

"They . . . they weren't sure. They thought he might be putting in with Astor, or maybe getting ready to tell Jefferson about the goings-on at Missouri Fur. They were certain it was one or the other. So they . . . made their little arrangement."

He paused and shook his head. "Later on, when they found out, well, it was too late of course. The man had already been sent. The killing was in progress."

He looked down with what passed for embarrassment from him, and I glared at him fiercely.

"Found out what?" I said.

"That Lewis was in it, of course. In Missouri Fur. He was the other silent partner. Along with General Clark."

I struggled for control: I didn't blurt anything out, and I believe I kept my expression blandly neutral.

"So they killed him for nothing?" I asked with a disbelieving whine. And he just stared blandly back at me.

And I thought: So Lewis was human, after all. So he wanted his share like everyone else. Except somehow he wound up dead because of it.

And then it was as if a bell went off in my head: *"What goings-on at Missouri Fur?"* I said.

Bradford closed his eyes and rubbed his hands over his forehead. "Stirring up the Indians, working with the British," he said with a yawn and a stretch.

"The *British?*" I said with a start. And I suddenly realized what I should have figured out long ago: that Charbonneau had lied (or been misled himself) about the meaning of at least a portion of the letters between Bates and Wilkinson—and that of course it had been the British all along.

"Yes, Hull, 'the British'," Bradford said in a mocking tone. "They're the ones with the money. Bates and Wilkinson got theirs."

"But not Lewis or Clark."

"I doubt it. First Bates seemed to think Lewis had found out about them—about the British bribes. Then, as I say, later on Bates learned Lewis was a partner and so he assumed that Lewis was in on the British bribes, too. So I think he would have stopped the killing if he could have—though for quite the wrong reason. Because I personally felt Lewis never knew the first thing about the British money—let alone took any of it. I doubt if Clark did, either." He stopped and shook his head wearily. "Either way, you're right, I suppose. Lewis almost certainly was killed for no reason."

"You are revolting," I said, and he suddenly stared at me with wide-eyed alarm.

"I . . . had nothing to do with that," he said. "That was Bates and Wilkinson and Burr and . . . maybe someone else . . . They arranged it. With that man, that Neelly. Nothing to do with me. Not that one, not on your life. I wouldn't have, couldn't have—"

I fired a load that nicked his right shoulder, and he squealed with pain.

"Oh please don't . . ."

"Not that one, eh?" I said with a faint smile, for he'd given me an unexpected little wedge of advantage. "Then what ones did you have to do with?" I looked at him with slightly puzzled indignation, almost as if I really didn't know the answer.

He gulped again. "What? I don't . . ."

"You didn't help with the Lewis killing. 'Not that one,' you just said. So?"

"I . . ."

"So which ones did you arrange, or do yourself?"

He breathed deeply for another minute or so, gradually regaining a bit of composure. He even regained the usual unctuous expression on his gloomy face.

"How did you . . . figure it out?" he asked, and I slowly raised my left hand from the ground up to as high as I could reach.

"You," I said, pointing at him. "So tall. Brahan and Phelps, they both died from above, so to speak. Your doing it made sense somehow."

He looked at me with a dismissive shrug. "That's nothing, that's not proof," he said. "Besides, you're as guilty as I am. It was your meddling that brought them into it in the first place. Made them a danger. To Bates. To Wilkinson. That's why they had to be . . . eliminated." He stopped, shook his head and shrugged again. "So? So now you know. So what? You can murder me if you want, but that's all you can do. You have nothing legal, nothing for the courts."

And right then another thought suddenly occurred to me. "You do them both yourself?" I asked. "Or with help?"

He snorted derisively. "Charbonneau didn't tell you?" And I shook my head. "He should speak for himself, really, but . . . well, he's strong as an ox, and between the two of us . . . Well, as you say, I'm tall enough." He looked around, squinting at the haze of the dying campfire, as if trying to see past it. "Say, what's wrong with Charbonneau, anyway?"

I took another swallow off the jug, while Bradford sat there staring toward the dead man with a look of growing alarm. And I thought, So that's why Charbonneau got into such a panic. And then, in the distance, there was a faint rustling sound in the trees. And then slowly, very slowly, it grew louder until finally it was very close by indeed, and then a man came walking out of the woods and right into the clearing.

It was Nyles Jackson.

"You hear that, Nyles?" I said.

"Every word," he answered, and Bradford looked up at him dumbfounded.

"You . . . were out there?" he gasped. "But Nyles, you . . . can't, you won't. It's absurd."

"I sent for him when I sent for you," I said. "You're as good as convicted of two murders."

Suddenly there was a wild new look of fear and confusion on Bradford's face. He started to get up, and I leapt to my feet. "Don't move!" I shouted, but he kept on till he was standing right there a few feet in front of me.

"Can't be, can't happen," he raved, more to himself than to me or Jackson. "Bates. Bates did it. I'll testify. I'll tell everything. He's the one you want. He gave the orders."

"Sorry, David," Jackson put in, and I started to say, Now wait a minute, Nyles, but before I could get a word in, Bradford was running toward me full speed with a demonic look in his eyes. And then Jackson stepped in front of me and suddenly there was a knife in his hand. And before I could speak or move, Jackson raised the dagger and Bradford simply ran his enormous frame onto the blade, and the next thing I knew he was slit clean up the middle and falling down dead.

Jackson pulled the knife out with a violent twist, wiped it clean and put it away.

"Henry Phelps was my best friend, Harry," he said, then turned and walked off.

A moment later, I faintly heard him ride away. And for some reason all I could think was that this was *not* the sort of night you could tell your grandchildren about, and besides that, I thought wildly, what would Betsy Grinder say if she saw me now?

Twenty-One

Frederick Bates's famous undulating upper lip was dripping with perspiration, but that meant nothing. It was almost always that way—wet with sweat. And it was hot, after all—another hot St. Louis summer day.

I had just shown Bates the documents—the letters and invoices—much as I had with Wilkinson before him. And now I watched as he read them, and I waited for him to react.

He read them carefully, methodically, with no posturing display of scowling indifference or bravado. There was, in point of fact, nothing at all revealing in his face.

A poker face, I thought. Or better yet a Yankee doctor's face, perhaps while delivering a baby.

"Interesting," he said, and pushed the papers back across the top of his desk. I picked them up and put them away in my bag.

"So this is what the president's 'special agent' has for me, eh?" he said. "This is what that man in the White House sends me. First, that Lewis. Oh, of course everybody loved Meriwether Lewis. He was special; he was the golden boy—the young prince, the heir apparent." Bates pulled a handkerchief out of his pocket and mopped away the sweat.

"Well, let me tell you," he went on, "he was a poser and a posturer, nothing more. Fred Bates did all the dirty work, sweated like a pig, but always in the background, while the fair-haired Lewis got all the credit. And now this is the thanks I get for all my years of dedication and toil, eh? No rewards, no thank yous. Just blame! That's what old Fred Bates gets. I'm the convenient scapegoat. Give the 'special agent' your 'fullest cooperation,' the note said. And this is what I get: a man comes in here with some silly scraps of paper, and I'm supposed to roll over for it. I'm a cheat, a swindler, a greedy power-grabber, and now a murderer on top of it. Is that it? Well, you can just forget that one, sonny, because I won't play. Far as I'm concerned, your papers aren't worth a pile of shit in an outhouse. Not without corroboration, and you have none. Why, they're all dead, for God's sake: Wilkinson, Bradford, Neelly, Boilvin, Charbonneau."

"And Lewis," I said. "Don't forget Lewis."

"Oh, you're always so clever, aren't you, Hull? Well, that's right, mister. Meriwether Lewis is goddamn good and dead, along with the rest of them, and it's goddamn good riddance as far as I'm concerned. And without him or the others you don't have anything. Nothing. Might as well burn that junk or wipe your ass with it because it's worthless, and you can take my word on that one."

I looked at him with a certain amazed admiration, for indeed I'd never heard an outburst quite like that before. Truth be told, I almost laughed in his face, then thought better of it and said:

"I have Nyles Jackson."

And Bates just stared at me quietly, evenly, for a long, long moment, once again revealing nothing—until he said:

"Nyles, come in here, will you," in a crisp tone of voice, and Nyles Jackson quietly slipped out from behind a partition in a far corner of the room, walked behind Bates's desk and quite pointedly stood just to his right and a little behind him.

"Nyles?" I said, but Jackson simply shook his head.

"I got the man I want, Harry," he said. "Bradford did the

deed; he was the killer. Him and Charbonneau. And you . . . well, Charbonneau's dead, too. So I'm satisfied."

"Nyles?" I said again, this time my voice more of a shriek than anything else. And I thought: Henry Phelps's best friend!

Bates leaned back in his chair, a clear message of contempt riding on his smile, while Jackson shook his head and pursed his lips—a grand gesture of infinite patience, I suppose, much as if he were indulging a small child.

"Harry, you got all the others," Jackson said. "All but one. You can't have everything. Nobody can. Be practical. Let it go. Accept the setback and relax. You're entitled."

The room was beginning to swirl around me, and I felt my heart pounding. "Good God, Nyles, he gave the orders. Lewis, Phelps, Brahan, the assault on Wilson, no doubt. Others actually did them, but he set it in motion. He can't just get away with it."

But they both just smiled calmly, and suddenly there was a candle burning bright inside me. "Ah, I see," I said, glaring at them through misty eyes.

"So how much, Nyles?" I went on. "What did you get? How big a piece of Missouri Fur did it take to let a bloodless killer walk away?"

"Now, Harry—"

"No, really, Nyles, I'm curious. Tell me. One percent. Two percent. Five. Ten. How much, Nyles, eh?"

"Be careful, Harry—"

"Why, I could ring that bell," Bates suddenly put in, "and two strapping privates would be in here in a minute flat dragging your ass to the stockade. I'd say you came in here, wild, making threats. Nyles would back me up—"

"Now take it easy, Governor. You're sounding like Harry, here," Jackson said with a forced little chuckle. He took a calming breath and held up both hands in a quieting gesture. "Let's all relax a minute, eh? No need to go crazy. We'll work it out, won't we, Harry? Don't you see, it's just . . . settled. It's fixed. It's the way it is."

I nodded and took a deep breath of my own, and then we all did sit quietly for a long moment. "How about a round of drinks, eh, gentlemen?" Jackson offered, then pulled out a flask of rum and poured us each a shot. I swallowed mine in one gulp, and Bates did the same with his.

"Now that's more like it," Jackson said, then drank down his own and poured a round of refills.

"By the way, Nyles, I meant to mention it," I said, leaning back in my chair with a grand smile, "but Winfield Scott and I became good friends during the Montreal business. Do you know him, he's—"

"No, Harry, I don't," Jackson said, a touch of confusion in his voice. Or maybe more than a touch.

"He's so terrifically bright," I went on, "and an outstanding officer. One of the few up there who could get anything right."

Bates smiled politely. Jackson scrutinized me, as if struggling to follow this sudden shift in conversation. And then I said:

"He's a protégé of Andrew Jackson's, you know."

And all of a sudden Bates, eyes widening just slightly, looked me over with new interest, and I knew that I had his attention at last.

"Look, Harry, that's all well and good, but what about—"

"Shut up, Nyles," Bates said, and nobody there was more stunned than I that my mad little bluff had gotten even this far in turning the tables. But of course there was still a long way to go.

"Well, well, well, Major Hull," Bates said with a sneering mixture of admiration and contempt. He leaned back in his chair, slid the tip of his right index finger along the point of his chin and carefully stole a glance at the man who was still standing just behind him and to his right.

"Uh, Colonel Jackson, could you excuse us for just a few minutes," Bates said silkily. "I have an important matter to talk over with Major Hull here."

And I thought: My God, he really has swallowed it, hasn't he?

Jackson, already more puzzled than ever, stared at Bates with growing agitation. "But, Governor," he stammered. "Are you sure, sir? Is it wise? I mean . . . what is this?"

"Nyles, please, we'll talk later," Bates said consolingly, but Jackson stubbornly shook his head.

"Harry, what is this?" he demanded, walking out from behind Bates's big desk. "What are you trying to pull now?"

He stood facing me, scowling angrily, no more than two feet away. "I have a right to be here, dammit. I won't be cut out. I've done too much; I know too much!"

"Nyles, please," Bates said.

"Nobody's cutting you out, Nyles," I said quietly. "It's nothing to do with you."

"Oh fuck that, Harry, I know damn well you're lying. I know damn well—"

"*Colonel Jackson!*" Bates suddenly shouted at positively the top of his voice. "*Get out!*"

Instantly, Jackson wheeled around to face the governor. Then he gave his most elaborate salute, did a formal about-face, marched from the room in the official military style and quietly closed the door behind him.

"More rum, Major Hull?" Bates said, barely waiting for the latch to catch, and I turned back toward him with a sigh.

"Of course," I said, and he filled our glasses to the top.

"I'm not sure you understand the enormity of what I'm offering, Major," Bates said. "I mean this is truly the opportunity of a lifetime, to get in at the start of something like this, where there's simply no limit to what you can make, how rich you can become."

We'd been talking (or I should say, *he'd* been talking) nearly two hours now and with no end in sight. Indeed, at the start he'd told the attendant outside he was not to be disturbed for any reason, and then he bolted the door against likely intruders. A moment later he grabbed the rum and two glasses, and beckoned me to join him in a pair of easy chairs beside an east-facing window with a handsome view of the town and the Mississippi beyond.

"I'm talking millions, Major. The kind of money men dream of. The kind that builds fiefdoms and kingdoms and empires." He paused, reached in his front coat pocket, fished out a pouch of tobacco and poured some in the bowl of his pipe.

"Smoke, Major?" he said, but I politely declined.

"Look at that town, Major Hull—double what it was three years ago. It's booming, and this is just the start." He fairly leapt from his chair and stepped right up to the window. "Look! Look at that river. That's our highway, Major. The men and money go out, the riches come back—riches beyond the dreams of any Oriental potentate hoarding his silks and his jewels. That's all out of date now, useless stuff. Our riches are what make things work, fur and whatever else is out there that makes the world go round—that turns riches into more riches. That's our secret, Hull. That's the secret the ancients never understood, and that's why we'll be richer and stronger and better than any of them."

Bates stood there a moment with the morning sun behind him, jaw thrust forward, eyes dark and serious, a picture of sheer determination—but also looking at that moment as if he might have wound down at last. Indeed, a minute later he quietly took his seat and poured himself another rum.

"And that's all out there for the taking, eh, Governor?" I said with a pleasant smile.

"In your case, Hull, just for the asking. Just say the word, we'll work it all out." He waited a moment, and when I didn't answer at once he began again on a slightly different tack.

"Look, Major," he said, his voice suddenly hushed and confidential. "You know as well as I do we don't want to bring that . . . man, the man you mentioned earlier—we don't want to bring him into this. Nobody wants that. Not you. Not the president. No one. It would be bad for everyone in the long run. I'm sure the president made that clear. And I *know* that Mrs. Madison—"

"She's the one who brought his name up," I interjected in what was undeniably a rather artless touch of dissimulation. But of course Bates had no way of knowing that.

"Aha," he said, and that was all he said for a good long couple of minutes.

And then I decided that that was as good a time as any to cut him short and press on with the thing at last.

"I don't need money, Governor, I have money," I said with a supercilious little twist of my head. "So I'm sorry, but . . ." I trailed off, finishing my sentence with an inconclusive flutter of my right hand. (And by the way I thought I was telling him the truth at that moment because I still didn't understand the full extent of my family's financial collapse.)

Bates just stared at me, blankly and blandly at first, as if he couldn't accept what I'd just told him because he couldn't believe after all his grand fervor that I remained so entirely unconvinced.

Then, very slowly, I saw his mouth twist up in anger, and for a moment I thought he might launch into another diatribe. Or maybe he'll simply pull out a pistol and murder me, I thought. After all, it was the one thing he hadn't actually done himself yet—at least so far as I knew. But soon enough the anger faded, too, and weary resignation crept into its place.

"What do you want, Hull?" he said in a tired voice. And I thought: Amazing the way everybody keeps asking me that same question lately. The answer, as well, was always the same of course, but I'd grown tired of giving it because what I spoke of somehow never occurred.

Justice. That's what I kept hoping for, but the best I ever got was revenge. Or so it seemed. So, I decided, I wouldn't waste my highfalutin answer on the likes of Frederick Bates. For him I had something else in mind, something infinitely more practical.

"You're out, Fred," I said, my tone suddenly crisp and assertive. "Out of politics. Out of fur."

"But—"

"You'll resign, Fred. Ill health or something. You'll do it by the end of the week. And Missouri Fur is out of business. The handwriting's on the wall, you'll say. You can't raise the money, can't compete with Astor and his men, which is probably true anyway in the long run."

"You fool. You—"

"Fred. Language. My God."

His lip was undulating full force again. Actually, it was positively quivering with anger and uncertainty.

"You can't make this stick, you son of a bitch. I just won't do it, I tell you. I won't. You're bluffing. You'll never do it, you won't bring Andrew Jackson into this."

"I can and I will," I said, lying with more conviction in my tone and demeanor than I ever have—before or since.

"Go ahead, Fred. Try me. Call my bluff. I'll bring in Jackson and Jefferson and even Madison, too, if I have to. You'll do what I tell you and do it fast, or I'll rock you out of your office and your get-rich schemes with the biggest goddamn scandal in history. And I don't care if it pulls the whole damn country down with it."

My eyes were on fire as I spoke, my mouth twisted up with anger, my voice filled with rage. I'd made a trade with James and Dolley Madison. They'd said I could do whatever I wanted to conclude my business in the West, and in return I promised never to bring Andrew Jackson into it. And I never would. But I never said I wouldn't lie about it a little along the way.

Bates hesitated, and in my mad state I almost pulled my famous dagger. But at the last minute I remembered where I was and who I was talking to and decided after all that even a criminal in a governor's chair deserves a little consideration.

"Well?" I demanded, being sure to hold on tightly to my anger as I spoke. It was, after all, all I had left: the very last card of the very last hand.

Bates, looking suddenly pale and worn out, breathed in an oddly heavy way for a long moment. I waited, watching him with some alarm at his condition, until at last he said, "All right," in a soft whisper.

And then I knew the game was up.

C H A P T E R

Twenty-Two

Bates kept his word: He quit his job a week later and announced the dissolution of Missouri Fur one week after that. I finished my work for the president (which as I say will have to await a later telling—and quite a tale it is, believe me!).

I never did achieve old Alexander Wilson's goal: the official redemption of Meriwether Lewis's good name. So I did the next best thing. I made a long overdue journey to Locust Hill, Lewis's family home in Virginia—not far from Monticello, in fact—and paid a call on his brother, Reuben, and mother, Lucy.

"I was a friend of your son's, of Meriwether's," I told her very softly.

It was winter by then, the snow piled high outside the rustic frame house. Inside, we talked before a roaring fire in the master bedroom where Lucy, bedridden now, propped herself up on some pillows and sipped hot tea while Reuben paced nervously behind me.

"Of Meriwether's?" she said in her creaky old woman's

voice. "Isn't that nice. You hear that, Reuben? This man knew Meriwether."

"Yes, Mother," he said.

"I've come to tell you—" I said, and then I stopped, not quite brave enough yet to blurt it out so suddenly.

"I've come to tell you something," I said. "Something important about your son."

"I know," she said with a kindly old woman's smile. "He was a wonderful boy, don't you think?"

"Wonderful," I said.

"How did you know him?" she asked. "Did you know him well?"

And I thought: My, what hard questions you ask, Mother Lewis, not unlike the disarmingly simple questions of little children.

So? I asked myself. So how well? I'd admired him, of course, and spent time with him. I'd been a good friend—both before he died and after, in a sense. For I'd spent months, or longer, of my life searching for the awful secrets behind his terrible death. In a way, I'd loved him. I said:

"I served under him once a long time ago, during the Whiskey Rebellion of '94. And then we studied birds together. We watched their colors and listened to their songs. We loved how beautiful and brutal and free they were. And we learned what we could about how they lived and died."

Her eyes burned with a sudden intensity—though a faint smile still played on her lips. She stared at me that way for a long time—long enough for the logs on the fire to crackle red hot and for Reuben Lewis to nearly wear himself out pacing little circles on the hard wood floor.

"Birds," Lucy Lewis finally said, her tone wistful, her eyes far away. "He loved birds, loved everything about the wild. That was what preoccupied him—the land, the wilderness, the animals, the plants. He was that sort of man—a frontiersman, I think they called him."

"He was an American," Reuben Lewis suddenly put in.

And for once I smiled admiringly at that statement of the obvious.

"Mrs. Lewis, your son did not commit suicide," I said at last.

And of course she said, "I know," quite matter-of-factly.

"I . . . know you know," I said. "But there's been a great deal of toil and risk and bloodshed along the way, and if you don't mind, ma'am, I'd like to explain to you why what you say you know is indeed the complete and absolute truth: that Meriwether Lewis was murdered."

I paused and bit my lower lip. "I think it will help you," I said. And at the very instant I said it I knew the largeness of the lie, for I suddenly realized that I had come here to tell her all this mainly for myself.

Reuben Lewis walked around to the far side of the bed, for no other reason that I could detect other than to let me see the expression of deep displeasure that was showing on his face.

Lucy Lewis stared at me silently for a very long time, her eyes uncertain, the rest of her face quivering with profound sadness.

"Go ahead," she finally said, very softly.

And as gently as I could I told her everything: about Wilkinson and Charbonneau and Bates and Bradford. And Boilvin and Neelly and Grinder, of course. It was hard, but I left nothing out, not even the part about Tilly and what happened to her.

Oddly enough, it was that that seemed to capture her attention in a whole new way. She pursed her lips and stared off with an oddly knowing look, then her eyes misted over and finally tears began to slip quietly down her face.

"You all right, ma'am?" I asked.

"Course," she snapped back at once. "Little nigger slave girl—what the hell do I care?" And I flinched at her unexpectedly savage answer, even though I felt that somehow or other at least part of it was a lie.

"Knew it all along," she said after I'd finally finished the whole sad story. "And they're all dead, you say?"

"All but one," I said, "and nobody'll hear from him again."

She nodded with seeming satisfaction in her eyes. "Have to do, I guess," she said. "Doesn't surprise me, though. Boy like that, been taking care of himself since he was twelve when his father died. Led fifty men through the unknown and back, lost hardly a one. And they tried to say he killed himself. How could that be? A boy like that."

"A man like that," Reuben Lewis said, and his mother smiled affectionately.

"Of course," she said.

She stared off, a bit misty-eyed for a long few minutes, then eyed Reuben tenderly.

"Glass of port," she said abruptly, and he obeyed with obvious reluctance.

He brought three glasses, and we sipped slowly, quietly. Indeed, it took only a sip or two for the old woman to get a pleasant glow about her.

"Paper," she said suddenly. "Pen, ink, tablet."

And poor Reuben scrambled to get them all, and then she scribbled a quick note, addressed the envelope, sealed it up and handed it to me.

"Don't look at that!" she insisted, and I quickly stuffed it in my inside coat pocket.

"Heading home, back to Philadelphia?" she asked me.

"Yes, ma'am," I said.

"Well, take that with you, and don't look at it till you get there," she said. "Not even the outside."

"Yes, ma'am."

"Promise me," she said, and of course I did so at once.

And then a few minutes later she quietly dozed off. Not surprisingly, the ordeal had sapped her strength.

Reuben Lewis motioned me out of the room and downstairs to the front parlor, ready, it seemed, to dismiss me with a terse goodbye. And in a way I couldn't blame him, for until then, what I'd said and done had been for his mother. And for me. But now at last I had something for him, as well. I opened my kit and handed him his brother's prize pistols.

He took them with something like the care a woman shows a newborn, fondling them tenderly.

"Thank you, Mr. Hull," he said, just a hint of tears showing in his eyes.

And I said, "No, Mr. Lewis, I'm the one who's thankful, and thank your mother, too." And then I walked out of there, got on my horse and headed home.

I kept my promise: I rode all the way to the town house in Philadelphia—we hadn't sold that just yet—before I finally pulled out the envelope from Lucy Lewis. It was addressed with just one word: "Tilly," it said.

So I walked the few blocks over to Emma Logan's house, paid my respects and asked to see her.

"You're lucky, she's home today," Emma said with a smile. "Usually she's studying over at the college."

A minute later, she came out into the little entranceway of the house, still no more than sixteen, but transformed beyond my wildest dreams: a cultured young lady in a handsome blue dress with a look of utter confidence in her eyes.

"Major Hull, so nice to see you again," she said with impeccable diction and an artful little curtsy.

"And you, Miss Tilly," I said with a bow. "You're well, I trust? And your studies?"

"Very well, yes thank you, Major. And your . . . adventures?"

"Splendid, thank you," I replied.

She hesitated then, and at second glance I realized there were tears slowly forming in her lovely brown eyes.

"I . . . missed you," she said, starting to cry, and I said, "Don't!" very sharply. Even so she melted into my arms and gave me a hug.

"It's all right," I said, "but don't. Be grateful—that's fine. But never miss me. It was all . . . too ugly, and missing me will only bring it back. Besides, I'll be leaving again soon. I'll always be leaving. So there's no point anyway, you see."

But she just hugged me more more tightly than ever. "Oh God, how can I ever thank you?" she said.

And I had no answer for that because there was no answer and because I simply didn't feel like telling her that it was beside the point and in any case not to worry about it—not now, not ever.

"I have something for you," I said, and handed her the note.

She carefully pulled it open, read it and said: "I'm not sure that I . . . *Who's* it from?"

She handed it to me and I read the brief message. It said: "Be strong, be brave. Always! No matter what!" Just below, the signature read: "Lucy Meriwether Marks Lewis."

"Is she . . ."

"Yes," I said.

"His widow?" she asked.

"His mother," I answered.

She glanced at the note again, studying it a moment, then looked up at me.

"That's nice, but I don't understand," she said. "I mean, why me?"

And wiping away a tear or two of my own, I smiled and said: "You know, that's a good question, but I just decided: that the older you get the less there is in life that makes any sense. So just take it for what it is—a bit of encouragement from an old lady of the South."

She looked at me closely for a long moment, and then very slowly a smile crept over her face. "Oh," she said with a delightful little-girl laugh. And that was all she said.

My mother died that winter, and then there wasn't much left for me in the East. Besides, the West had got under my skin, as they say. The West, and another kind of life, and maybe something else, as well. Or some*one* else.

On top of all that the roof really caved in at last, financially speaking, and we had to sell the town house and just about everything else that was left. So I said my farewells to Tilly and the Logans and Edward and my sisters, and traveled on.

I headed south to Virginia, then west on the Old Wilderness Road and finally back into Tennessee, of all places. I rode once again through that gloomy country of fallen timbers and craggy cliffs and smelly swamps—still listening warily for the mockingbird but never hearing it, thank God.

Until finally one day I rode up on a slight rise of land, no more than a bump, really, and looked down over a funny little place: a hardscrabble farm with a stand in the center—a barn and a ramshackle shed and a couple of cabins.

It was all decrepit and sad enough, except that even from there I could see a figure hard at work: a woman bossing two men and somehow getting done what she needed to, no matter what.

The woman was handsome in a way—strong and sturdy, yet voluptuous, as well. Watching her, I nodded to myself with no small satisfaction. Then I kicked my heels and the horse ambled slowly down there.

"Morning, Mrs. Grinder," I said.

She looked up at me, squinting into the sun, and even that way, in the harshness of that light with her eyes all scrunched up, there was something about her that captured my attention.

"Captain . . . Hull, is it?" she said.

"Major—" I started to say, but cut myself short. "Just mister," I said. "In fact, just call me Harry."

"Been a long time, Harry," she said with a trace of a smile.

"Been lots to do," I answered.

"Imagine so," she said. "And call me Betsy, Harry."

I dismounted, tied the horse and stood there awkwardly in the barnyard.

"What brings you here, Harry?" she said, suddenly with a touch of sternness in her tone. "What brings you back to Grinder's Stand?"

"Well . . ." I said, then stopped, at a rare loss for words.

She is, I decided, trying to keep me guessing. And she always will, I thought with a smile. So what else can I do, I asked myself, but keep her guessing, too—at least for a little while.

Author's Note

The death of Meriwether Lewis remains a mystery to this day, but modern historians who have studied the subject now agree that suicide is virtually out of the question. What is known about the immediate circumstances of his demise, including the variations in Betsy Grinder's three published accounts, are accurately presented in this volume. In addition, the intrigue and double-dealing that took place while Lewis was governor at St. Louis are, if anything, understated; James Wilkinson and Frederick Bates are factual characters accurately portrayed, as are Alexander Wilson and Big White. Harrison Hull is my own invention, and while it is speculative to link the plotting over the fur trade with Lewis's death, some historians believe it to be at least within the realm of plausibility.

All the names of birds, including the Latin terms, were taken from *The Life and Letters of Alexander Wilson,* edited by Clark Hunter and published by the American Philosophical Society in Philadelphia;

Wilson's letters were also an invaluable resource in the writing of this book. Other sources include: *The Shaping of America* by Page Smith; *Suicide or Murder? The Strange Death of Governor Meriwether Lewis* by Vardis Fisher; *Meriwether Lewis, A Biography* by Richard Dillon; *Thomas Jefferson: Writings* edited by Merrill D. Peterson; *Tarnished Warrior, Major General James Wilkinson* by James Ripley Jacobs; and *To His Excellency Thomas Jefferson, Letters to a President* edited by Jack McLaughlin. My thanks also to the librarians at the Missouri Historical Society in St. Louis for their generous assistance.